KEYSTONE WESTERN AMERICANA SERIES

William H. Goetzmann and Archibald Hanna, General Editors

ASTORIA

D1736302

ASTORIA

OR

ANECDOTES OF AN ENTERPRISE
BEYOND THE ROCKY MOUNTAINS

BY

WASHINGTON IRVING

⋙⋘

The 1836 Edition, Unabridged
in two volumes

Introduction by William H. Goetzmann

Volume II

J. B. LIPPINCOTT COMPANY
PHILADELPHIA AND NEW YORK

CONTENTS

A map of the routes of Hunt and Stuart follows the listing of chapters in each volume.

CONTENTS

Volume II

CHAPTER XXXI

CHAPTER XXXII

CHAPTER XXXIII

CHAPTER XXXIV

Determination of the party to proceed on foot—dreary deserts
between Snake river and the Columbia—distribution of effects

CHAPTER XXXIX

CHAPTER XL

CHAPTER XLI

CHAPTER XLII

CHAPTER XLIII

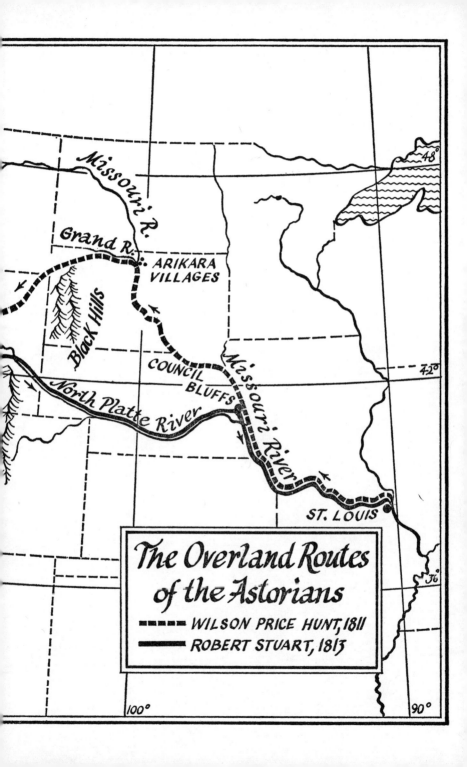

48°

Missouri R.

Grand R.

ARIKARA
VILLAGES

Black Hills

42°

COUNCIL
BLUFFS

Missouri River

North Platte River

ST. LOUIS

36°

The Overland Routes
of the Astorians
-------- WILSON PRICE HUNT, 1811
———— ROBERT STUART, 1813

100°

90°

Astoria

CHAPTER XXXI

ON the banks of Mad river Mr.
Hunt held a consultation with the other partners as to their future
movements. The wild and impetuous current of the river rendered
him doubtful whether it might not abound with impediments lower
down, sufficient to render the navigation of it slow and perilous, if
not impracticable. The hunters who had acted as guides, knew nothing of the character of the river below; what rocks, and shoals, and
rapids might obstruct it, or through what mountains and deserts it
might pass. Should they then abandon their horses, cast themselves
loose in fragile barks upon this wild, doubtful, and unknown river;
or should they continue their more toilsome and tedious, but perhaps more certain wayfaring by land?

The vote, as might have been expected, was almost unanimous
for embarcation; for when men are in difficulties every change
seems to be for the better. The difficulty now was to find timber of

sufficient size for the construction of canoes, the trees in these high mountain regions being chiefly a scrubbed growth of pines and cedars, aspens, haws and service berries, and a small kind of cotton tree with a leaf resembling that of the willow. There was a species of large fir, but so full of knots as to endanger the axe in hewing it. After searching for some time, a growth of timber, of sufficient size, was found lower down the river, whereupon the encampment was moved to the vicinity.

The men were now set to work to fell trees, and the mountains echoed to the unwonted sound of their axes. While preparations were thus going on for a voyage down the river, Mr. Hunt, who still entertained doubts of its practicability, despatched an exploring party, consisting of John Reed, the clerk, John Day the hunter, and Pierre Dorion the interpreter, with orders to proceed several days march along the stream, and notice its course and character.

After their departure, Mr. Hunt turned his thoughts to another object of importance. He had now arrived at the head waters of the Columbia, which were among the main points embraced by the enterprize of Mr. Astor. These upper streams were reputed to abound in beaver, and had as yet been unmolested by the white trapper. The numerous signs of beaver met with during the recent search for timber, gave evidence that the neighborhood was a good "trapping ground." Here then it was proper to begin to cast loose those leashes of hardy trappers, that are detached from trading parties, in the very heart of the wilderness. The men detached in the present instance were Alexander Carson, Louis St. Michel, Pierre Detayé, and Pierre Delaunay. Trappers generally go in pairs, that they may assist, protect and comfort each other in their lonely and perilous occupations. Thus Carson and St. Michel formed one couple, and Detayé and Delaunay another. They were fitted out with traps, arms, ammunition, horses and every other requisite, and were to trap upon the upper part of Mad river, and upon the neighboring streams of the mountains. This would probably occupy them for some months; and, when they should have collected a sufficient quantity of peltries, they

were to pack them upon their horses and make the best of their way
to the mouth of Columbia river, or to any intermediate post which
might be established by the company. They took leave of their comrades and started off on their several courses with stout hearts, and
cheerful countenances; though these lonely cruisings into a wild
and hostile wilderness seem to the uninitiated equivalent to being
cast adrift in the ship's yawl in the midst of the ocean.

Of the perils that attend the lonely trapper, the reader will have
sufficient proof, when he comes, in the after part of this work, to
learn the hard fortunes of these poor fellows in the course of their
wild peregrinations.

The trappers had not long departed, when two Snake Indians wandered into the camp. When they perceived that the strangers were
fabricating canoes, they shook their heads and gave them to understand that the river was not navigable. Their information, however,
was scoffed at by some of the party, who were obstinately bent on
embarcation, but was confirmed by the exploring party who returned
after several days absence. They had kept along the river with great
difficulty for two days, and found it a narrow, crooked, turbulent
stream, confined in a rocky channel, with many rapids, and occasionally overhung with precipices. From the summit of one of these they
had caught a bird's eye view of its boisterous career, for a great
distance, through the heart of the mountain, with impending rocks
and cliffs. Satisfied, from this view, that it was useless to follow
its course either by land or water, they had given up all further in-
vestigation.

These concurring reports determined Mr. Hunt to abandon Mad
river, and seek some more navigable stream. This determination was
concurred in by all his associates excepting Mr. Miller, who had become impatient of the fatigue of land travel, and was for immediate
embarcation at all hazards. This gentleman had been in a gloomy
and irritated state of mind for some time past, being troubled with a
bodily malady that rendered travelling on horseback extremely irksome to him, and being, moreover, discontented with having a

smaller share in the expedition than his comrades. His unreasonable objections to a further march by land were overruled, and the party prepared to decamp.

Robinson, Hoback, and Rezner, the three hunters who had hitherto served as guides among the mountains, now stepped forward, and advised Mr. Hunt to make for the post established during the preceding year by Mr. Henry, of the Missouri Fur Company. They had been with Mr. Henry, and, as far as they could judge by the neighboring landmarks, his post could not be very far off. They presumed there could be but one intervening ridge of mountains, which might be passed without any great difficulty. Henry's post, or fort, was on an upper branch of the Columbia, down which they made no doubt it would be easy to navigate in canoes.

The two Snake Indians being questioned in the matter, showed a perfect knowledge of the situation of the post, and offered, with great alacrity, to guide them to the place. Their offer was accepted, greatly to the displeasure of Mr. Miller, who seemed obstinately bent upon braving the perils of Mad river.

The weather for a few days past had been stormy; with rain and sleet. The Rocky mountains are subject to tempestuous winds from the west; these, sometimes, come in flaws or currents, making a path through the forests many yards in width, and whirling off trunks and branches to a great distance. The present storm subsided on the third of October, leaving all the surrounding heights covered with snow; for, while rain had fallen in the valley, it had snowed on the hill tops.

On the 4th, they broke up their encampment, and crossed the river, the water coming up to the girths of their horses. After travelling four miles, they encamped at the foot of the mountain, the last, as they hoped, which they should have to traverse. Four days more took them across it, and over several plains, watered by beautiful little streams, tributaries of Mad river. Near one of their encampments there was a hot spring continually emitting a cloud of vapor. These elevated plains, which give a peculiar character to the mountains, are frequented by large gangs of antelopes, fleet as the wind.

On the evening of the 8th October, after a cold wintry day, with gusts of westerly wind and flurries of snow, they arrived at the sought for post of Mr. Henry. Here he had fixed himself, after being compelled by the hostilities of the Blackfeet, to abandon the upper waters of the Missouri. The post, however, was deserted, for Mr. Henry had left it in the course of the preceding spring, and, as it afterwards appeared, had fallen in with Mr. Lisa, at the Arickara village on the Missouri, sometime after the separation of Mr. Hunt and his party.

The weary travellers gladly took possession of the deserted log huts which had formed the post, and which stood on the bank of a stream upwards of a hundred yards wide, on which they intended to embark. There being plenty of suitable timber in the neighborhood, Mr. Hunt immediately proceeded to construct canoes. As he would have to leave his horses and their accoutrements here, he determined to make this a trading post, where the trappers and hunters, to be distributed about the country, might repair; and where the traders might touch on their way through the mountains to and from the establishment at the mouth of the Columbia. He informed the two Snake Indians of this determination, and engaged them to remain in that neighborhood and take care of the horses until the white men should return, promising them ample rewards for their fidelity. It may seem a desperate chance to trust to the faith and honesty of two such vagabonds; but, as the horses would have, at all events, to be abandoned, and would otherwise become the property of the first vagrant horde that should encounter them, it was one chance in favor of their being regained.

At this place another detachment of hunters prepared to separate from the party for the purpose of trapping beaver. Three of these had already been in this neighborhood, being the veteran Robinson and his companions, Hoback and Rezner, who had accompanied Mr. Henry across the mountains, and who had been picked up by Mr. Hunt on the Missouri, on their way home to Kentucky. According to agreement they were fitted out with horses, traps, ammunition, and every thing requisite for their undertaking, and were to bring in all the peltries

they should collect, either to this trading post, or to the establishment at the mouth of Columbia river. Another hunter, of the name
of Cass, was associated with them in their enterprise. It is in this way
that small knots of trappers and hunters are distributed about the
wilderness by the fur companies, and like cranes and bitterns,
haunt its solitary streams. Robinson the Kentuckian, the veteran
of the "bloody ground," who, as has already been noted, had been
scalped by the Indians in his younger days, was the leader of this little
band. When they were about to depart, Mr. Miller called the partners together, and threw up his share in the company, declaring his
intention of joining the party of trappers.

This resolution struck every one with astonishment, Mr. Miller
being a man of education and of cultivated habits, and little fitted
for the rude life of a hunter. Besides, the precarious and slender
profits arising from such a life were beneath the prospects of one
who held a share in the general enterprise. Mr. Hunt was especially
concerned and mortified at his determination, as it was through his
advice and influence he had entered into the concern. He endeavored,
therefore, to dissuade him from this sudden resolution; representing
its rashness, and the hardships and perils to which it would expose
him. He earnestly advised him, however he might feel dissatisfied
with the enterprise, still to continue on in company until they should
reach the mouth of Columbia river. There they would meet the
expedition that was to come by sea; when, should he still feel disposed to relinquish the undertaking, Mr. Hunt pledged himself to
furnish him a passage home in one of the vessels belonging to the
company.

To all this, Miller replied abruptly, that it was useless to argue
with him, as his mind was made up. They might furnish him, or not,
as they pleased, with the necessary supplies, but he was determined
to part company here, and set off with the trappers. So saying, he
flung out of their presence without vouchsafing any further conversation.

Much as this wayward conduct gave them anxiety, the partners
saw it was in vain to remonstrate. Every attention was paid to fit him

out for his headstrong undertaking. He was provided with four horses, and all the articles he required. The two Snakes undertook to conduct him and his companions to an encampment of their tribe, lower down among the mountains, from whom they would receive information as to the best trapping grounds. After thus guiding them, the Snakes were to return to Fort Henry, as the new trading post was called, and take charge of the horses which the party would leave there, of which, after all the hunters were supplied, there remained seventy-seven. These matters being all arranged, Mr. Miller set out with his companions, under guidance of the two Snakes, on the 10th of October; and much did it grieve the friends of that gentleman to see him thus wantonly casting himself loose upon savage life. How he and his comrades feared in the wilderness, and how the Snakes acquitted themselves of their trust, respecting the horses, will hereafter appear in the course of these rambling anecdotes.

CHAPTER XXXII

WHILE the canoes were in prepara- tion, the hunters ranged about the neighborhood, but with little suc- cess. Tracks of buffaloes were to be seen in all directions, but none of a fresh date. There were some elk, but extremely wild; two only were killed. Antelopes were likewise seen, but too shy and fleet to be approached. A few beavers were taken every night, and salmon trout of a small size, so that the camp had principally to subsist upon dried buffalo meat.

On the 14th, a poor, half-naked Snake Indian, one of that forlorn caste called the Shuckers, or diggers, made his appearance at the camp. He came from some lurking place among the rocks and cliffs, and presented a picture of that famishing wretchedness to which these lonely fugitives among the mountains are sometimes reduced. Having received wherewithal to allay his hunger, he disappeared, but in the course of a day or two returned to the camp bringing with him his son, a miserable boy, still more naked and forlorn than him- self. Food was given to both; they skulked about the camp like hungry hounds, seeking what they might devour, and having gathered up the feet and entrails of some beavers that were lying about, slunk off with them to their den among the rocks.

236

By the 18th of October, fifteen canoes were completed, and on the following day the party embarked with their effects; leaving their horses grazing about the banks, and trusting to the honesty of the two Snakes, and some special turn of good luck for their future recovery.

The current bore them along at a rapid rate; the light spirits of the Canadian voyageurs, which had occasionally flagged upon land, rose to their accustomed buoyancy on finding themselves again upon the water. They wielded their paddles with their wonted dexterity, and for the first time made the mountains echo with their favorite boat songs.

In the course of the day the little squadron arrived at the confluence of Henry and Mad rivers, which, thus united, swelled into a beautiful stream of a light pea-green color, navigable for boats of any size, and which, from the place of junction, took the name of Snake river, a stream doomed to be the scene of much disaster to the travellers. The banks were here and there fringed with willow thickets and small cotton-wood trees. The weather was cold, and it snowed all day, and great flocks of ducks and geese, sporting in the water or streaming through the air, gave token that winter was at hand; yet the hearts of the travellers were light, and, as they glided down the little river, they flattered themselves with the hope of soon reaching the Columbia. After making thirty miles in a southerly direction, they encamped for the night in a neighborhood which required some little vigilance, as there were recent traces of grizzly bears among the thickets.

On the following day the river increased in width and beauty; flowing parallel to a range of mountains on the left, which at times were finely reflected in its light green waters. The three snowy summits of the Pilot Knobs or Tetons, were still seen towering in the distance. After pursuing a swift but placid course for twenty miles, the current began to foam and brawl, and assume the wild and broken character common to the streams west of the Rocky mountains. In fact the rivers which flow from those mountains to the Pacific, are essentially different from those which traverse the great prairies on their eastern declivities. The latter, though sometimes boisterous, are generally free from obstructions, and easily navigated; but the rivers to the west of the mountains descend more steeply and impetuously, and are continually liable to cascades and rapids. The latter abounded in the part of the river which the travellers were now descending. Two of the canoes filled among the breakers; the crews were saved, but much of the lading was lost or damaged, and one of the canoes drifted down the stream and was broken among the rocks.

On the following day, October 21st, they made but a short distance when they came to a dangerous strait, where the river was compressed for nearly half a mile between perpendicular rocks, reducing it to the width of twenty yards, and increasing its violence. Here they were obliged to pass the canoes down cautiously by a line from the impending banks. This consumed a great part of a day; and after they had re-embarked they were soon again impeded by rapids, when they had to unload their canoes and carry them and their cargoes for some distance by land. It is at these places, called "portages," that the Canadian voyageur exhibits his most valuable qualities; carrying heavy burdens, and toiling to and fro, on land and in the water, over rocks and precipices, among brakes and brambles, not only without a murmur, but with the greatest cheerfulness and alacrity, joking and laughing and singing scraps of old French ditties.

The spirits of the party, however, which had been elated on first varying their journeying from land to water, had now lost some of their buoyancy. Every thing ahead was wrapped in uncertainty. They knew nothing of the river on which they were floating. It had never before been navigated by a white man, nor could they meet with an Indian to give them any information concerning it. It kept on its course through a vast wilderness of silent and apparently uninhabited mountains without a savage wigwam upon its banks, or bark upon its waters. The difficulties and perils they had already passed, made them apprehend others before them, that might effectually bar their progress. As they glided onward, however, they regained heart and hope. The current continued to be strong; but it was steady, and though they met with frequent rapids, none of them were bad. Mountains were constantly to be seen in different directions, but sometimes the swift river glided through prairies, and was bordered by small cotton-wood trees and willows. These prairies at certain seasons are ranged by migratory herds of the wide-wandering buffalo, the tracks of which, though not of recent date, were frequently to be seen. Here, too, were to be found the prickly pear or Indian fig, a plant which loves a more southern climate. On the land were large flights of magpies, and American robins; whole fleets of ducks and geese navigated the river, or flew off in long streaming files at the approach of the canoes; while the frequent establishments of the pains-taking and quiet-loving beaver, showed that the solitude of these waters was rarely disturbed, even by the all-pervading savage.

They had now come near two hundred and eighty miles since leaving Fort Henry, yet without seeing a human being, or a human habitation; a wild and desert solitude extended on either side of the river, apparently almost destitute of animal life. At length, on the 24th of October, they were gladdened by the sight of some savage tents, and hastened to land, and visit them, for they were anxious to procure information to guide them on their route. On their approach, however, the savages fled in consternation. They proved to be a wandering band of Shoshonies. In their tents were great quantities of small fish about two inches long, together with roots and seeds, or grain, which they were drying for winter provisions. They appeared to be destitute of tools of any kind, yet there were bows and arrows very well made; the former were formed of pine, cedar or bone, strengthened by sinews, and the latter of the wood of rose bushes, and other crooked plants, but carefully straightened, and tipped with stone of a bottle-green color.

There were also vessels of willow and grass, so closely wrought as to hold water, and a seine neatly made with meshes, in the ordinary manner, of the fibres of wild flax or nettle. The humble effects of the poor savages remained unmolested by their visiters, and a few small articles, with a knife or two, were left in the camp, and were no doubt regarded as invaluable prizes.

Shortly after leaving this deserted camp, and re-embarking in the canoes, the travellers met with three of the Snakes on a triangular raft made of flags or reeds; such was their rude mode of navigating the river. They were entirely naked excepting small mantles of hare skins over their shoulders. The canoes approached near enough to gain a full view of them, but they were not to be brought to a parley.

All further progress for the day was barred by a fall in the river of about thirty feet perpendicular; at the head of which the party encamped for the night.

The next day was one of excessive toil and but little progress: the river winding through a wild rocky country, and being interrupted by frequent rapids, among which the canoes were in great peril. On the succeeding day they again visited a camp of wandering Snakes, but the inhabitants fled with terror at the sight of a fleet of canoes, filled with white men, coming down their solitary river.

As Mr. Hunt was extremely anxious to gain information concerning his route, he endeavored by all kinds of friendly signs to entice back the fugitives. At length one, who was on horseback, ventured back with fear and trembling. He was better clad, and in better condition than most of his vagrant tribe that Mr. Hunt had yet seen. The chief object of his return appeared to be to intercede for a quantity of dried meat and salmon trout, which he had left behind; on which, probably, he depended for his winter's subsistence. The poor wretch approached with hesitation, the alternate dread of famine and of white men operating upon his mind. He made the most abject signs, imploring Mr. Hunt not to carry off his food. The latter tried in every way to reassure him, and offered him knives in exchange for his provisions; great as was the temptation, the poor Snake could only prevail upon himself to spare a part; keeping a feverish watch over the rest, lest it should be taken away. It was in vain Mr. Hunt made inquiries of him concerning his route, and the course of the river. The Indian was too much frightened and bewildered to comprehend him or to reply; he did nothing but alternately commend himself to the protection of the Good Spirit, and supplicate

Mr. Hunt not to take away his fish and buffalo meat; and in this
state they left him, trembling about his treasures.

In the course of that and the next day they made nearly eighty
miles; the river inclining to the south of west, and being clear and
beautiful, nearly half a mile in width, with many populous commu-
nities of the beaver along its banks. The 28th of October, however, was a day of disaster. The river again become rough and impetuous, and was chafed and broken by numerous rapids. These grew
more and more dangerous, and the utmost skill was required to
steer among them. Mr. Crooks was seated in the second canoe of the
squadron, and had an old experienced Canadian for steersman,
named Antoine Clappine, one of the most valuable of the voyageurs.
The leading canoe had glided safely among the turbulent and roaring surges, but in following it, Mr. Crooks perceived that his canoe
was bearing towards a rock. He called out to the steersman, but his
warning voice was either unheard or unheeded. In the next moment
they struck upon the rock. The canoe was split and overturned. There
were five persons on board. Mr. Crooks and one of his companions
were thrown amidst roaring breakers and a whirling current, but
succeeded, by strong swimming, to reach the shore. Clappine and
two others clung to the shattered bark, and drifted with it to a rock.
The wreck struck the rock with one end, and swinging round flung
poor Clappine off into the raging stream, which swept him away, and
he perished. His comrades succeeded in getting upon the rock, from
whence they were afterwards taken off.

This disastrous event brought the whole squadron to a halt, and
struck a chill into every bosom. Indeed, they had arrived at a terrific strait, that forbade all further progress in the canoes, and dismayed the most experienced voyageur. The whole body of the river
was compressed into a space of less than thirty feet in width, between two ledges of rocks, upwards of two hundred feet high, and
formed a whirling and tumultuous vortex, so frightfully agitated, as
to receive the name of "The Caldron Linn." Beyond this fearful
abyss, the river kept raging and roaring on, until lost to sight among
impending precipices.

CHAPTER XXXIII

Mr. Hunt and his companions en-
camped upon the borders of the Caldron Linn, and held gloomy
council as to their future course. The recent wreck had dismayed even
the voyageurs, and the fate of their popular comrade, Clappine, one of
the most adroit and experienced of their fraternity, had struck sor-
row to their hearts, for, with all their levity, these thoughtless beings
have great kindness towards each other.

The whole distance they had navigated since leaving Henry's fort,
was computed to be about three hundred and forty miles; strong
apprehensions were now entertained that the tremendous impediments before them would oblige them to abandon their canoes. It
was determined to send exploring parties on each side of the river,
to ascertain whether it was possible to navigate it further. Accordingly, on the following morning three men were despatched along
the south bank, while Mr. Hunt and three others proceeded along
the north. The two parties returned after a weary scramble among
swamp, rocks, and precipices, and with very disheartening accounts.
For nearly forty miles that they had explored, the river foamed and
roared along through a deep and narrow channel, from twenty to
thirty yards wide, which it had worn, in the course of ages, through

the heart of a barren rocky country. The precipices on each side, were often two and three hundred feet high, sometimes perpendicular and sometimes overhanging, so that it was impossible, excepting in one or two places, to get down to the margin of the stream. This dreary strait was rendered the more dangerous by frequent rapids, and occasionally perpendicular falls from ten to forty feet in height; so that it seemed almost hopeless to attempt to pass the canoes down it. The party, however, who had explored the south side of the river had found a place, about six miles from the camp, where they thought it possible the canoes might be carried down the bank and launched upon the stream, and from whence they might make their way with the aid of occasional portages. Four of the best canoes were accordingly selected for the experiment, and were transported to the place on the shoulders of sixteen of the men. At the same time, Mr. Reed the clerk, and three men, were detached to explore the river still further down than the previous scouting parties had been, and at the same time to look out for Indians from whom provisions might be obtained, and a supply of horses, should it be found necessary to proceed by land.

The party who had been sent with the canoes returned on the following day, weary and dejected. One of the canoes had been swept away with all the weapons and effects of four of the voyageurs, in attempting to pass it down a rapid by means of a line. The other three had stuck fast among the rocks, so that it was impossible to move them; the men returned, therefore, in despair, and declared the river unnavigable.

The situation of the unfortunate travellers was now gloomy in the extreme. They were in the heart of an unknown wilderness, untraversed as yet by a white man. They were at a loss what route to take, and how far they were from the ultimate place of their destination, nor could they meet, in these uninhabited wilds, with any human being to give them information. The repeated accidents to their canoes had reduced their stock of provisions to five days allowance, and there was now every appearance of soon having famine added to their other sufferings.

This last circumstance rendered it more perilous to keep together than to separate. Accordingly, after a little anxious but bewildered council, it was determined that several small detachments should start off in different directions, headed by the several partners. Should any of them succeed in falling in with friendly Indians, within a reasonable distance, and obtaining a supply of provisions and horses, they were to return to the aid of the main body: otherwise, they were to shift for themselves, and shape their course according to circumstances; keeping the mouth of Columbia river as the ultimate point of their wayfaring. Accordingly, three several parties set off from the camp at Caldron Linn, in opposite directions. Mr. M'Lellan, with three men, kept down along the bank of the river. Mr. Crooks, with five others, turned their steps up it; retracing by land the weary course they had made by water, intending, should they not find relief nearer at hand, to keep on until they should reach Henry's fort, where they hoped to find the horses they had left there, and to return with them to the main body.

The third party, composed of five men, was headed by Mr. M'Kenzie, who struck to the northward, across the desert plains, in hopes of coming upon the main stream of the Columbia.

Having seen these three adventurous bands depart upon their forlorn expeditions, Mr. Hunt turned his thoughts to provide for the subsistence of the main body left to his charge, and to prepare for their future march. There remained with him thirty-one men, beside the squaw and two children of Pierre Dorion. There was no game to be met with in the neighborhood; but beavers were occasionally trapped about the river banks, which afforded a scanty supply of food; in the meantime they comforted themselves that some one or other of the foraging detachments would be successful, and return with relief.

Mr. Hunt now set to work with all diligence, to prepare *caches*, in which to deposit the baggage and merchandize, of which it would be necessary to disburthen themselves, preparatory to their weary march by land; and here we shall give a brief description of those contrivances, so noted in the wilderness.

A cache is a term common among traders and hunters, to designate a hiding place for provisions and effects. It is derived from the French word *cacher*, to conceal, and originated among the early colonists of Canada and Louisiana; but the secret depository which it designates was in use among the aboriginals long before the intrusion of the white men. It is, in fact, the only mode that migratory hordes have of preserving their valuables from robbery, during their long absences from their villages or accustomed haunts, on hunting expeditions, or during the vicissitudes of war. The utmost skill and caution are required to render these places of concealment invisible to the lynx eye of an Indian. The first care is to seek out a proper situation, which is generally some dry low bank of clay, on the margin of a water course. As soon as the precise spot is pitched upon, blankets, saddle cloths, and other coverings, are spread over the surrounding grass and bushes, to prevent foot tracks, or any other derangement; and as few hands as possible are employed. A circle of about two feet in diameter is then nicely cut in the sod, which is carefully removed, with the loose soil immediately beneath it, and laid aside in a place where it will be safe from any thing that may change its appearance. The uncovered area is then digged perpendicularly to the depth of about three feet, and is then gradually widened so as to form a conical chamber six or seven feet deep. The whole of the earth displaced by this process, being of a different color from that on the surface, is handed up in a vessel, and heaped into a skin or cloth, in which it is conveyed to the stream and thrown into the midst of the current, that it may be entirely carried off. Should the cache not be formed in the vicinity of a stream, the earth thus thrown up is carried to a distance, and scattered in such manner as not to leave the minutest trace. The cave being formed, is well lined with dry grass, bark, sticks, and poles, and occasionally a dried hide. The property intended to be hidden is then laid in, after having been well aired: a hide is spread over it, and dried grass, brush, and stones, thrown in, and trampled down until the pit is filled to the neck. The loose soil, which had been put aside, is then brought, and rammed down firmly, to prevent its caving in, and is frequently sprinkled with water, to destroy the scent, lest the wolves and bears should be attracted to the place, and root up the concealed treasure. When the neck of the cache is nearly level with the surrounding surface, the sod is again fitted in with the utmost exactness, and any bushes, stocks, or stones, that may have originally been about the spot, are restored to their former places. The blankets and other coverings are then removed from the surrounding herbage: all tracks are obliterated: the grass is gently raised by the hand to its natural position, and the minutest chip or straw is scrupulously gleaned up and thrown into the stream. After all is done, the place is abandoned for the night, and, if all be right next morning, is not visited again, until there be a necessity for re-opening the cache. Four men are sufficient in this way, to conceal the amount of three tons weight of provisions or merchandize, in the course of two days. Nine caches were required to contain the goods and baggage which Mr. Hunt found it necessary to leave at this place.

Three days had been thus employed since the departure of the several detachments, when that of Mr. Crooks unexpectedly made its appearance. A momentary joy was diffused through the camp, for they supposed succor to be at hand. It was soon dispelled. Mr. Crooks and his companions had become completely disheartened by this retrograde march through a bleak and barren country; and had found, computing from their progress and the accumulating difficulties besetting every step, that it would be impossible to reach Henry's fort, and return to the main body in the course of the winter. They had determined, therefore, to rejoin their comrades, and share their lot.

One avenue of hope was thus closed upon the anxious sojourners at the Caldron Linn; their main expectation of relief was now from the two parties under Reed and M'Lellan, which had proceeded down the river; for, as to Mr. M'Kenzie's detachment, which had struck across the plains, they thought it would have sufficient difficulty in struggling forward through the trackless wilderness. For five days they continued to support themselves by trapping and fishing. Some fish of tolerable size were speared at night by the light of cedar torches; others, that were very small, were caught in nets with fine meshes. The product of their fishing, however, was very scanty. Their trapping was also precarious; and the tails and bellies of the beavers were dried and put by for the journey.

At length, two of the companions of Mr. Reed returned, and were hailed with the most anxious eagerness. Their report served but to increase the general despondency. They had followed Mr. Reed for some distance below the point to which Mr. Hunt had explored, but had met with no Indians, from whom to obtain information and relief. The river still presented the same furious aspect, brawling and boiling along a narrow and rugged channel, between rocks that rose like walls.

A lingering hope, which had been indulged by some of the party, of proceeding by water, was now finally given up: the long and terrific strait of the river set all further progress at defiance, and in their disgust at the place, and their vexation at the disasters sustained there, they gave it the indignant, though not very decorous appellation, of the Devil's Scuttle Hole.

CHAPTER XXXIV

DETERMINATION OF THE PARTY TO PROCEED ON FOOT—DREARY
DESERTS BETWEEN SNAKE RIVER AND THE COLUMBIA—DISTRIBU-
TION OF EFFECTS PREPARATORY TO A MARCH—DIVISION OF THE
PARTY—RUGGED MARCH ALONG THE RIVER—WILD AND BROKEN
SCENERY—SHOSHONIES—ALARM OF A SNAKE ENCAMPMENT—IN-
TERCOURSE WITH THE SNAKES—HORSE DEALING—VALUE OF A TIN
KETTLE—SUFFERINGS FROM THIRST—A HORSE RECLAIMED—FORTI-
TUDE OF AN INDIAN WOMAN—SCARCITY OF FOOD—DOG'S FLESH
A DAINTY—NEWS OF MR. CROOKS AND HIS PARTY—PAINFUL
TRAVELLING AMONG THE MOUNTAINS—SNOW STORMS—A DREARY
MOUNTAIN PROSPECT—A BIVOUACK DURING A WINTRY NIGHT—RE-
TURN TO THE RIVER BANK

THE resolution of Mr. Hunt and his
companions was now taken to set out immediately on foot. As to the
other detachments that had in a manner gone forth to seek their fortunes, there was little chance of their return; they would probably
make their own way through the wilderness. At any rate, to linger in
the vague hope of relief from them, would be to run the risk of perishing with hunger. Besides, the winter was rapidly advancing, and
they had a long journey to make through an unknown country, where
all kinds of perils might await them. They were yet, in fact, a thousand miles from Astoria, but the distance was unknown to them at
the time: every thing before and around them was vague and con-
jectural, and wore an aspect calculated to inspire despondency.

In abandoning the river, they would have to launch forth upon
vast trackless plains destitute of all means of subsistence, where they

might perish of hunger and thirst. A dreary desert of sand and gravel extends from Snake river almost to the Columbia. Here and there is a thin and scanty herbage, insufficient for the pasturage of horse or buffalo. Indeed these treeless wastes between the Rocky mountains and the Pacific, are even more desolate and barren than the naked, upper prairies on the Atlantic side; they present vast desert tracts that must ever defy cultivation, and interpose dreary and thirsty wilds between the habitations of man, in traversing which, the wanderer will often be in danger of perishing.

Seeing the hopeless character of these wastes, Mr. Hunt and his companions determined to keep along the course of the river, where they would always have water at hand and would be able occasionally to procure fish, and beaver, and might perchance meet with Indians, from whom they could obtain provisions.

They now made their final preparations for the march. All their remaining stock of provisions consisted of forty pounds of Indian corn, twenty pounds of grease, about five pounds of portable soup, and a sufficient quantity of dried meat to allow each man a pittance of five pounds and a quarter, to be reserved for emergencies. This being properly distributed, they deposited all their goods and superfluous articles in the caches, taking nothing with them but what was indispensible to the journey. With all their management, each man had to carry twenty pound's weight beside his own articles and equipments.

That they might have the better chance of procuring subsistence in the scanty regions they were to traverse, they divided their party into two bands, Mr. Hunt, with eighteen men beside Pierre Dorion and his family, was to proceed down the north side of the river, while Mr. Crooks with eighteen men, kept along the south side.

On the morning of the 9th of October, the two parties separated and set forth on their several courses. Mr. Hunt and his companions followed along the right bank of the river, which made its way far below them, brawling at the foot of perpendicular precipices of solid rock, two and three hundred feet high. For twenty-eight miles that they travelled this day, they found it impossible to get down to the margin of the stream. At the end of this distance they encamped for the night at a place which admitted a scrambling descent. It was with the greatest difficulty, however, that they succeeded in getting up a kettle of water from the river for the use of the camp. As some rain had fallen in the afternoon, they passed the night under the shelter of the rocks.

The next day they continued thirty-two miles to the northwest, keeping along the river, which still ran in its deep cut channel. Here and there a sandy beach or a narrow strip of soil, fringed with dwarf willows, would extend for a little distance along the foot of the cliffs, and sometimes a reach of still water would intervene like a smooth mirror between the foaming rapids.

As through the preceding day, they journeyed on without finding, except in one instance, any place where they could get down to the river's edge, and they were fain to allay the thirst caused by hard travelling, with the water collected in the hollow of the rocks.

In the course of their march on the following morning, they fell into a beaten horse path leading along the river, which showed that they were in the neighborhood of some Indian village or encampment. They had not proceeded far along it, when they met with two Shoshonies, or Snakes. They approached with some appearance of uneasiness, and accosting Mr. Hunt, held up a knife, which by signs they let him know they had received from some of the white men of the advance parties. It was with some difficulty that Mr. Hunt prevailed upon one of the savages to conduct him to the lodges of his people. Striking into a trail or path which led up from the river, he guided them for some distance in the prairie, until they came in sight of a number of lodges made of straw, and shaped like hay stacks. Their approach, as on former occasions, caused the wildest affright among the inhabitants. The women hid such of their children as were too large to be carried, and too small to take care of themselves, under straw, and clasping their infants to their breasts, fled across the prairie. The men awaited the approach of the strangers, but evidently in great alarm.

Mr. Hunt entered the lodges, and, as he was looking about, ob-

served where the children were concealed; their black eyes glistening
like those of snakes, from beneath the straw. He lifted up the cover-
ing to look at them; the poor little beings were horribly frightened,
and their fathers' stood trembling, as if a beast of prey were about
to pounce upon the brood.

The friendly manner of Mr. Hunt soon dispelled these apprehensions; he succeeded in purchasing some excellent dried salmon, and
a dog, an animal much esteemed as food, by the natives; and when
he returned to the river one of the Indians accompanied him. He
now came to where lodges were frequent along the banks, and, after
a day's journey of twenty-six miles to the northwest, encamped in a
populous neighborhood. Forty or fifty of the natives soon visited
the camp, conducting themselves in a very amicable manner. They
were well clad, and all had buffalo robes, which they procured from
some of the hunting tribes in exchange for salmon. Their habitations
were very comfortable; each had its pile of wormwood at the door
for fuel, and within was abundance of salmon, some fresh, but the
greater part cured. When the white men visited the lodges, however,
the women and children hid themselves through fear. Among the
supplies obtained here were two dogs, on which our travellers break-
fasted, and found them to be very excellent, well-flavored, and hearty
food.

In the course of the three following days, they made about sixty-
three miles, generally in a north-west direction. They met with many
of the natives in their straw-built cabins who received them without
alarm. About their dwellings were immense quantities of the heads
and skins of salmon, the best parts of which had been cured, and
hidden in the ground. The women were badly clad; the children
worse; their garments were buffalo robes, or the skins of foxes, wolves,
hares and badgers, and sometimes the skins of ducks, sewed together,
with the plumage on. Most of the skins must have been procured by
traffic with other tribes, or in distant hunting excursions, for the
naked prairies in the neighborhood afforded few animals, excepting
horses, which were abundant. There were signs of buffaloes having
been there, but a long time before.

On the 15th of November, they made twenty-eight miles along the river which was entirely free from rapids. The shores were lined with dead salmon, which tainted the whole atmosphere. The natives whom they met spoke of Mr. Reed's party having passed through that neighborhood. In the course of the day Mr. Hunt saw a few horses, but the owners of them took care to hurry them out of the way. All the provisions they were able to procure, were two dogs and a salmon. On the following day they were still worse off, having to subsist on parched corn, and the remains of their dried meat. The river this day had resumed its turbulent character, forcing its way through a narrow channel between steep rocks, and down violent rapids. They made twenty miles over a rugged road, gradually approaching a mountain in the northwest, covered with snow, which had been in sight for three days past.

On the 17th, they met with several Indians, one of whom had a horse. Mr. Hunt was extremely desirous of obtaining it as a pack horse; for the men, worn down by fatigue and hunger, found the loads of twenty pound's weight which they had to carry, daily growing heavier and more galling. The Indians, however, along this river, were never willing to part with their horses, having none to spare. The owner of the steed in question seemed proof against all temptation; article after article of great value in Indian eyes was offered and refused. The charms of an old tin kettle, however, were irresistible, and a bargain was concluded.

A great part of the following morning was consumed in lightening the packages of the men and arranging the load for the horse. At this encampment there was no wood for fuel, even the wormwood on which they had frequently depended, having disappeared. For the two last days they had made thirty miles to the northwest.

On the 19th of November, Mr. Hunt was lucky enough to purchase another horse for his own use, giving in exchange a tomahawk, a knife, a fire steel, and some beads and gartering. In an evil hour, however, he took the advice of the Indians to abandon the river, and follow a road or trail, leading into the prairies. He soon had cause to repent the change. The road led across a dreary waste, without verdure; and where there was neither fountain, nor pool, nor running stream. The men now began to experience the torments of thirst, aggravated by their usual diet of dried fish. The thirst of the Canadian voyageurs became so insupportable as to drive them to the most revolting means of allaying it. For twenty-five miles did they toil on across this dismal desert, and laid themselves down at night, parched and disconsolate, beside their wormwood fires; looking forward to still greater sufferings on the following day. Fortunately it began to rain in the night, to their infinite relief; the water soon collected in puddles and afforded them delicious draughts.

Refreshed in this manner, they resumed their wayfaring as soon as the first streaks of dawn gave light enough for them to see their path. The rain continued all day so that they no longer suffered from thirst, but hunger took its place, for, after travelling thirty-three miles they had nothing to sup on but a little parched corn.

The next day brought them to the banks of a beautiful little stream, running to the west, and fringed with groves of cottonwood and willow. On its borders was an Indian camp, with a great many horses grazing around it. The inhabitants, too, appeared to be better clad than usual. The scene was altogether a cheering one to the poor half-famished wanderers. They hastened to the lodges, but on arriving at them, met with a check that at first dampened their cheerfulness. An Indian immediately laid claim to the horse of Mr. Hunt, saying that it had been stolen from him. There was no disproving a fact, supported by numerous bystanders, and which the horse stealing habits of the Indians rendered but too probable; so Mr. Hunt relinquished his steed to the claimant; not being able to retain him by a second purchase.

At this place they encamped for the night and made a sumptuous repast upon fish and a couple of dogs, procured from their Indian neighbors. The next day they kept along the river, but came to a halt after ten miles march, on account of the rain. Here they again got a supply of fish and dogs from the natives; and two of the men were fortunate enough each to get a horse in exchange for a buffalo robe. One of these men was Pierre Dorion, the half-breed interpreter, to whose suffering family the horse was a most timely acquisition. And here we cannot but notice the wonderful patience, perseverance and hardihood of the Indian women, as exemplified in the conduct of the poor squaw of the interpreter. She was now far advanced in her pregnancy, and had two children to take care of; one four, and the other two years of age. The latter of course she had frequently to carry on her back, in addition to the burthen usually imposed upon the squaw, yet she had borne all her hardships without a murmur and throughout this weary and painful journey, had kept pace with the best of the pedestrians. Indeed on various occasions in the course of this enterprise, she displayed a force of character that won the respect and applause of the white men.

Mr. Hunt endeavored to gather some information from these Indians concerning the country, and the course of the rivers. His communications with them had to be by signs, and a few words which he had learnt, and of course were extremely vague. All that he could learn from them was, that the great river, the Columbia, was still far distant, but he could ascertain nothing as to the route he ought to take to arrive at it. For the two following days they continued westward upward of forty miles along the little stream, until they crossed it just before its junction with Snake river, which they found still running to the north. Before them was a wintry looking mountain covered with snow on all sides.

In three days more they made about seventy miles; fording two small rivers, the waters of which were very cold. Provisions were extremely scarce; their chief sustenance was portable soup; a meagre diet for weary pedestrians.

On the 27th of November the river led them into the mountains through a rocky defile where there was scarcely room to pass. They were frequently obliged to unload the horses to get them by the narrow places; and sometimes to wade through the water in getting round rocks and butting cliffs. All their food this day was a beaver which they had caught the night before; by evening, the cravings of hunger were so sharp, and the prospect of any supply among the mountains so faint, that they had to kill one of the horses. "The men," says Mr. Hunt, in his journal, "find the meat very good, and indeed, so should I, were it not for the attachment I have to the animal."

Early in the following day, after proceeding ten miles to the north, they came to two lodges of Shoshonies: who seemed in nearly as great an extremity as themselves, having just killed two horses for food. They had no other provisions excepting the seed of a weed which they gather in great quantities, and pound fine. It resembles hemp seed. Mr. Hunt purchased a bag of it and also some small pieces of horse flesh which he began to relish, pronouncing them "fat and tender."

From these Indians he received information that several white men had gone down the river, some one side, and a good many on the other; these last he concluded to be Mr. Crooks and his party. He was thus released from much anxiety about their safety, especially as the Indians spoke of Mr. Crooks having one of his dogs yet, which showed that he and his men had not been reduced to extremity of hunger.

As Mr. Hunt feared that he might be several days in passing through this mountain defile, and run the risk of famine, he encamped in the neighborhood of the Indians, for the purpose of bartering with them for a horse. The evening was expended in ineffectual trials. He offered a gun, a buffalo robe, and various other articles. The poor fellows had, probably, like himself, the fear of starvation before their eyes. At length the women, learning the object of his pressing solicitations, and tempting offers, set up such a terrible hue and cry, that he was fairly howled and scolded from the ground.

The next morning early, the Indians seemed very desirous to get rid of their visiters, fearing, probably for the safety of their horses. In reply to Mr. Hunt's enquiries about the mountains, they told him that he would have to sleep but three nights more among them; and that six days travelling would take him to the falls of the Columbia; information in which he put no faith, believing it was only given to induce him to set forward. These, he was told, were the last Snakes he would meet with, and that he would soon come to a nation called Sciatogas.

Forward then did he proceed on his tedious journey, which, at every step grew more painful. The road continued for two days, through narrow defiles, where they were repeatedly obliged to unload the horses. Sometimes the river passed through such rocky chasms and under such steep precipices that they had to leave it, and make their way, with excessive labor, over immense hills, almost impassable for horses. On some of these hills were a few pine trees, and their summits were covered with snow. On the second day of this scramble one of the hunters killed a black-tailed deer, which afforded the half-starved travellers a sumptuous repast. Their progress these two days was twenty-eight miles, a little to the northward of east.

The month of December set in drearily, with rain in the vallies, and snow upon the hills. They had to climb a mountain with snow to the midleg, which increased their painful toil. A small beaver supplied them with a scanty meal, which they eked out with frozen blackberries, haws, and chokecherries, which they found in the course of their scramble. Their journey this day, though excessively fatiguing, was but thirteen miles; and all the next day they had to remain encamped, not being able to see half a mile ahead, on account of a snow storm. Having nothing else to eat, they were compelled to kill another of their horses. The next day they resumed their march in snow and rain, but with all their efforts could only get forward nine miles, having for a part of the distance to unload the horses and carry the packs themselves. On the succeeding morning they were obliged to leave the river, and scramble up the hills. From the summit of these, they got a wide view of the surrounding country, and it was a prospect almost sufficient to make them despair. In every direction they beheld snowy mountains, partially sprinkled with pines and other evergreens, and spreading a desert and toilsome world around them. The wind howled over the bleak and wintry landscape, and seemed to penetrate to the marrow of their bones. They waded on through the snow which at every step was more than knee deep.

After toiling in this way all day, they had the mortification to find that they were but four miles distant from the encampment of the preceding night, such was the meandering of the river among these dismal hills. Pinched with famine, exhausted with fatigue, with evening approaching, and a wintry wild still lengthening as they advanced; they began to look forward with sad forebodings to the night's exposure upon this frightful waste. Fortunately they succeeded in reaching a cluster of pines about sunset. Their axes were immediately at work; they cut down trees, piled them up in great heaps, and soon had huge fires "to cheer their cold and hungry hearts."

About three o'clock in the morning it again began to snow, and at daybreak they found themselves, as it were, in a cloud; scarcely being able to distinguish objects at the distance of a hundred yards. Guiding themselves by the sound of running water, they set out for the river, and by slipping and sliding contrived to get down to its bank. One of the horses, missing his footing, rolled down several hundred yards with his load, but sustained no injury. The weather in the valley was less rigorous than on the hills. The snow lay but ankle deep, and there was a quiet rain now falling. After creeping along for six miles, they encamped on the border of the river. Being utterly destitute of provisions, they were again compelled to kill one of their horses to appease their famishing hunger.

CHAPTER XXXV

THE wanderers had now accom-
plished four hundred and seventy-two miles of their dreary journey since leaving the Caldron Linn, how much further they had yet
to travel, and what hardships to encounter, no one knew.

On the morning of the 6th of December, they left their dismal
encampment, but had scarcely begun their march, when, to their
surprise, they beheld a party of white men coming up along the
opposite bank of the river. As they drew nearer, they were recognised for Mr. Crooks and his companions. When they came opposite, and could make themselves heard across the murmuring of
the river, their first cry was for food; in fact, they were almost
starved. Mr. Hunt immediately returned to the camp, and had a
kind of canoe made out of the skin of the horse, killed on the preceding night. This was done after the Indian fashion, by drawing
up the edges of the skin with thongs, and keeping them distended
by sticks or thwarts pieces. In this frail bark, Sardepie, one of the
Canadians, carried over a portion of the flesh of the horse to the
famishing party on the opposite side of the river, and brought back
with him Mr. Crooks, and the Canadian, Le Clerc. The forlorn and

wasted looks, and starving condition of these two men, struck dismay to the hearts of Mr. Hunt's followers. They had been accustomed to each other's appearance, and to the gradual operation of hunger and hardship upon their frames, but the change in the looks of these men, since last they parted, was a type of the famine and desolation of the land; and they now began to indulge the horrible presentiment that they would all starve together, or be reduced to the direful alternative of casting lots!

When Mr. Crooks had appeased his hunger, he gave Mr. Hunt some account of his wayfaring. On the side of the river, along which he had kept, he had met with but few Indians, and those were too miserably poor to yield much assistance. For the first eighteen days, after leaving the Caldron Linn, he and his men had been confined to half a meal in twenty-four hours; for three days following, they had subsisted on a single beaver, a few wild cherries, and the soles of old moccasins, and for the last six days, their only animal food had been the carcass of a dog. They had been three days' journey further down the river than Mr. Hunt, always keeping as near to its banks as possible, and frequently climbing over sharp and rocky ridges that projected into the stream. At length they had arrived to where the mountains increased in height, and came closer to the river, with perpendicular precipices, which rendered it impossible to keep along the stream. The river here rushed with incredible velocity through a defile not more than thirty yards wide, where cascades and rapids succeeded each other almost without intermission. Even had the opposite banks, therefore, been such as to permit a continuance of their journey, it would have been madness to attempt to pass the tumultuous current, either on rafts or otherwise. Still bent, however, on pushing forward, they attempted to climb the opposing mountains; and struggled on through the snow for half a day until, coming to where they could command a prospect, they found that they were not half way to the summit, and that mountain upon mountain lay piled beyond them, in wintry desolation. Famished and emaciated as they were, to continue forward would be to perish; their only chance seemed to be to regain the river, and retrace their steps up its banks. It was in this forlorn and retrograde march that they had met with Mr. Hunt and his party.

Mr. Crooks also gave information of some others of their fellow adventurers. He had spoken several days previously with Mr. Reed and Mr. M'Kenzie, who with their men were on the opposite side of the river, where it was impossible to get over to them. They informed him that Mr. M'Lellan had struck across from the little river above the mountains, in the hope of falling in with some of the tribe of Flatheads, who inhabit the western skirts of the Rocky range. As the companions of Reed and M'Kenzie were picked men, and had found provisions more abundant on their side of the river, they were in better condition, and more fitted to contend with the difficulties of the country, than those of Mr. Crooks, and when he lost sight of them, were pushing onward, down the course of the river.

Mr. Hunt took a night to revolve over his critical situation, and to determine what was to be done. No time was to be lost; he had twenty men and more, in his own party, to provide for, and Mr. Crooks and his men to relieve. To linger would be to starve. The idea of retracing his steps was intolerable, and, notwithstanding all the discouraging accounts of the ruggedness of the mountains lower down the river, he would have been disposed to attempt them, but the depth of the snow with which they were covered, deterred him; having already experienced the impossibility of forcing his way against such an impediment.

The only alternative, therefore, appeared to be, to return and seek the Indian bands scattered along the small rivers above the mountains. Perhaps, from some of these he might procure horses enough to support him until he could reach the Columbia; for he still cherished the hope of arriving at that river in the course of the winter, though he was apprehensive that few of Mr. Crooks' party would be sufficiently strong to follow him. Even in adopting this course, he had to make up his mind to the certainty of several days of famine at the outset, for it would take that time to reach the

last Indian lodges from which he had parted, and until they should
arrive there, his people would have nothing to subsist upon but
haws and wild berries, excepting one miserable horse, which was
little better than skin and bone.

After a night of sleepless cogitation, Mr. Hunt announced to his
men the dreary alternative he had adopted, and preparations were
made to take Mr. Crooks and Le Clerc across the river, with the remainder of the meat, as the other party were to keep up along the
opposite bank. The skin canoe had unfortunately been lost in the
night, a raft was constructed, therefore, after the manner of the natives, of bundles of willows, but it could not be floated across the
impetuous current. The men were directed, in consequence, to
keep on along the river by themselves, while Mr. Crooks and Le
Clerc would proceed with Mr. Hunt. They all, then, took up their
retrograde march with drooping spirits.

In a little while, it was found that Mr. Crooks and Le Clerc were
so feeble as to walk with difficulty, so that Mr. Hunt was obliged to
retard his pace, that they might keep up with him. His men grew
impatient at the delay. They murmured that they had a long and
desolate region to traverse, before they could arrive at the point
where they might expect to find horses; that it was impossible for
Crooks and Le Clerc, in their feeble condition, to get over it; that
to remain with them would only be to starve in their company.
They importuned Mr. Hunt, therefore, to leave these unfortunate
men to their fate, and think only of the safety of himself and his
party. Finding him not to be moved, either by entreaties or their
clamors, they began to proceed without him, singly and in parties.
Among those who thus went off was Pierre Dorion, the interpreter.
Pierre owned the only remaining horse; which was now a mere skeleton. Mr. Hunt had suggested, in their present extremity, that it
should be killed for food; to which the half-breed flatly refused
his assent, and cudgelling the miserable animal forward, pushed on
sullenly, with the air of a man doggedly determined to quarrel for
his right. In this way Mr. Hunt saw his men, one after another,
break away, until but five remained to bear him company.

On the following morning, another raft was made, on which Mr. Crooks and Le Clerc again attempted to ferry themselves across the river, but after repeated trials, had to give up in despair. This caused additional delay: after which, they continued to crawl forward at a snail's pace. Some of the men who had remained with Mr. Hunt now became impatient of these incumbrances, and urged him, clamorously, to push forward, crying out that they should all starve. The night which succeeded was intensely cold, so that one of the men was severely frost-bitten. In the course of the night, Mr. Crooks was taken ill, and in the morning was still more incompetent to travel. Their situation was now desperate, for their stock of provisions was reduced to three beaver skins. Mr. Hunt, therefore, resolved to push on, overtake his people, and insist upon having the horse of Pierre Dorion sacrificed for the relief of all hands. Accordingly, he left two of his men to help Crooks and Le Clerc on their way, giving them two of the beaver skins for their support; the remaining skin he retained, as provision for himself and the three other men who struck forward with him.

CHAPTER XXXVI

ALL that day, Mr. Hunt and his
three comrades travelled without eating. At night they made a tantalizing supper on their beaver skin, and were nearly starved with
hunger and cold. The next day, December 10th, they overtook the
advance party, who were all as much famished as themselves,
some of them not having eaten since the morning of the seventh.
Mr. Hunt now proposed the sacrifice of Pierre Dorion's skeleton
horse. Here he again met with positive and vehement opposition
from the half-breed, who was too sullen and vindictive a fellow to
be easily dealt with. What was singular, the men, though suffering
such pinching hunger, interfered in favor of the horse. They represented, that it was better to keep on as long as possible without re-
sorting to this last resource. Possibly the Indians, of whom they
were in quest, might have shifted their encampment, in which case
it would be time enough to kill the horse to escape starvation.
Mr. Hunt, therefore, was prevailed upon to grant Pierre Dorion's
horse a reprieve.

Fortunately, they had not proceeded much further, when, towards evening, they came in sight of a lodge of Shoshonies, with a number of horses grazing around it. The sight was as unexpected as it was joyous. Having seen no Indians in this neighborhood as they passed down the river; they must have subsequently come out from among the mountains. Mr. Hunt, who first descried them, checked the eagerness of his companions, knowing the unwillingness of these Indians to part with their horses, and their aptness to hurry them off and conceal them, in case of alarm. This was no time to risk such a disappointment. Approaching, therefore, stealthily and silently, they came upon the savages by surprise, who fled in terror. Five of their horses were eagerly seized, and one was despatched upon the spot. The carcass was immediately cut up, and a part of it hastily cooked and ravenously devoured. A man was now sent on horseback with a supply of the flesh to Mr. Crooks and his companions. He reached them in the night: they were so famished that the supply sent them seemed but to aggravate their hunger, and they were almost tempted to kill and eat the horse that had brought the messenger. Availing themselves of the assistance of the animal, they reached the camp early in the morning.

On arriving there, Mr. Crooks was shocked to find that, while the people on this side of the river, were amply supplied with provisions, none had been sent to his own forlorn and famishing men on the opposite bank. He immediately caused a skin canoe to be constructed, and called out to his men to fill their camp kettles with water and hang them over the fire, that no time might be lost in cooking the meat the moment it should be received. The river was so narrow, though deep, that every thing could be distinctly heard and seen across it. The kettles were placed on the fire, and the water was boiling by the time the canoe was completed. When all was ready, however, no one would undertake to ferry the meat across. A vague, and almost superstitious, terror had infected the minds of Mr. Hunt's followers, enfeebled and rendered imaginative of horrors by the dismal scenes and sufferings through which they had passed. They regarded the haggard crew, hovering like spectres of famine on the opposite bank, with indefinite feelings of awe and apprehension, as if something desperate and dangerous was to be feared from them.

Mr. Crooks tried in vain to reason or shame them out of this singular state of mind. He then attempted to navigate the canoe himself, but found his strength incompetent to brave the impetuous current. The good feelings of Ben Jones the Kentuckian, at length overcame his fears, and he ventured over. The supply he brought was received with trembling avidity. A poor Canadian, however, named Jean Baptiste Prevost, whom famine had rendered wild and desperate, ran frantically about the bank, after Jones had returned, crying out to Mr. Hunt to send the canoe for him, and take him from that horrible region of famine, declaring that otherwise he would never march another step, but would lie down there and die.

The canoe was shortly sent over again, under the management of Joseph Delaunay, with further supplies. Prevost immediately pressed forward to embark. Delaunay refused to admit him, telling him that there was now a sufficient supply of meat on his side of the river. He replied that it was not cooked, and he should starve before it was ready; he implored, therefore, to be taken where he could get something to appease his hunger immediately. Finding the canoe putting off without him, he forced himself aboard. As he drew near the opposite shore, and beheld meat roasting before the fires, he jumped up, shouted, clapped his hands, and danced in a delirium of joy, until he upset the canoe. The poor wretch was swept away by the current and drowned, and it was with extreme difficulty that Delaunay reached the shore.

Mr. Hunt now sent all his men forward excepting two or three. In the evening, he caused another horse to be killed, and a canoe to be made out of the skin, in which he sent over a further supply of meat to the opposite party. The canoe brought back John Day, the Kentucky hunter, who came to join his former employer and commander, Mr. Crooks. Poor Day, once so active and vigorous, was now reduced to a condition even more feeble and emaciated than his companions. Mr. Crooks had such a value for the man, on account of his past services and faithful character, that he determined not to quit him; he exhorted Mr. Hunt, however, to proceed forward, and join the party, as his presence was all important to the conduct of the expedition. One of the Canadians, Jean Baptiste Dubreuil, likewise remained with Mr. Crooks.

Mr. Hunt left two horses with them, and a part of the carcass of the last that had been killed. This, he hoped, would be sufficient to sustain them until they should reach the Indian encampment.

One of the chief dangers attending the enfeebled condition of Mr. Crooks and his companions, was their being overtaken by the Indians whose horses had been seized: though Mr. Hunt hoped that he had guarded against any resentment on the part of the savages, by leaving various articles in their lodge, more than sufficient to compensate for the outrage he had been compelled to commit.

Resuming his onward course, Mr. Hunt came up with his people in the evening. The next day, December 13th, he beheld several Indians, with three horses, on the opposite side of the river, and after a time came to the two lodges which he had seen on going down. Here he endeavored in vain to barter a rifle for a horse, but again succeeded in effecting the purchase with an old tin kettle, aided by a few beads.

The two succeeding days were cold and stormy; the snow was augmenting, and there was a good deal of ice running in the river. Their road, however, was becoming easier; they were getting out of the hills, and finally emerged into the open country, after twenty days of fatigue, famine, and hardship of every kind, in the ineffectual attempt to find a passage down the river.

They now encamped on a little willowed stream, running from the east, which they had crossed on the 26th of November. Here they found a dozen lodges of Shoshonies, recently arrived, who informed them that had they persevered along the river, they would have found their difficulties augment until they became absolutely insurmountable. This intelligence added to the anxiety of Mr. Hunt for the fate of Mr. M'Kenzie and his people, who had kept on.

Mr. Hunt now followed up the little river, and encamped at some lodges of Shoshonies, from whom he procured a couple of horses, a dog, a few dried fish, and some roots and dried cherries. Two or three days were exhausted in obtaining information about the route, and what time it would take to get to the Sciatogas, a hospitable tribe, on the west side of the mountains, represented as having many horses. The replies were various, but concurred in saying that the distance was great, and would occupy from seventeen to twenty-one nights. Mr. Hunt then tried to procure a guide; but though he sent to various lodges up and down the river, offering articles of great value in Indian estimation, no one would venture. The snow they said was waist deep in the mountains; and to all his offers they shook their heads, gave a shiver, and replied, "we shall freeze! we shall freeze!" at the same time they urged him to remain and pass the winter among them.

Mr. Hunt was in a dismal dilemma. To attempt the mountains without a guide, would be certain death to him and all his people; to remain there, after having already been so long on the journey, and at such great expense, was worse to him he said than "two deaths." He now changed his tone with the Indians, charged them with deceiving him in respect to the mountains, and talking with a "forked tongue," or, in other words, with lying. He upbraided them with their want of courage, and told them they were women, to shrink from the perils of such a journey. At length one of them, piqued by his taunts, or tempted by his offers, agreed to be his guide; for which he was to receive a gun, a pistol, three knives, two horses, and a little of every article in possession of the party; a reward sufficient to make him one of the wealthiest of his vagabond nation.

Once more then, on the 21st of December, they set out upon their wayfaring, with newly excited spirits. Two other Indians accompanied their guide, who led them immediately back to Snake river, which they followed down for a short distance, in search of

some Indian rafts made of reeds, on which they might cross. Finding none, Mr. Hunt caused a horse to be killed, and a canoe to be
made out of its skin. Here, on the opposite bank, they saw the
thirteen men of Mr. Crooks' party, who had continued up along
the river. They told Mr. Hunt, across the stream, that they had not
seen Mr. Crooks, and the two men who had remained with him,
since the day that he had separated from them.

The canoe proving too small, another horse was killed, and the
skin of it joined to that of the first. Night came on before the little
bark had made more than two voyages. Being badly made, it was
taken apart and put together again, by the light of the fire. The
night was cold; the men were weary and disheartened with such
varied and incessant toil and hardship. They crouched, dull and
drooping, around their fires; many of them began to express a wish
to remain where they were for the winter. The very necessity of
crossing the river dismayed some of them in their present enfeebled and dejected state. It was rapid and turbulent, and filled
with floating ice, and they remembered that two of their comrades
had already perished in its waters. Others looked forward with mis-
givings to the long and dismal journey through lonesome regions
that awaited them, when they should have passed this dreary flood.

At an early hour of the morning, December 23d, they began to
cross the river. Much ice had formed during the night, and they
were obliged to break it for some distance on each shore. At length
they all got over in safety to the west side; and their spirits rose
on having achieved this perilous passage. Here they were rejoined
by the people of Mr. Crooks, who had with them a horse and a dog,
which they had recently procured. The poor fellows were in the
most squalid and emaciated state. Three of them were so completely prostrated in strength and spirits, that they expressed a
wish to remain among the Snakes. Mr. Hunt, therefore, gave them
the canoe, that they might cross the river, and a few articles, with
which to procure necessaries, until they should meet with Mr.
Crooks. There was another man, named Michael Carriere, who was
almost equally reduced, but he determined to proceed with his

comrades, who were now incorporated with the party of Mr. Hunt. After the day's exertions they encamped together on the banks of the river. This was the last night they were to spend upon its borders. More than eight hundred miles of hard travelling, and many weary days, had it cost them; and the sufferings connected with it, rendered it hateful in their remembrance, so that the Canadian voyageurs always spoke of it as "La maudite riviere enragée" —the accursed mad river: thus coupling a malediction with its name.

CHAPTER XXXVII

On the 24th of December, all
things being arranged, Mr. Hunt turned his back upon the disastrous banks of Snake river, and struck his course westward for the
mountains. His party, being augmented by the late followers of Mr.
Crooks, amounted now to thirty-two white men, three Indians, and
the squaw and two children of Pierre Dorion. Five jaded, half-
starved horses were laden with their luggage, and, in case of need,
were to furnish them with provisions. They travelled painfully
about fourteen miles a day, over plains and among hills, rendered
dreary by occasional falls of snow and rain. Their only sustenance
was a scanty meal of horse flesh once in four and twenty hours.

On the third day the poor Canadian, Carriere, one of the famished party of Mr. Crooks, gave up in despair, and lying down upon
the ground declared he could go no further. Efforts were made to
cheer him up, but it was found that the poor fellow was absolutely

exhausted and could not keep on his legs. He was mounted, therefore, upon one of the horses, though the forlorn animal was in little
better plight than himself.

On the 28th, they came upon a small stream winding to the
north, through a fine level valley; the mountains receding on each
side. Here their Indian friends pointed out a chain of woody
mountains to the left, running north and south, and covered with
snow; over which they would have to pass. They kept along the
valley for twenty-one miles on the 29th, suffering much from a
continued fall of snow and rain, and being twice obliged to ford
the icy stream. Early in the following morning the squaw of Pierre
Dorion, who had hitherto kept on without murmuring or flinching,
was suddenly taken in labour, and enriched her husband with
another child. As the fortitude and good conduct of the poor
woman had gained for her the good will of the party, her situation
caused concern and perplexity. Pierre, however, treated the matter
as an occurrence that could soon be arranged and need cause no
delay. He remained by his wife in the camp, with his other children
and his horse, and promised soon to rejoin the main body, who
proceeded on their march.

Finding that the little river entered the mountains, they abandoned it and turned off for a few miles among hills. Here another
Canadian, named La Bonté gave out, and had to be helped on
horseback. As the horse was too weak to bear both him and his
pack, Mr. Hunt took the latter upon his own shoulders. Thus, with
difficulties augmenting at every step, they urged their toilsome way
among the hills half famished, and faint at heart, when they came
to where a fair valley spread out before them of great extent, and
several leagues in width, with a beautiful stream meandering
through it. A genial climate seemed to prevail here, for though the
snow lay upon all the mountains within sight, there was none to
be seen in the valley. The travellers gazed with delight upon this
serene sunny landscape, but their joy was complete on beholding
six lodges of Shoshonies pitched upon the borders of the stream,
with a number of horses and dogs about them. They all pressed

forward with eagerness and soon reached the camp. Here their first
attention was to obtain provisions. A rifle, an old musket, a tomahawk, a tin kettle, and a small quantity of ammunition soon procured them four horses, three dogs, and some roots. Part of the
live stock was immediately killed, cooked with all expedition, and
as promptly devoured. A hearty meal restored every one to good
spirits. In the course of the following morning the Dorion family,
made its re-appearance. Pierre came trudging in the advance, followed by his valued, though skeleton steed, on which was mounted
his squaw with the new born infant in her arms, and her boy of two
years old, wrapped in a blanket and slung at her side. The mother
looked as unconcerned as if nothing had happened to her; so easy
is nature in her operations in the wilderness, when free from the
enfeebling refinements of luxury, and the tamperings and appli-
ances of art.

The next morning ushered in the new year, (1812). Mr. Hunt
was about to resume his march, when his men requested permission to celebrate the day. This was particularly urged by the Canadian voyageurs, with whom new year's day is a favorite festival;
and who never willingly give up a holiday, under any circumstances. There was no resisting such an application; so the day was
passed in repose and revelry; the poor Canadians contrived to sing
and dance in defiance of all their hardships; and there was a sumptuous new year's banquet of dog's meat and horse flesh.

After two days of welcome rest, the travellers addressed themselves once more to their painful journey. The Indians of the lodges
pointed out a distant gap through which they must pass in traversing the ridge of mountains. They assured them that they would
be but little incommoded by snow, and in three days would arrive
among the Sciatogas. Mr. Hunt, however, had been so frequently
deceived by Indian accounts of routes and distances, that he gave
but little faith to this information.

The travellers continued their course due west for five days,
crossing the valley and entering the mountains. Here the travelling
became excessively toilsome, across rough stony ridges, and amidst

fallen trees. They were often knee deep in snow, and sometimes in the hollows between the ridges sank up to their waists. The weather was extremely cold; the sky covered with clouds, so that for days they had not a glimpse of the sun. In traversing the highest ridge they had a wide but chilling prospect over a wilderness of snowy mountains.

On the 6th of January, however, they had crossed the dividing summit of the chain, and were evidently under the influence of a milder climate. The snow began to decrease; the sun once more emerged from the thick canopy of clouds, and shone cheeringly upon them, and they caught a sight of what appeared to be a plain, stretching out in the west. They hailed it as the poor Israelites hailed the first glimpse of the promised land, for they flattered themselves that this might be the great plain of the Columbia, and that their painful pilgrimage might be drawing to a close.

It was now five days since they had left the lodges of the Shoshonies, during which they had come about sixty miles, and their guide assured them that in the course of the next day they would see the Sciatogas.

On the following morning, therefore, they pushed forward with eagerness, and soon fell upon a small stream which led them through a deep, narrow defile, between stupendous ridges. Here among the rocks and precipices they saw gangs of that mountain-loving animal, the black-tailed deer, and came to where great tracks of horses were to be seen in all directions, made by the Indian hunters.

The snow had entirely disappeared, and the hopes of soon coming upon some Indian encampment induced Mr. Hunt to press on. Many of the men, however, were so enfeebled that they could not keep up with the main body, but lagged, at intervals, behind; and some of them did not arrive at the night encampment. In the course of this day's march the recently born child of Pierre Dorion died.

The march was resumed early the next morning, without waiting for the stragglers. The stream which they had followed throughout the preceding day was now swollen by the influx of another river; the declivities of the hills were green and the valleys were clothed with grass. At length the jovial cry was given of "an Indian camp!" It was yet in the distance, in the bosom of the green valley, but they could perceive that it consisted of numerous lodges, and that hundreds of horses were grazing the grassy meadows around it. The prospect of abundance of horse flesh diffused universal joy, for by this time the whole stock of travelling provisions was reduced to the skeleton steed of Pierre Dorion, and another wretched animal, equally emaciated, that had been repeatedly reprieved during the journey.

A forced march soon brought the weary and hungry travellers to the camp. It proved to be a strong party of Sciatogas and Tus-che-pas. There were thirty-four lodges, comfortably constructed of mats; the Indians, too, were better clothed than any of the wandering bands they had hitherto met on this side of the Rocky mountains. Indeed they were as well clad as the generality of the wild hunter tribes. Each had a good buffalo or deer skin robe; and a deer skin hunting shirt and leggins. Upwards of two thousand horses were ranging the pastures around their encampment; but what delighted Mr. Hunt was, on entering the lodges, to behold brass kettles, axes, copper tea kettles, and various other articles of civilized manufacture, which showed that these Indians had an indirect communication with the people of the sea-coast who traded with the whites. He made eager enquiries of the Sciatogas, and gathered from them that the great river (the Columbia,) was but two day's march distant, and that several white people had recently descended it; who he hoped might prove to be M'Lellan, M'Kenzie and their companions.

It was with the utmost joy and the most profound gratitude to heaven, that Mr. Hunt found himself and his band of weary and famishing wanderers, thus safely extricated from the most perilous part of their long journey, and within the prospect of a termination of their toils. All the stragglers who had lagged behind arrived, one after another, excepting the poor Canadian voyageur,

Carriere. He had been seen late in the preceding afternoon, riding behind a Snake Indian, near some lodges of that nation, a few miles distant from the last night's encampment; and it was expected that he would soon make his appearance.

The first object of Mr. Hunt was to obtain provisions for his men. A little venison of an indifferent quality and some roots were all that could be procured that evening; but the next day he succeeded in purchasing a mare and colt, which were immediately killed, and the cravings of the half-starved people in some degree appeased.

For several days they remained in the neighborhood of these Indians, reposing after all their hardships, and feasting upon horse flesh and roots, obtained in subsequent traffic. Many of the people ate to such excess as to render themselves sick, others were lame from their past journey; but all gradually recruited in the repose and abundance of the valley. Horses were obtained here much more readily, and at a cheaper rate, than among the Snakes. A blanket, a knife, or a half pound of blue beads would purchase a steed, and at this rate many of the men bought horses for their individual use.

This tribe of Indians, who are represented as a proud-spirited race, and uncommonly cleanly, never eat horses nor dogs, nor would they permit the raw flesh of either to be brought into their huts. They had a small quantity of venison in each lodge, but set so high a price upon it that the white men, in their impoverished state, could not afford to purchase it. They hunted the deer on horseback; "ringing," or surrounding them, and running them down in a circle. They were admirable horsemen, and their weapons were bows and arrows, which they managed with great dexterity. They were altogether primitive in their habits, and seemed to cling to the usages of savage life, even when possessed of the aids of civilization. They had axes among them, yet they generally made use of a stone mallet wrought into the shape of a bottle, and wedges of elk horn, in splitting their wood. Though they might have two or three brass kettles hanging in their lodges, yet they would frequently use vessels made of willow, for carrying water, and would even boil their meat in them, by means of hot stones. Their women wore caps of willow neatly worked and figured.

As Carriere, the Canadian straggler did not make his appearance for two or three days after the encampment in the valley, two men were sent out on horseback in search of him. They returned, however, without success. The lodges of the Snake Indians near which he had been seen, were removed, and they could find no trace of him. Several days more elapsed, yet nothing was seen or heard of him, or of the Snake horseman, behind whom he had been last observed. It was feared, therefore, that he had either perished through hunger and fatigue; had been murdered by the Indians; or, being left to himself, had mistaken some hunting tracks for the trail of the party, and been led astray and lost.

The river on the banks of which they were encamped, emptied into the Columbia, was called by the natives the Eu-o-tal-la, or Umatalla, and abounded with beaver. In the course of their sojourn in the valley which it watered, they twice shifted their camp, proceeding about thirty miles down its course, which was to the west. A heavy fall of rain caused the river to overflow its banks, dislodged them from their encampment, and drowned three of their horses, which were tethered in the low ground.

Further conversation with the Indians satisfied them that they were in the neighborhood of the Columbia. The number of the white men who they said had passed down the river, agreed with that of M'Lellan, M'Kenzie and their companions, and increased the hope of Mr. Hunt that they might have passed through the wilderness with safety.

These Indians had a vague story that white men were coming to trade among them; and they often spoke of two great men named Ke-Koosh and Jacquean, who gave them tobacco, and smoked with them. Jacquean, they said, had a house somewhere upon the great river. Some of the Canadians supposed they were speaking of one Jacquean Finlay a clerk of the North-west Company, and inferred that the house must be some trading post on one of the tributary streams of the Columbia. The Indians were overjoyed when they found this band of white men intended to return and trade with them. They promised to use all diligence in collecting quantities of beaver skins, and no doubt proceeded to make deadly war upon that sagacious, but ill-fated animal, who, in general, lived in peaceful insignificance among his Indian neighbors, before the intrusion of the white trader. On the 20th of January, Mr. Hunt took leave of these friendly Indians, and of the river on which they were encamped, and continued westward.

At length, on the following day, the wayworn travellers lifted up their eyes and beheld before them the long-sought waters of the Columbia. The sight was hailed with as much transport as if they had already reached the end of their pilgrimage; nor can we wonder at their joy. Two hundred and forty miles had they marched, through wintry wastes and rugged mountains, since leaving Snake river; and six months of perilous wayfaring had they experienced since their departure from the Arickara village on the Missouri. Their whole route by land and water from that point, had been, according to their computation, seventeen hundred and fifty-one miles, in the course of which they had endured all kinds of hardships. In fact, the necessity of winding the dangerous country of the Blackfeet, had obliged them to make a bend to the south, and to traverse a great additional extent of unknown wilderness.

The place where they struck the Columbia was some distance below the junction of its two great branches, Lewis, and Clarke rivers, and not far from the influx of the Wallah-Wallah. It was a beautiful stream, three quarters of a mile wide, totally free from trees; bordered in some places with steep rocks, in others with pebbled shores.

On the banks of the Columbia they found a miserable horde of Indians, called Akai-chies, with no clothing but a scanty mantle of the skins of animals, and sometimes a pair of sleeves of wolf's skin. Their lodges were shaped like a tent, and very light and warm, being covered with mats of rushes; beside which they had excavations on the ground, lined with mats, and occupied by the women, who were even more slightly clad than the men. These people subsisted chiefly by fishing; having canoes of a rude construction, being merely the trunks of pine trees split and hollowed out by fire. Their lodges were well stored with dried salmon, and they had great quantities of fresh salmon trout, of an excellent flavor, taken at the mouth of the Umatalla; of which the travellers obtained a most acceptable supply.

Finding that the road was on the north side of the river, Mr. Hunt crossed, and continued five or six days travelling rather slowly down along its banks, being much delayed by the straying of the horses, and the attempts made by the Indians to steal them. They frequently passed lodges, where they obtained fish and dogs. At one place the natives had just returned from hunting, and had brought back a large quantity of elk and deer meat, but asked so high a price for it as to be beyond the funds of the travellers, so they had to content themselves with dog flesh. They had by this time, however, come to consider it very choice food, superior to horse flesh, and the minutes of the expedition speak rather exultingly now and then, of their having made a "famous repast," where this viand happened to be unusually plenty.

They again learnt tidings of some of the scattered members of the expedition, supposed to be M'Kenzie, M'Lellan and their men, who had preceded them down the river, and had overturned one of their canoes, by which they lost many articles. All these floating pieces of intelligence of their fellow adventurers, who had separated from them in the heart of the wilderness, they received with eager interest.

The weather continued to be temperate, marking the superior softness of the climate on this side of the mountains. For a great part of the time, the days were delightfully mild and clear, like the serene days of October, on the Atlantic borders. The country in general, in the neighborhood of the river, was a continual plain, low, near the water, but rising gradually; destitute of trees, and almost without shrubs or plants of any kind, excepting a few willow bushes. After travelling about sixty miles, they came to where the country became very hilly and the river made its way between rocky banks, and down numerous rapids. The Indians in this vicinity were better clad and altogether in more prosperous condition than those above, and, as Mr. Hunt thought, showed their consciousness of ease by something like sauciness of manner. Thus prosperity is apt to produce arrogance in savage as well as in civilized life. In both conditions, man is an animal that will not bear pampering.

From these people Mr. Hunt for the first time received vague, but deeply interesting intelligence of that part of the enterprise which had proceeded by sea to the mouth of the Columbia. The Indians spoke of a number of white men who had built a large house at the mouth of the great river, and surrounded it with palisades. None of them had been down to Astoria themselves; but rumors spread widely and rapidly from mouth to mouth among the Indian tribes, and are carried to the heart of the interior, by hunting parties, and migratory hordes.

The establishment of a trading emporium at such a point, also, was calculated to cause a sensation to the most remote parts of the vast wilderness beyond the mountains. It, in a manner, struck the pulse of the great vital river, and vibrated up all its tributary streams.

It is surprising to notice how well this remote tribe of savages had learnt through intermediate gossips, the private feelings of the colonists at Astoria; it shows that Indians are not the incurious and indifferent observers that they have been represented. They told Mr. Hunt that the white people at the large house had been looking anxiously for many of their friends, whom they had expected to descend the great river; and had been in much affliction, fearing that they were lost. Now, however, the arrival of him and his party would wipe away all their tears and they would dance and sing for joy.

On the 31st of January, Mr. Hunt arrived at the falls of the Columbia, and encamped at the village of Wish-ram, situated at the head of that dangerous pass of the river called "the long narrows."

CHAPTER XXXVIII

OF the village of Wish-ram, the aborigines' fishing mart of the Columbia, we have given some account in an early chapter of this work. The inhabitants held a traffic in the productions of the fisheries of the falls, and their village was the trading resort of the tribes from the coast and from the mountains. Mr. Hunt found the inhabitants shrewder and more intelligent than any Indians he had met with. Trade had sharpened their wits, though it had not improved their honesty; for they were a community of arrant rogues and freebooters. Their habitations comported with their circumstances, and were superior to any the travellers had yet seen west of the Rocky mountains. In general, the dwellings of the savages on the Pacific side of that great barrier, were mere tents and cabins of mats, or skins, or straw, the country being destitute of timber. In Wish-ram, on the contrary, the houses were built of wood, with long sloping roofs. The floor was sunk about six feet below the surface of the ground, with a low door at the gabel end, extremely narrow and partly sunk. Through this it was necessary to crawl, and then to descend a short ladder. This inconvenient entrance was probably for the purpose of defence; there were loop holes also under the eaves, apparently for the discharge of arrows. The houses were larger, generally containing two or three families. Immediately within the door were sleeping places, ranged along the walls, like berths in a ship; and furnished with pallets of matting. These extended along one half of the building; the remaining half was appropriated to the storing of dried fish.

The trading operations of the inhabitants of Wish-ram had given them a wider scope of information, and rendered their village a kind of head quarters of intelligence. Mr. Hunt was able, therefore, to collect more distinct tidings concerning the settlement of Astoria and its affairs. One of the inhabitants had been at the trading post established by David Stuart on the Oakinagan, and had picked up a few words of English there. From him, Mr. Hunt gleaned various particulars about that establishment, as well as about the general concerns of the enterprise. Others repeated the name of Mr. M'Kay, the partner who perished in the massacre on board of the Tonquin, and gave some account of that melancholy affair. They said, Mr. M'Kay was a chief among the white men, and had built a great house at the mouth of the river, but had left it, and sailed away in a large ship to the northward, where he had been attacked by bad Indians in canoes. Mr. Hunt was startled by this intelligence, and made further inquiries. They informed him that the Indians had lashed their canoes to the ship, and fought until they killed him and all his people. This is another instance of the clearness with which intelligence is transmitted from mouth to mouth among the Indian tribes. These tidings, though but partially credited by Mr. Hunt, filled his mind with anxious forebodings. He now endeavored to procure canoes, in which to descend the Columbia, but none suitable for the purpose were to be obtained above the narrows; he continued on, therefore, the distance of twelve miles, and encamped on the bank of the river. The camp was soon surrounded by loitering savages, who went prowling about, seeking what they might pilfer. Being baffled by the vigilance of the guard, they endeavored to compass their ends by other means. To-wards evening, a number of warriors entered the camp in ruffling style; painted and dressed out as if for battle, and armed with lances, bows and arrows, and scalping knives. They informed Mr. Hunt that a party of thirty or forty braves were coming up from a village below to attack the camp and carry off the horses, but that they were determined to stay with him, and defend him. Mr. Hunt received them with great coldness, and, when they had finished their story, gave them a pipe to smoke. He then called up all hands, stationed sentinels in different quarters, but told them to keep as vigilant an eye within the camp as without.

The warriors were evidently baffled by these precautions, and, having smoked their pipe, and vapored off their valor, took their departure. The farce, however, did not end here. After a little while, the warriors returned, ushering in another savage, still more hero-ically arrayed. This they announced as the chief of the belligerent village, but as a great pacificator. His people had been furiously bent upon the attack, and would have doubtless carried it into ef-fect, but this gallant chief had stood forth as the friend of white men, and had dispersed the throng by his own authority and prow-ess. Having vaunted this signal piece of service, there was a signifi-cant pause; all evidently expecting some adequate reward. Mr. Hunt again produced the pipe, smoked with the chieftain and his worthy compeers; but made no further demonstrations of grati-tude. They remained about the camp all night, but at daylight returned, baffled and crest-fallen, to their homes, with nothing but smoke for their pains.

Mr. Hunt now endeavored to procure canoes, of which he saw several about the neighborhood, extremely well made, with ele-vated stems and sterns, some of them capable of carrying three thousand pounds weight. He found it extremely difficult, however, to deal with these slippery people, who seemed much more in-clined to pilfer. Notwithstanding a strict guard maintained round the camp, various implements were stolen, and several horses car-ried off. Among the latter, we have to include the long cherished steed of Pierre Dorion. From some wilful caprice, that worthy pitched his tent at some distance from the main body, and tethered his invaluable steed beside it, from whence it was abstracted in the night, to the infinite chagrin and mortification of the hybrid interpreter.

Having, after several days' negociation, procured the requisite number of canoes, Mr. Hunt would gladly have left this thievish neighborhood, but was detained until the 5th of February, by violent head winds, accompanied by snow and rain. Even after he was enabled to get under way, he had still to struggle against contrary winds and tempestuous weather. The current of the river, however, was in his favor; having made a portage at the grand rapid, the canoes met with no further obstruction, and, on the afternoon of the 15th of February, swept round an intervening cape, and came in sight of the infant settlement of Astoria. After eleven months wandering in the wilderness, a great part of the time over trackless wastes, where the sight of a savage wigwam was a rarity, we may imagine the delight of the poor weatherbeaten travellers, at beholding the embryo establishment, with its magazines, habitations, and picketed bulwarks, seated on a high point of land, dominating a beautiful little bay, in which was a trim-built shallop riding quietly at anchor. A shout of joy burst from each canoe at the long wished for sight. They urged their canoes across the bay, and pulled with eagerness for shore, where all hands poured down from the settlement to receive and welcome them. Among the first to greet them on their landing, were some of their old comrades and fellow-sufferers, who, under the conduct of Reed, M'Lellan, and M'Kenzie, had parted from them at the Caldron Linn. These had reached Astoria nearly a month previously, and, judging from their own narrow escape from starvation, had given up Mr. Hunt and his followers as lost. Their greeting was the more warm and cordial. As to the Canadian voyageurs, their mutual felicitations, as usual, were loud and vociferous, and it was almost ludicrous to behold these ancient "comrades" and "confreres," hugging and kissing each other on the river bank.

When the first greetings were over, the different bands interchanged accounts of their several wanderings, after separating at Snake river; we shall briefly notice a few of the leading particulars. It will be recollected by the reader, that a small exploring detachment had proceeded down the river, under the conduct of Mr. John Reed, a clerk of the company: that another had set off under M'Lellan, and a third in a different direction, under M'Kenzie. After wandering for several days without meeting with Indians, or obtaining any supplies, they came together fortuitously among the Snake river mountains, some distance below that disastrous pass or strait, which had received the appellation of the Devil's Scuttle Hole.

When thus united, their party consisted of M'Kenzie, M'Lellan, Reed, and eight men, chiefly Canadians. Being all in the same predicament, without horses, provisions, or information of any kind, they all agreed that it would be worse than useless to return to Mr. Hunt and encumber him with so many starving men, and that their only course was to extricate themselves as soon as possible from this land of famine and misery, and make the best of their way for the Columbia. They accordingly continued to follow the downward course of Snake river; clambering rocks and mountains, and defying all the difficulties and dangers of that rugged defile, which subsequently, when the snows had fallen, was found impassable by Messrs. Hunt and Crooks.

Though constantly near to the borders of the river, and for a great part of the time within sight of its current, one of their greatest sufferings was thirst. The river had worn its way in a deep channel through rocky mountains, destitute of brooks or springs. Its banks were so high and precipitous, that there was rarely any place where the travellers could get down to drink of its waters. Frequently they suffered for miles the torments of Tantalus; water continually within sight, yet fevered with the most parching thirst. Here and there they met with rain water collected in the hollows of the rocks, but more than once they were reduced to the utmost extremity; and some of the men had recourse to the last expedient to avoid perishing.

Their sufferings from hunger were equally severe. They could meet with no game, and subsisted for a time on strips of beaver skin, broiled on the coals. These were doled out in scanty allowances, barely sufficient to keep up existence, and at length failed them altogether. Still they crept feebly on, scarce dragging one limb after another, until a severe snow storm brought them to a pause. To struggle against it, in their exhausted condition, was impossible, so cowering under an impending rock at the foot of a steep mountain, they prepared themselves for that wretched fate which seemed inevitable.

At this critical juncture, when famine stared them in the face, M'Lellan casting up his eyes, beheld an ahsahta, or bighorn, sheltering itself under a shelving rock on the side of the hill above them. Being in more active plight than any of his comrades, and an excellent marksman, he set off to get within shot of the animal. His companions watched his movements with breathless anxiety, for their lives depended upon his success. He made a cautious circuit; scrambled up the hill with the utmost silence, and at length arrived, unperceived, within a proper distance. Here levelling his rifle he took so sure an aim, that the bighorn fell dead on the spot; a fortunate circumstance, for, to pursue it, if merely wounded, would have been impossible in his emaciated state. The declivity of the hill enabled him to roll the carcass down to his companions, who were too feeble to climb the rocks. They fell to work to cut it up; yet exerted a remarkable self-denial for men in their starving condition, for they contented themselves for the present with a soup made from the bones, reserving the flesh for future repasts. This providential relief gave them strength to pursue their journey, but they were frequently reduced to almost equal straits, and it was only the smallness of their party, requiring a small supply of provisions, that enabled them to get through this desolate region with their lives.

At length, after twenty-one days of toil and suffering, they got through these mountains, and arrived at a tributary stream of that branch of the Columbia called Lewis river, of which Snake river forms the southern fork. In this neighborhood they met with wild horses, the first they had seen west of the Rocky mountains. From hence they made their way to Lewis river, where they fell in with a friendly tribe of Indians, who freely administered to their necessities. On this river they procured two canoes, in which they dropped down the stream to its confluence with the Columbia, and then down that river to Astoria, where they arrived haggard and emaciated, and perfectly in rags.

Thus, all the leading persons of Mr. Hunt's expedition were once more gathered together, excepting Mr. Crooks, of whose safety they entertained but little hope, considering the feeble condition in which they had been compelled to leave him in the heart of the wilderness.

A day was now given up to jubilee, to celebrate thc arrival of Mr. Hunt and his companions, and the joyful meeting of the various scattered bands of adventurers at Astoria. The colors were hoisted; the guns, great and small, were fired; there was a feast of fish, of beaver, and venison, which relished well with men who had so long been glad to revel on horse flesh and dogs' meat; a genial allowance of grog was issued, to increase the general animation, and the festivities wound up, as usual, with a grand dance at night, by the Canadian voyageurs.*

* The distance from St. Louis to Astoria, by the route travelled by Hunt and M'Kenzie, was upwards of thirty-five hundred miles, though in a direct line, it does not exceed eighteen hundred.

CHAPTER XXXIX

SCANTY FARE DURING THE WINTER—A POOR HUNTING GROUND—
THE RETURN OF THE FISHING SEASON—THE UTHLECAN OR SMELT
—ITS QUALITIES—VAST SHOALS OF IT—STURGEON—INDIAN MODES
OF TAKING IT—THE SALMON—DIFFERENT SPECIES—NATURE OF
THE COUNTRY ABOUT THE COAST—FORESTS AND FOREST TREES
—A REMARKABLE FLOWERING VINE—ANIMALS—BIRDS—REPTILES
—CLIMATE WEST OF THE MOUNTAINS—MILDNESS OF THE TEM-
PERATURE—SOIL OF THE COAST AND THE INTERIOR

THE winter had passed away tranquilly at Astoria. The apprehensions of hostility from the natives had subsided; indeed, as the season advanced, the Indians for the most part had disappeared from the neighborhood, and abandoned the sea coast, so that, for want of their aid, the colonists had at times suffered considerably for want of provisions. The hunters belonging to the establishment made frequent and wide excursions, but with very moderate success. There were some deer and a few bears to be found in the vicinity, and elk in great numbers; the country, however, was so rough, and the woods so close and entangled, that it was almost impossible to beat up the game. The prevalent rains of winter, also, rendered it difficult for the hunter to keep his arms in order. The quantity of game, therefore, brought in by the hunters was extremely scanty, and it was frequently necessary to put all hands on very moderate allowance. Towards spring, however, the fishing season commenced,—the season of plenty on the Columbia. About the beginning of February, a small kind of fish, about six inches long, called by the natives the uthlecan, and resembling the smelt, made its appearance at the mouth of the river. It is said to be of delicious flavor, and so fat as to burn like a candle, for which it is often used by the natives. It enters the river in immense shoals, like solid columns, often extending to the depth of five or more feet, and is scooped up by the natives with small nets at the end of poles. In this way they will soon fill a canoe, or form a great heap upon the river banks. These fish constitute a principal article of their food; the women drying them and stringing them on cords.

As the uthlecan is only found in the lower part of the river, the arrival of it soon brought back the natives to the coast; who again resorted to the factory to trade, and from that time furnished plentiful supplies of fish.

The sturgeon makes its appearance in the river shortly after the uthlecan, and is taken in different ways, by the natives: sometimes they spear it; but oftener they use the hook and line, and the net. Occasionally, they sink a cord in the river by a heavy weight, with a buoy at the upper end, to keep it floating. To this cord several hooks are attached by short lines, a few feet distant from each other, and baited with small fish. This apparatus is often set towards night, and by the next morning several sturgeon will be found hooked by it; for though a large and strong fish, it makes but little resistance when ensnared.

The salmon, which are the prime fish of the Columbia, and as important to the piscatory tribes as are the buffaloes to the hunters of the prairies, do not enter the river until towards the latter part of May, from which time, until the middle of August, they abound, and are taken in vast quantities, either with the spear or seine, and mostly in shallow water. An inferior species succeeds, and continues from August to December. It is remarkable for having a double row of teeth, half an inch long and extremely sharp, from whence it has received the name of the dog-toothed salmon. It is generally killed with the spear in small rivulets, and smoked for winter provision. We have noticed in a former chapter the mode in which the salmon are taken and cured at the falls of the Columbia; and put up in parcels for exportation. From these different fisheries of the river tribes, the establishment at Astoria had to derive much of its precarious supplies of provisions.

A year's residence at the mouth of the Columbia, and various expeditions in the interior, had now given the Astorians some idea of the country. The whole coast is described as remarkably rugged and mountainous; with dense forests of hemlock, spruce, white and red cedar, cotton-wood, white oak, white and swamp ash, willow, and a few walnut. There is likewise an undergrowth of aromatic shrubs, creepers, and clambering vines, that render the forests almost impenetrable; together with berries of various kinds, such as gooseberries, strawberries, raspberries, both red and yellow, very large and finely flavored whortleberries, cranberries, serviceberries, blackberries, currants, sloes, and wild and choke cherries.

Among the flowering vines is one deserving of particular notice. Each flower is composed of six leaves or petals, about three inches in length, of a beautiful crimson, the inside spotted with white. Its leaves, of a fine green, are oval, and disposed by threes. This plant climbs upon the trees without attaching itself to them; when it has reached the topmost branches, it descends perpendicularly, and as it continues to grow, extends from tree to tree, until its various stalks interlace the grove like the rigging of a ship. The stems or trunks of this vine are tougher and more flexible than willow, and are from fifty to one hundred fathoms in length. From the fibres, the Indians manufacture baskets of such close texture as to hold water.

The principal quadrupeds that had been seen by the colonists in their various expeditions, were the stag, fallow deer, hart, black and grizzly bear, antelope, ahsahta or bighorn, beaver, sea and river otter, muskrat, fox, wolf, and panther, the latter extremely rare. The only domestic animals among the natives were horses and dogs.

The country abounded with aquatic and land birds, such as swans, wild geese, brant, ducks of almost every description, pelicans, herons, gulls, snipes, curlews, eagles, vultures, crows, ravens, magpies, woodpeckers, pigeons, partridges, pheasants, grouse, and a great variety of singing birds.

There were few reptiles; the only dangerous kinds were the rattlesnake, and one striped with black, yellow, and white, about four feet long. Among the lizard kind was one about nine or ten inches in length, exclusive of the tail, and three inches in circumference. The tail was round, and of the same length as the body. The head was triangular, covered with small square scales. The upper part of the body was likewise covered with small scales, green, yellow, black and blue. Each foot had five toes, furnished with strong nails, probably to aid it in burrowing, as it usually lived under ground on the plains.

A remarkable fact, characteristic of the country west of the Rocky mountains, is the mildness and equability of the climate. That great mountain barrier seems to divide the continent into different climates, even in the same degrees of latitude. The rigorous winters and sultry summers, and all the capricious inequalities of temperature prevalent on the Atlantic side of the mountains, are but little felt on their western declivities. The countries between them and the Pacific are blest with milder and steadier temperature, resembling the climates of parallel latitudes in Europe. In the plains and valleys, but little snow falls throughout the winter, and usually melts while falling. It rarely lies on the ground more than two days at a time, except on the summits of the mountains. The winters are rainy rather than cold. The rains for five months, from the middle of October to the middle of March, are almost incessant, and often accompanied by tremendous thunder and lightning. The winds prevalent at this season are from the south and southeast, which usually bring rain. Those from the north to the southwest are the harbingers of fair weather and a clear sky. The residue of the year, from the middle of March to the middle of October, an interval of seven months, is serene and delightful. There is scarcely any rain throughout this time, yet the face of the country is kept fresh and verdant by nightly dews, and occasionally by humid fogs in the mornings. These are not considered prejudicial to health, since both the natives and the whites sleep in the open air with perfect impunity. While this equable and bland temperature prevails throughout the lower country, the peaks and ridges of the vast mountains by which it is dominated, are covered with perpetual snow. This renders them discernable at a great distance, shining at times like bright summer clouds, at other times assuming the most aerial tints, and always forming brilliant and striking features in the vast landscape. The mild temperature prevalent throughout the country is attributed by some to the succession of winds from the Pacific ocean, extending from latitude twenty degrees to at least fifty degrees north. These temper the heat of summer, so that in the shade no one is incommoded by perspiration; they also soften the rigors of winter, and produce such a moderation in the climate, that the inhabitants can wear the same dress throughout the year.

The soil in the neighborhood of the sea coast is of a brown color, inclining to red, and generally poor; being a mixture of clay and gravel. In the interior, and especially in the valleys of the Rocky mountains, the soil is generally blackish; though sometimes yellow. It is frequently mixed with marl and with marine substances, in a state of decomposition. This kind of soil extends to a considerable depth, as may be perceived in the deep cuts made by ravines, and by the beds of rivers. The vegetation in these valleys is much more abundant than near the coast; in fact, it is in these fertile intervals, locked up between rocky sierras, or scooped out from barren wastes, that population must extend itself, as it were, in veins and ramifications, if ever the regions beyond the mountains should become civilized.

CHAPTER XL

A BRIEF mention has already been made of the tribes or hordes existing about the lower part of the Columbia at the time of the settlement; a few more particulars concerning them may be acceptable. The four tribes nearest to Astoria, and with whom the traders had most intercourse, were, as has heretofore been observed, the Chinooks, the Clatsops, the Wahkiacums, and the Cathlamets. The Chinooks resided chiefly along the banks of a river of the same name, running parallel to the sea coast, through a low country studded with stagnant pools, and emptying itself into Baker's bay, a few miles from Cape Disappointment. This was the tribe over which Comcomly, the one eyed chieftain, held sway; it boasted two hundred and fourteen fighting men. Their chief subsistence was on fish, with an occasional regale of the flesh of elk and deer, and of wild fowl from the neighboring ponds.

The Clatsops resided on both sides of Point Adams; they were the mere reliques of a tribe which had been nearly swept off by the smallpox, and did not number more than one hundred and eighty fighting men.

The Wahkiacums, or Waak-i-cums, inhabited the north side of the Columbia, and numbered sixty-six warriors. They and the Chinooks were originally the same; but a dispute arising about two generations previous to the time of the settlement between the ruling chief and his brother Wahkiacum; the latter seceded, and with his adherents, formed the present horde which continues to go by his name. In this way new tribes or clans are formed, and lurking causes of hostility engendered.

The Cathlemets lived opposite to the lower village of the Wahkiacums, and numbered ninety-four warriors.

These four tribes, or rather clans, have every appearance of springing from the same origin, resembling each other in person, dress, language and manners. They are rather a diminutive race, generally below five feet, five inches, with crooked legs and thick ankles; a deformity caused by their passing so much of their time sitting or squatting upon the calves of their legs, and their heels, in the bottom of their canoes; a favorite position, which they retain, even when on shore. The women increase the deformity by wearing tight bandages round the ankles, which prevent the circulation of the blood, and cause a swelling of the muscles of the leg.

Neither sex can boast of personal beauty. Their faces are round, with small, but animated eyes. Their noses are broad and flat at top, and fleshy at the end, with large nostrils. They have wide mouths, thick lips, and short, irregular and dirty teeth. Indeed, good teeth are seldom to be seen among the tribes west of the Rocky mountains, who live chiefly on fish.

In the early stages of their intercourse with white men, these savages were but scantily clad. In summer time the men went entirely naked; in the winter and in bad weather, the men wore a small robe, reaching to the middle of the thigh, made of the skins of animals, or of the wool of the mountain sheep. Occasionally, they wore a kind of mantle of matting, to keep off the rain; but, having thus protected the back and shoulders, they left the rest of the body naked.

The women wore similar robes, though shorter, not reaching below the waist; beside which, they had a kind of petticoat, or fringe,
reaching from the waist to the knee, formed of the fibres of Cedar
bark, broken into strands, or a tissue of silk grass twisted and knotted
at the ends. This was the usual dress of the women in summer; should
the weather be inclement, they added a vest of skins, similar to the
robe.

The men carefully eradicated every vestige of a beard, considering
it a great deformity. They looked with disgust at the whiskers and
well furnished chins of the white men, and in derision called them
Long beards. Both sexes, on the other hand, cherished the hair
of the head, which with them is generally black and rather coarse.
They allowed it to grow to a great length, and were very proud and
careful of it, sometimes wearing it plaited, sometimes wound round
the head in fanciful tresses. No greater affront could be offered to
them than to cut off their treasured locks.

They had conical hats with narrow rims, neatly woven of bear
grass or of the fibres of cedar bark, interwoven with designs of
various shapes and colors; sometimes merely squares and triangles, at
other times rude representations of canoes, with men fishing and har-
pooning. These hats were nearly water proof, and extremely durable.

The favorite ornaments of the men were collars of bears' claws,
the proud trophies of hunting exploits; while the women and children
wore similar decorations of elk's tusks. An intercourse with the white
traders, however, soon effected a change in the toilets of both sexes.
They became fond of arraying themselves in any article of civilized
dress which they could procure, and often made a most grotesque appearance. They adapted many articles of finery, also, to their own
previous tastes. Both sexes were fond of adorning themselves with
bracelets of iron, brass or copper. They were delighted, also, with blue
and white beads, particularly the former, and wore broad tight bands
of them round the waist and ancles; large rolls of them round the
neck, and pendants of them in the ears. The men, especially, who, in
savage life carry a passion for personal decoration farther than the females, did not think their gala equipments complete, unless they had

a jewel of haiqua, or wampum, dangling at the nose. Thus arrayed, their hair besmeared with fish oil, and their bodies bedaubed with red clay, they considered themselves irresistible.

When on warlike expeditions, they painted their faces and bodies in the most hideous and grotesque manner, according to the universal practice of American savages. Their arms were bows and arrows, spears, and war clubs. Some wore a corslet, formed of pieces of hard wood, laced together with bear grass, so as to form a light coat of mail, pliant to the body; and a kind of casque of cedar bark, leather, and bear grass, sufficient to protect the head from an arrow or a war club. A more complete article of defensive armor was a buff jerkin or shirt of great thickness, made of doublings of elk skin, and reaching to the feet, holes being left for the head and arms. This was perfectly arrow proof; add to which, it was often endowed with charmed virtues, by the spells and mystic ceremonials of the medicine man, or conjurer.

Of the peculiar custom, prevalent among these people, of flattening the head, we have already spoken. It is one of those instances of human caprice, like the crippling of the feet of females in China, which are quite incomprehensible. This custom prevails principally among the tribes on the sea coast, and about the lower parts of the rivers. How far it extends along the coast we are not able to ascertain. Some of the tribes, both north and south of the Columbia, practice it; but they all speak the Chinook language, and probably originated from the same stock. As far as we can learn, the remoter tribes, which speak an entirely different language, do not flatten the head. This absurd custom declines, also, in receding from the shores of the Pacific; few traces of it are to be found among the tribes of the Rocky mountains, and after crossing the mountains it disappears altogether. Those Indians, therefore, about the head waters of the Columbia, and in the solitary mountain regions, who are often called Flatheads, must not be supposed to be characterized by this deformity. It is an appellation often given by the hunters east of the mountain chain, to all the western Indians, excepting the Snakes.

The religious belief of these people was extremely limited and confined; or rather, in all probability, their explanations were but little understood by their visiters. They had an idea of a benevolent and omnipotent spirit, the creator of all things. They represent him as assuming various shapes at pleasure, but generally that of an immense bird. He usually inhabits the sun, but occasionally wings his way through the aerial regions, and sees all that is doing upon earth. Should any thing displease him, he vents his wrath in terrific storms and tempests, the lightning being the flashes of his eyes, and the thunder the clapping of his wings. To propitiate his favor they offer to him annual sacrifices of salmon and venison, the first fruits of their fishing and hunting.

Beside this aerial spirit they believe in an inferior one, who inhabits the fire, and of whom they are in perpetual dread, as, though he possesses equally the power of good and evil, the evil is apt to predominate. They endeavor, therefore, to keep him in good humor by frequent offerings. He is supposed also to have great influence with the winged spirit, their sovereign protector and benefactor. They implore him, therefore, to act as their interpreter and procure them all describable things, such as success in fishing and hunting, abundance of game, fleet horses, obedient wives, and male children

These Indians have likewise their priests, or conjurers, or medicine men, who pretend to be in the confidence of the deities, and the expounders and enforcers of their will. Each of these medicine men has his idols carved in wood, representing the spirits of the air and of the fire, under some rude and grotesque form of a horse, a bear, a beaver, or other quadruped, or that of a bird or fish. These idols are hung round with amulets and votive offerings, such as beaver's teeth, and bear's and eagle's claws.

When any chief personage is on his death bed, or dangerously ill, the medicine men are sent for. Each brings with him his idols, with which he retires into a canoe to hold a consultation. As doctors are prone to disagree, so these medicine men have now and then a violent altercation as to the malady of the patient, or the treatment of it. To settle this they beat their idols soundly against each other; which ever first loses a tooth or a claw is considered as confuted, and his votary retires from the field.

Polygamy is not only allowed, but considered honorable, and the greater number of wives a man can maintain, the more important is he in the eyes of the tribe. The first wife, however, takes rank of all the others, and is considered mistress of the house. Still the domestic establishment is liable to jealousies and cabals, and the lord and master has much difficulty in maintaining harmony in his jangling household.

In the manuscript from which we draw many of these particulars, it is stated that he who exceeds his neighbors in the number of his wives, male children and slaves, is elected chief of the village; a title to office which we do not recollect ever before to have met with.

Feuds are frequent among these tribes, but are not very deadly. They have occasionally pitched battles, fought on appointed days, and at specified places, which are generally the banks of a rivulet. The adverse parties post themselves on the opposite sides of the stream, and at such distances that the battles often last a long while before any blood is shed. The number of killed and wounded seldom exceed half a dozen. Should the damage be equal on each side, the war is considered as honorably concluded; should one party lose more than the other, it is entitled to a compensation in slaves or other property, otherwise hostilities are liable to be renewed at a future day. They are much given also to predatory inroads into the territories of their enemies, and sometimes of their friendly neighbors. Should they fall upon a band of inferior force, or upon a village, weakly defended, they act with the ferocity of true poltroons, slaying all the men and carrying off the women and children as slaves. As to the property, it is packed upon horses which they bring with them for the purpose. They are mean and paltry as warriors, and altogether inferior in heroic qualities to the savages of the buffalo plains on the east side of the mountains.

A great portion of their time is passed in revelry, music, dancing and gambling. Their music scarcely deserves the name; the instruments being of the rudest kind. Their singing is harsh and discordant, the songs are chiefly extempore, relating to passing circumstances, the persons present, or any trifling object that strikes the attention of the singer. They have several kinds of dances, some of them lively and pleasing. The women are rarely permitted to dance with the men, but form groups apart, dancing to the same instrument and song.

They have a great passion for play, and a variety of games. To such a pitch of excitement are they sometimes roused, that they gamble away every thing they possess, even to their wives and children. They are notorious thieves, also, and proud of their dexterity. He who is frequently successful, gains much applause and popularity; but the clumsy thief, who is detected in some bungling attempt, is scoffed at and despised, and sometimes severely punished.

Such are a few leading characteristics of the natives in the neighborhood of Astoria. They appear to us inferior in many respects to the tribes east of the mountains, the bold rovers of the prairies; and to partake much of the Esquimaux character; elevated in some degree by a more genial climate, and more varied style of living.

The habits of traffic engendered at the cataracts of the Columbia, have had their influence along the coast. The Chinooks and other Indians at the mouth of the river, soon proved themselves keen traders, and in their early dealings with the Astorians, never hesitated to ask three times what they considered the real value of an article. They were inquisitive, also, in the extreme, and impertinently intrusive; and were prone to indulge in scoffing and ridicule, at the expense of the strangers.

In one thing, however, they showed superior judgment and self-command, to most of their race; this was, in their abstinence from ardent spirits, and the abhorrence and disgust with which they regarded a drunkard. On one occasion, a son of Comcomly had been induced to drink freely at the factory, and went home in a state of intoxication, playing all kinds of mad pranks, until he sank into a stupor, in which he remained for two days. The old chieftain repaired to his friend, M'Dougal, with indignation flaming in his countenance, and bitterly reproached him for having permitted his son to degrade himself into a beast, and to render himself an object of scorn and laughter to his slave.

CHAPTER XLI

As the spring opened, the little settlement of Astoria was in agitation, and prepared to send forth various expeditions. Several important things were to be done. It was necessary to send a supply of goods to the trading post of Mr. David Stuart, established in the preceding autumn on the Oakinagan. The cache, or secret deposit made by Mr. Hunt at the Caldron Linn, was likewise to be visited, and the merchandize and other effects left there, to be brought to Astoria. A third object of moment was to send despatches overland to Mr. Astor at New York, informing him of the state of affairs at the settlement, and the fortunes of the several expeditions.

The task of carrying supplies to Oakinagan was assigned to Mr. Robert Stuart, a spirited and enterprising young man, nephew to the one who had established the post. The cache was to be sought out by two of the clerks, named Russell Farnham and Donald M'Gilles, conducted by a guide, and accompanied by eight men, to assist in bringing home the goods.

As to the despatches, they were confided to Mr. John Reed, the clerk, the same who had conducted one of the exploring detachments of Snake river. He was now to trace back his way across the mountains by the same route by which he had come, with no other companions or escort than Ben Jones, the Kentucky hunter, and two Canadians. As it was still hoped that Mr. Crooks might be in existence, and that Mr. Reed and his party might meet with him in the course of their route, they were charged with a small supply of goods and provisions, to aid that gentleman on his way to Astoria.

When the expedition of Reed was made known, Mr. M'Lellan announced his determination to accompany it. He had long been dissatisfied with the smallness of his interest in the copartnership, and had requested an additional number of shares; his request not being complied with, he resolved to abandon the company. M'Lellan was a man of a singularly self-willed and decided character, with whom persuasion was useless; he was permitted, therefore, to take his own course without opposition.

As to Reed, he set about preparing for his hazardous journey with the zeal of a true Irishman. He had a tin case made, in which the letters and papers addressed to Mr. Astor were carefully soldered up. This case he intended to strap upon his shoulders, so as to bear it about with him, sleeping and waking, in all changes and chances, by land or by water, and never to part with it but with his life!

As the route of these several parties would be the same for nearly four hundred miles up the Columbia, and within that distance would lie through the piratical pass of the rapids, and among the freebooting tribes of the river, it was thought advisable to start about the same time, and to keep together. Accordingly, on the 22d of March, they all set off, to the number of seventeen men, in two canoes;—and here we cannot but pause to notice the hardihood of these several expeditions, so insignificant in point of force, and severally destined to traverse immense wildernesses, where larger parties had experienced so much danger and distress. When recruits were sought in the preceding year among experienced hunters and voyageurs at Montreal and St. Louis, it was considered dangerous to attempt to cross the Rocky mountains with less than sixty men; and yet here we find Reed ready to push his way across those barriers with merely three companions. Such is the fearlessness, the insensibility to danger, which men acquire by the habitude of constant risk. The mind, like the body, becomes callous by exposure.

The little associated band proceeded up the river, under the command of Mr. Robert Stuart, and arrived early in the month of April at the Long Narrows, that notorious plundering place. Here it was necessary to unload the canoes, and to transport both them and their cargoes to the head of the Narrows by land. Their party was too few in number for the purpose. They were obliged, therefore, to seek the assistance of the Cathlasco Indians, who undertook to carry the goods on their horses. Forward then they set, the Indians with their horses well freighted, and the first load convoyed by Reed and five men, well armed; the gallant Irishman striding along at the head, with his tin case of despatches glittering on his back. In passing, however, through a rocky and intricate defile, some of the freebooting vagabonds turned their horses up a narrow path and galloped off, carrying with them two bales of goods, and a number of smaller articles. To follow them was useless; indeed, it was with much ado that the convoy got into port with the residue of the cargoes; for some of the guards were pillaged of their knives and pocket handkerchiefs, and the lustrous tin case of Mr. John Reed was in imminent jeopardy.

Mr. Stuart heard of these depredations, and hastened forward to the relief of the convoy, but could not reach them before dusk, by which time they had arrived at the village of Wish-ram, already noted for its great fishery, and the knavish propensities of its inhabitants. Here they found themselves benighted in a strange place, and surrounded by savages bent on pilfering, if not upon open robbery. Not knowing what active course to take, they remained under arms all night, without closing an eye, and at the very first peep of dawn, when objects were yet scarce visible, every thing was hastily embarked, and, without seeking to recover the stolen effects, they pushed off from shore; "Glad to bid adieu," as they said, "to this abominable nest of miscreants."

The worthies of Wish-ram, however, were not disposed to part so

easily with their visiters. Their cupidity had been quickened by
the plunder which they had already taken, and their confidence increased by the impunity with which their outrage had passed. They
resolved, therefore, to take further toll of the travellers, and, if possible, to capture the tin case of despatches; which, shining conspicu-
ously from afar, and being guarded by John Reed with such especial
care, must, as they supposed, be "a great medicine."

Accordingly, Mr. Stuart and his comrades had not proceeded far
in the canoes, when they beheld the whole rabble of Wish-ram
stringing in groups along the bank, whooping and yelling, and gibber-
ing in their wild jargon, and when they landed below the falls, they
were surrounded by upwards of four hundred of these river ruffians,
armed with bows and arrows, war clubs, and other savage weapons.
These now pressed forward, with offers to carry the canoes and effects up the portage. Mr. Stuart declined forwarding the goods, alleging the lateness of the hour; but, to keep them in good-humor, informed them that, if they conducted themselves well, their offered
services might probably be accepted in the morning; in the meanwhile, he suggested that they might carry up the canoes. They accordingly set off with the two canoes on their shoulders, accompanied
by a guard of eight men well armed.

When arrived at the head of the falls, the mischievous spirit of
the savages broke out, and they were on the point of destroying the
canoes, doubtless with a view to impede the white men from carrying
forward their goods, and laying them open to further pilfering. They
were with some difficulty prevented from committing this outrage by
the interference of an old man, who appeared to have authority
among them; and, in consequence of his harangue, the whole of the
hostile band, with the exception of about fifty, crossed to the north
side of the river, where they lay in wait, ready for further mischief.

In the meantime, Mr. Stuart, who had remained at the foot of the
falls with the goods, and who knew that the proffered assistance of the
savages was only for the purpose of having an opportunity to plunder,
determined, if possible, to steal a march upon them, and defeat their
machinations. In the dead of the night, therefore, about one o'clock,

the moon shining brightly, he roused his party, and proposed that they should endeavor to transport the goods themselves, above the falls, before the sleeping savages could be aware of their operations. All hands sprang to the work with zeal, and hurried it on in the hope of getting all over before daylight. Mr. Stuart went forward with the first loads, and took his station at the head of the portage, while Mr. Reed and Mr. M'Lellan remained at the foot to forward the remainder.

The day dawned before the transportation was completed. Some of the fifty Indians who had remained on the south side of the river, perceived what was going on, and, feeling themselves too weak for an attack, gave the alarm to those on the opposite side, upwards of a hundred of whom embarked in several large canoes. Two loads of goods yet remained to be brought up. Mr. Stuart despatched some of the people for one of the loads, with a request to Mr. Reed to retain with him as many men as he thought necessary to guard the remaining load, as he suspected hostile intentions on the part of the Indians. Mr. Reed, however, refused to retain any of them, saying that M'Lellan and himself were sufficient to protect the small quantity that remained. The men accordingly departed with the load, while Reed and M'Lellan continued to mount guard over the residue. By this time, a number of the canoes had arrived from the opposite side. As they approached the shore, the unlucky tin box of John Reed, shining afar like the brilliant helmet of Euryalus, caught their eyes. No sooner did the canoes touch the shore, than they leaped forward on the rocks, set up a war-whoop, and sprang forward to secure the glittering prize. Mr. M'Lellan, who was at the river bank, advanced to guard the goods, when one of the savages attempted to hoodwink him with his buffalo robe with one hand, and to stab him with the other. M'Lellan sprang back just far enough to avoid the blow, and raising his rifle, shot the ruffian through the heart.

In the meantime, Reed, who with the want of forethought of an Irishman, had neglected to remove the leathern cover from the lock of his rifle, was fumbling at the fastenings, when he received a blow on the head with a war club that laid him senseless on the ground.

In a twinkling he was stripped of his rifle and pistols, and the tin box, the cause of all this onslaught, was borne off in triumph.

At this critical juncture, Mr. Stuart, who had heard the war-whoop, hastened to the scene of action with Ben Jones, and seven others, of the men. When he arrived, Reed was weltering in his blood, and an Indian standing over him and about to despatch him with a tomahawk. Stuart gave the word, when Ben Jones levelled his rifle, and shot the miscreant on the spot. The men then gave a cheer, and charged upon the main body of the savages, who took to instant flight. Reed was now raised from the ground, and borne senseless and bleeding to the upper end of the portage. Preparations were made to launch the canoes and embark in all haste, when it was found that they were too leaky to be put in the water, and that the oars had been left at the foot of the falls. A scene of confusion now ensued. The Indians were whooping and yelling, and running about like fiends. A panic seized upon the men, at being this suddenly checked, the hearts of some of the Canadians died within them, and two young men actually fainted away. The moment they recovered their senses, Mr. Stuart ordered that they should be deprived of their arms, their under garments taken off, and that a piece of cloth should be tied round their waists, in imitation of a squaw; an Indian punishment for cowardice. Thus equipped, they were stowed away among the goods in one of the canoes. This ludicrous affair excited the mirth of the bolder spirits, even in the midst of their perils, and roused the pride of the wavering. The Indians having crossed back again to the north side, order was restored, some of the hands were sent back for the oars, others set to work to caulk and launch the canoes, and in a little while all were embarked and were continuing their voyage along the southern shore.

No sooner had they departed, than the Indians returned to the scene of action, bore off their two comrades, who had been shot, one of whom was still living, and returned to their village. Here they killed two horses; and drank the hot blood to give fierceness to their courage. They painted and arrayed themselves hideously for battle; performed the dead dance round the slain, and raised the war song of vengeance. Then mounting their horses, to the number of four hundred and fifty men, and brandishing their weapons, they set off along the northern bank of the river, to get ahead of the canoes, lie in wait for them, and take a terrible revenge on the white men.

They succeeded in getting some distance above the canoes without being discovered, and were crossing the river to post themselves on the side along which the white men were coasting, when they were fortunately descried. Mr. Stuart and his companions were immediately on the alert. As they drew near to the place where the savages had crossed, they observed them posted among steep and overhanging rocks, close along which, the canoes would have to pass. Finding that the enemy had the advantage of the ground, the whites stopped short when within five hundred yards of them, and discharged and reloaded their pieces. They then made a fire, and dressed the wounds of Mr. Reed, who had received five severe gashes in the head. This being done, they lashed the canoes together, fastened them to a rock at a small distance from the shore, and there awaited the menaced attack.

They had not been long posted in this manner, when they saw a canoe approaching. It contained the war-chief of the tribe, and three of his principal warriors. He drew near, and made a long harangue, in which he informed them that they had killed one and wounded another of his nation; that the relations of the slain cried out for vengeance, and he had been compelled to lead them to the fight. Still he wished to spare unnecessary bloodshed, he proposed, therefore, that Mr. Reed, who, he observed, was little better than a dead man, might be given up to be sacrificed to the manes of the deceased warrior. This would appease the fury of his friends; the hatchet would then be buried, and all thenceforward would be friends. The answer was a stern refusal and a defiance, and the war-chief saw that the canoes were well prepared for a vigorous defence. He withdrew, therefore, and, returning to his warriors among the rocks held long deliberations. Blood for blood is a principle in Indian equity and Indian honor; but though the inhabitants of Wish-ram were men of war, they were likewise men of traffic, and it was suggested that honor for once

might give way to profit. A negotiation was accordingly opened with
the white men, and after some diplomacy, the matter was compro-
mised for a blanket to cover the dead, and some tobacco to be smoked
by the living. This being granted, the heroes of Wish-ram crossed the
river once more, returned to their village to feast upon the horses
whose blood they had so vaingloriously drunk, and the travellers pursued their voyage without further molestation.

The tin case, however, containing the important despatches for
New York, was irretrievably lost; the very precaution taken by the
worthy Hibernian to secure his missives, had, by rendering them con-
spicuous, produced their robbery. The object of his over-land journey,
therefore, being defeated, he gave up the expedition. The whole party
repaired with Mr. Robert Stuart to the establishment of Mr. David
Stuart, on the Oakinagan river. After remaining here two or three
days, they all set out on their return to Astoria, accompanied by Mr.
David Stuart. This gentleman, had a large quantity of beaver skins at
his establishment, but did not think it prudent to take them with
him, fearing the levy of "black mail" at the falls.

On their way down, when below the forks of the Columbia, they
were hailed one day from the shore in English. Looking around, they
descried two wretched men, entirely naked. They pulled to shore; the
men came up and made themselves known. They proved to be Mr.
Crooks and his faithful follower, John Day.

The reader will recollect, that Mr. Crooks, with Day and four
Canadians, had been so reduced by famine and fatigue, that Mr.
Hunt was obliged to leave them, in the month of December, on the
banks of the Snake river. Their situation was the more critical, as they
were in the neighborhood of a band of Shoshonies, whose horses had
been forcibly seized by Mr. Hunt's party for provisions. Mr. Crooks
remained here twenty days, detained by the extremely reduced state
of John Day, who was utterly unable to travel, and whom he would
not abandon, as Day had been in his employ on the Missouri, and had
always proved himself most faithful. Fortunately the Shoshonies did
not offer to molest them. They had never before seen white men, and

seemed to entertain some superstitions with regard to them, for, though they would encamp near them in the day time, they would move off with their tents in the night; and finally disappeared, without taking leave.

When Day was sufficiently recovered to travel, they kept feebly on, sustaining themselves as well as they could, until in the month of February, when three of the Canadians, fearful of perishing with want, left Mr. Crooks on a small river, on the road by which Mr. Hunt had passed in quest of Indians. Mr. Crooks followed Mr. Hunt's track in the snow for several days, sleeping as usual in the open air, and suffering all kinds of hardships. At length, coming to a low prairie, he lost every appearance of the "trail," and wandered during the remainder of the winter in the mountains, subsisting sometimes on horse meat, sometimes on beavers and their skins, and a part of the time on roots.

About the last of March, the other Canadian gave out, and was left with a lodge of Shoshonies; but Mr. Crooks and John Day still kept on, and finding the snow sufficiently diminished, undertook, from Indian information, to cross the last mountain ridge. They happily succeeded, and afterwards fell in with the Wallah-Wallahs, a tribe of Indians inhabiting the banks of a river of the same name, and reputed as being frank, hospitable and sincere. They proved worthy of the character, for they received the poor wanderers kindly, killed a horse for them to eat, and directed them on their way to the Columbia. They struck the river about the middle of April, and advanced down it one hundred miles, until they came within about twenty miles of the falls.

Here they met with some of the "chivalry" of that noted pass, who received them in a friendly way, and set food before them; but, while they were satisfying their hunger, perfidiously seized their rifles. They then stripped them naked, and drove them off, refusing the entreaties of Mr. Crooks for a flint and steel of which they had robbed him; and threatening his life if he did not instantly depart.

In this forlorn plight, still worse off than before, they renewed their wanderings. They now sought to find their way back to the hospitable Wallah-Wallahs, and had advanced eighty miles along the river, when fortunately, on the very morning that they were going to leave the Columbia, and strike inland, the canoes of Mr. Stuart hove in sight.

It is needless to describe the joy of these poor men at once more finding themselves among countrymen and friends, or of the honest and hearty welcome with which they were received by their fellow adventurers. The whole party now continued down the river, passed all the dangerous places without interruption, and arrived safely at Astoria on the 11th of May.

CHAPTER XLII

HAVING traced the fortune of the two expeditions by sea and land to the mouth of the Columbia, and presented a view of affairs at Astoria, we will return for a moment to the master spirit of the enterprise, who regulated the springs of Astoria, at his residence in New York.

It will be remembered, that a part of the plan of Mr. Astor was to furnish the Russian fur establishment on the north-west coast with regular supplies, so as to render it independent of those casual vessels which cut up the trade and supplied the natives with arms. This plan had been countenanced by our own government, and likewise by Count Pahlen, the Russian minister at Washington. As its views, however, were important and extensive, and might eventually affect a wide course of commerce, Mr. Astor was desirous of establishing a complete arrangement on the subject with the Russian American Fur Company, under the sanction of the Russian government. For this purpose, in March, 1811, he despatched a confidential agent to St. Petersburgh, fully empowered to enter into the requisite negotiations. A passage was given to this gentleman by the government of the United States, in the John Adams, one of its armed vessels, bound to a European port.

The next step of Mr. Astor was, to despatch the annual ship contemplated on his general plan. He had as yet heard nothing of the
success of the previous expeditions, and had to proceed upon the pre-
sumption that every thing had been affected according to his instructions. He accordingly fitted out a fine ship of four hundred and ninety
tons, called the Beaver, and freighted her with a valuable cargo destined for the factory, at the mouth of the Columbia, the trade along
the coast, and the supply of the Russian establishment. In this ship
embarked a reinforcement, consisting of a partner, five clerks, fifteen
American laborers, and six Canadian voyageurs. In choosing his agents
for his first expedition, Mr. Astor had been obliged to have recourse
to British subjects experienced in the Canadian fur trade; henceforth
it was his intention, as much as possible, to select Americans, so as to
secure an ascendancy of American influence in the management of
the company, and to make it decidedly national.

Accordingly, Mr. John Clarke, the partner who took the lead in
the present expedition, was a native of the United States, though he
had passed much of his life in the northwest, having been employed
in the fur trade since the age of sixteen. Most of the clerks were young
gentlemen of good connections in the American cities, some of whom
embarked in the hope of gain, others through the mere spirit of ad-
venture incident to youth.

The instructions given by Mr. Astor to Captain Sowle, the commander of the Beaver, were, in some respects, hypothetical, in consequence of the uncertainty resting upon the previous steps of the enterprise.

He was to touch at the Sandwich islands, enquire about the fortunes of the Tonquin, and whether an establishment had been formed
at the mouth of the Columbia. If so, he was to take as many Sandwich
islanders as his ship would accommodate, and proceed thither. On
arriving at the river, he was to observe great caution, for even if an
establishment should have been formed, it might have fallen into hostile hands. He was, therefore, to put in as if by casualty or distress, to
give himself out as a coasting trader, and to say nothing about his ship
being owned by Mr. Astor, until he had ascertained that every thing

was right. In that case, he was to land such part of his cargo as was intended for the establishment, and to proceed to New Archangel with the supplies intended for the Russian post at that place, where he could receive peltries in payment. With these he was to return to Astoria; take in the furs collected there, and, having completed his cargo by trading along the coast, was to proceed to Canton. The captain received the same injunctions that had been given to Captain Thorn of the Tonquin, of great caution and circumspection in his intercourse with the natives, and that he should not permit more than one or two to be on board at a time.

The Beaver sailed from New York on the 10th of October, 1811, and reached the Sandwich islands without any occurrence of moment. Here a rumor was heard of the disastrous fate of the Tonquin. Deep solicitude was felt by every one on board for the fate of both expeditions, by sea and land. Doubts were entertained whether any establishment had been formed at the mouth of the Columbia, or whether any of the company would be found there. After much deliberation, the captain took twelve Sandwich islanders on board, for the service of the factory, should there be one in existence, and proceeded on his voyage.

On the 6th of May he arrived off of the mouth of the Columbia, and running as near as possible, fired two signal guns. No answer was returned, nor was there any signal to be descried. Night coming on, the ship stood out to sea, and every heart drooped as the land faded away. On the following morning they again ran in within four miles of the shore, and fired other signal guns, but still without reply. A boat was then despatched, to sound the channel, and attempt an entrance; but returned without success, there being a tremendous swell, and breakers. Signal guns were fired again in the evening, but equally in vain, and once more the ship stood off to sea for the night. The captain now gave up all hope of finding any establishment at the place, and indulged in the most gloomy apprehensions. He feared his predecessors had been massacred before they had reached their place of destination; or if they should have erected a factory, that it had been surprised and destroyed by the natives.

In this moment of doubt and uncertainty, Mr. Clarke announced his determination, in case of the worst, to found an establishment with the present party, and all hands bravely engaged to stand by him in the undertaking. The next morning the ship stood in for the third time, and fired three signal guns, but with little hope of reply. To the great joy of the crew, three distinct guns were heard in answer. The apprehensions of all but Captain Sowle were now at rest. That cautious commander recollected the instructions given him by Mr. Astor, and determined to proceed with great circumspection. He was well aware of Indian treachery and cunning. It was not impossible, he observed, that these cannon might have been fired by the savages themselves. They might have surprised the fort, massacred its inmates; and these signal guns might only be decoys to lure him across the bar, that they might have a chance of cutting him off, and seizing his vessel.

At length a white flag was descried hoisted as a signal on cape Disappointment. The passengers pointed to it in triumph, but the captain did not yet dismiss his doubts. A beacon fire blazed through the night on the same place, but the captain observed that all these signals might be treacherous.

On the following morning, May 9th, the vessel came to anchor off cape Disappointment, outside of the bar. Towards noon an Indian canoe was seen making for the ship, and all hands were ordered to be on the alert. A few moments afterwards, a barge was perceived following the canoe. The hopes and fears of those on board of the ship were in tumultuous agitation, as the boat drew nigh that was to let them know the fortunes of the enterprise, and the fate of their predecessors. The captain, who was haunted with the idea of possible treachery, did not suffer his curiosity to get the better of his caution, but ordered a party of his men under arms, to receive the visiters. The canoe came first along side, in which were Comcomly and six Indians; in the barge were M'Dougal, M'Lellan, and eight Canadians. A little conversation with these gentlemen dispelled all the captain's fears, and the Beaver crossing the bar under their pilotage, anchored safely in Baker's bay.

CHAPTER XLIII

THE arrival of the Beaver with a re-
inforcement and supplies, gave new life and vigor to affairs at Astoria.
These were means for extending the operations of the establishment,
and founding interior trading posts. Two parties were immediately
set on foot to proceed severally under the command of Messrs.
M'Kenzie and Clarke, and establish posts above the forks of the
Columbia, at points where most rivalry and opposition were apprehended from the North-west Company.

A third party, headed by Mr. David Stuart, was to repair with supplies to the post of that gentleman on the Oakinagan. In addition to
these expeditions, a fourth was necessary to convey despatches to Mr.
Astor, at New York, in place of those unfortunately lost by John Reed.
The safe conveyance of these despatches were highly important, as by
them Mr. Astor would receive an account of the state of the factory,
and regulate his reinforcements and supplies accordingly. The mission
was one of peril and hardship, and required a man of nerve and vigor.
It was confided to Robert Stuart, who, though he had never been
across the mountains, and a very young man, had given proofs of his

competency to the task. Four trusty and well-tried men, who had come over land in Mr. Hunt's expedition, were given as his guides and hunters. These were Ben Jones and John Day, the Kentuckians, and Andri Vallar and Francis Le Clerc, Canadians. Mr. M'Lellan again expressed his determination to take this opportunity of returning to the Atlantic states. In this he was joined by Mr. Crooks, who, notwithstanding all that he had suffered in the dismal journey of the preceding winter, was ready to retrace his steps and brave every danger and hardship, rather than remain at Astoria. This little handful of adventurous men we propose to accompany in its long and perilous peregrinations.

The several parties we have mentioned all set off in company on the 29th of June, under a salute of cannon from the fort. They were to keep together, for mutual protection, through the piratical passes of the river, and to separate, on their different destinations, at the forks of the Columbia. Their number, collectively, was nearly sixty, consisting of partners and clerks, Canadian voyageurs, Sandwich islanders, and American hunters; and they embarked in two barges and ten canoes.

They had scarcely got under way, when John Day, the Kentucky hunter, became restless, and uneasy, and extremely wayward in his deportment. This caused surprise, for in general he was remarked for his cheerful, manly deportment. It was supposed that the recollection of past sufferings might harrass his mind in undertaking to retrace the scenes where they had been experienced. As the expedition advanced, however, his agitation increased. He began to talk wildly and incoherently, and to show manifest symptoms of derangement.

Mr. Crooks now informed his companions that in his desolate wanderings through the Snake river country during the preceding winter, in which he had been accompanied by John Day, the poor fellow's wits had been partially unsettled by the sufferings and horrors through which they had passed, and he doubted whether they had ever been restored to perfect sanity. It was still hoped that this agitation of spirit might pass away as they proceeded; but, on the contrary, it grew more and more violent. His comrades endeavored to divert his mind and to draw him into rational conversation, but he only became the more exasperated, uttering wild and incoherent ravings. The sight of any of the natives put him in an absolute fury, and he would heap on them the most opprobrious epithets; recollecting, no doubt, what he had suffered from Indian robbers.

On the evening of the 2d of July he became absolutely frantic, and attempted to destroy himself. Being disarmed, he sank into quietude, and professed the greatest remorse for the crime he had meditated. He then pretended to sleep, and having thus lulled suspicion, suddenly sprang up, just before daylight, seized a pair of loaded pistols, and endeavored to blow out his brains. In his hurry he fired too high, and the balls passed over his head. He was instantly secured, and placed under a guard in one of the boats. How to dispose of him was now the question, as it was impossible to keep him with the expedition. Fortunately Mr. Stuart met with some Indians accustomed to trade with Astoria. These undertook to conduct John Day back to the factory, and deliver him there in safety. It was with the utmost concern that his comrades saw the poor fellow depart; for, independent of his invaluable services as a first rate hunter, his frank loyal qualities had made him a universal favorite. It may be as well to add that the Indians executed their task faithfully, and landed John Day among his friends at Astoria; but his constitution was completely broken by the hardships he had undergone, and he died within a year.

On the evening of the 6th of July the party arrived at the piratical pass of the river, and encamped at the foot of the first rapid. The next day, before the commencement of the portage, the greatest precautions were taken to guard against lurking treachery, or open attack. The weapons of every man were put in order, and his cartridge-box replenished. Each one wore a kind of surcoat made of the skin of the elk, reaching from his neck to his knees, and answering the purpose of a shirt of mail, for it was arrow proof, and could even resist a musket ball at the distance of ninety yards. Thus armed and equipped, they posted their forces in military style. Five of the officers took their stations at each end of the portage, which was between three and four miles in length; a number of men mounted guard at short distances along the heights immediately overlooking the river, while the residue thus protected from surprise, employed themselves below in dragging up the barges and canoes, and carrying up the goods along the narrow margin of the rapids. With these precautions they all passed unmolested. The only accident that happened was the upsetting of one of the canoes, by which some of the goods sunk, and others floated down the stream. The alertness and rapacity of the hordes which infest these rapids, were immediately apparent. They pounced upon the floating merchandise with the keenness of regular wreckers. A bale of goods which landed upon one of the islands was immediately ripped open, one half of its contents divided among the captives, and the other half secreted in a lonely hut in a deep ravine. Mr. Robert Stuart, however, set out in a canoe with five men and an interpreter, ferreted out the wreckers in their retreat, and succeeded in wresting from them their booty.

Similar precautions to those already mentioned, and to a still greater extent, were observed in passing the long narrows, and the falls, where they would be exposed to the depredations of the chivalry of Wishram, and its freebooting neighborhood. In fact, they had scarcely set their first watch one night, when an alarm of "Indians!" was given. "To arms!" was the cry, and every man was at his post in an instant. The alarm was explained; a war party of Shoshonies had surprised a canoe of the natives just below the encampment, had murdered four men and two women, and it was apprehended they would attack the camp. The boats and canoes were immediately hauled up, a breastwork was made of them, and the packages, forming three sides of a square, with the river in the rear, and thus the party remained fortified throughout the night.

The dawn, however, dispelled the alarm; the portage was conducted in peace; the vagabond warriors of the vicinity hovered about them while at work, but were kept at a wary distance. They regarded the loads of merchandise with wistful eyes, but seeing the "long beards" so formidable in number, and so well prepared for action, they made no attempt either by open force or sly pilfering to collect their usual toll, but maintained a peaceful demeanor, and were afterwards rewarded for their good conduct with presents of tobacco.

Fifteen days were consumed in ascending from the foot of the first rapid, to the head of the falls, a distance of about eighty miles, but full of all kinds of obstructions. Having happily accomplished these difficult portages, the party, on the 19th of July, arrived at a smoother part of the river, and pursued their way up the stream with greater speed and facility.

They were now in the neighborhood where Mr. Crooks and John Day had been so perfidiously robbed and stripped a few months previously, when confiding in the proffered hospitality of a ruffian band. On landing at night, therefore, a vigilant guard was maintained about the camp. On the following morning a number of Indians made their appearance, and came prowling round the party while at breakfast. To his great delight, Mr. Crooks recognized among them two of the miscreants by whom he had been robbed. They were instantly seized, bound hand and foot, and thrown into one of the canoes. Here they lay in doleful fright, expecting summary execution. Mr. Crooks, however, was not of a revengeful disposition, and agreed to release the culprits as soon as the pillaged property should be restored. Several savages immediately started off in different directions, and before night the rifles of Crooks and Day were produced; several of the smaller articles pilfered from them, however, could not be recovered.

The bands of the culprits were then removed, and they lost no time in taking their departure, still under the influence of abject terror, and scarcely crediting their senses that they had escaped the merited punishment of their offences.

The country on each side of the river now began to assume a different character. The hills, and cliffs, and forests, disappeared; vast sandy plains, scantily clothed here and there with short tufts of grass, parched by the summer sun, stretched far away to the north and south. The river was occasionally obstructed with rocks and rapids, but often there were smooth placid intervals, where the current was gentle, and the boatmen were enabled to lighten their labors with the assistance of the sail.

The natives in this part of the river resided entirely on the north-

ern side. They were hunters, as well as fishermen, and had horses in
plenty. Some of these were purchased by the party, as provisions, and
killed on the spot, though they occasionally found a difficulty in procuring fuel wherewith to cook them. One of the greatest dangers that
beset the travellers in this part of their expedition, was the vast number of rattlesnakes which infested the rocks about the rapids and portages, and on which the men were in danger of treading. They were
often found, too, in quantities about the encampments. In one place,
a nest of them lay coiled together, basking in the sun. Several guns
loaded with shot were discharged at them, and thirty-seven killed and
wounded. To prevent any unwelcome visits from them in the night,
tobacco was occasionally strewed around the tents, a weed for which
they have a very proper abhorrence.

On the 28th of July the travellers arrived at the mouth of the
Wallah-Wallah, a bright, clear stream, about six feet deep, and fifty-
five yards wide, which flows rapidly over a bed of sand and gravel, and
throws itself into the Columbia, a few miles below Lewis river. Here
the combined parties that had thus far voyaged together, were to separate, each for its particular destination.

On the banks of the Wallah-Wallah lived the hospitable tribe of
the same name who had succored Mr. Crooks and John Day in the
time of their extremity. No sooner did they hear of the arrival of the
party, than they hastened to greet them. They built a great bonfire
on the bank of the river, before the camp, and men and women
danced round it to the cadence of their songs, in which they sang the
praises of the white men, and welcomed them to their country.

On the following day a traffic was commenced, to procure horses
for such of the party as intended to proceed by land. The Wallah-
Wallahs are an equestrian tribe. The equipments of their horses were
rude and inconvenient. High saddles, roughly made of deer skin,
stuffed with hair, which chafe the horse's back, and leave it raw;
wooden stirrups, with a thong of raw hide wrapped round them; and
for bridles they have cords of twisted horse hair, which they tie round
the under jaw. They are like most Indians, bold, but hard riders, and
when on horseback gallop about the most dangerous places, without

fear for themselves, or pity for their steeds.

From these people Mr. Stuart purchased twenty horses for his party; some for the saddle, and others to transport the baggage. He was fortunate in procuring a noble animal for his own use, which was praised by the Indians for its great speed and bottom, and a high price set upon it. No people understand better the value of a horse, than these equestrian tribes; and no where is speed a greater requisite, as they frequently engage in the chase of the antelope, one of the fleetest of animals. Even after the Indian who sold this boasted horse to Mr. Stuart had concluded his bargain, he lingered about the animal, seeming loth to part from him, and to be sorry for what he had done.

A day or two were employed by Mr. Stuart in arranging packages and pack saddles, and making other preparations for his long and arduous journey. His party, by the loss of John Day, was now reduced to six, a small number for such an expedition. They were young men, however, full of courage, health, and good spirits, and stimulated, rather than appalled by danger.

On the morning of the 31st of July, all preparation being concluded, Mr. Stuart and his little band mounted their steeds and took a farewell of their fellow travellers, who gave them three hearty cheers as they set out on their dangerous journey. The course they took was to the southeast, towards the fated region of the Snake river. At an immense distance rose a chain of craggy mountains, which they would have to traverse; they were the same among which the travellers had experienced such sufferings from cold during the preceding winter, and from their azure tints, when seen at a distance, had received the name of the Blue mountains.

CHAPTER XLIV

In retracing the route which had
proved so disastrous to Mr. Hunt's party during the preceding winter,
Mr. Stuart had trusted, in the present more favorable season, to find
easy travelling and abundant supplies. On these great wastes and
wilds, however, each season has its peculiar hardships. The travellers
had not proceded far, before they found themselves among naked and
arid hills, with a soil composed of sand and clay, baked and brittle,
that to all appearance had never been visited by the dews of heaven.

Not a spring, or pool, or running stream was to be seen; the sunburnt country was seamed and cut up by dry ravines, the beds of winter torrents, serving only to balk the hopes of man and beast, with the
sight of dusty channels where water had once poured along in floods.

For a long summer day they continued onward without halting; a
burning sky above their heads, a parched desert beneath their feet,
with just wind enough to raise the light sand from the knolls, and en-
velope them in stifling clouds. The sufferings from thirst became
intense; a fine young dog, their only companion of the kind, gave out,

and expired. Evening drew on without any prospect of relief, and they were almost reduced to despair, when they descried something that looked like a fringe of forest, along the horizon. All were inspired with new hope, for they knew that on these arid wastes, in the neighborhood of trees, there is always water.

They now quickened their pace; the horses seemed to understand their motives, and to partake of their anticipations, for, though before, almost ready to give out, they now required neither whip nor spur. With all their exertions, it was late in the night before they drew near to the trees. As they approached, they heard, with transport, the rippling of a shallow stream. No sooner did the refreshing sound reach the ears of the horses, than the poor animals snuffed the air, rushed forward with ungovernable eagerness, and, plunging their muzzles into the water, drank until they seemed in danger of bursting. Their riders had but little more discretion, and required repeated draughts to quench their excessive thirst. Their weary march that day had been forty-five miles, over a tract that might rival the deserts of Africa for aridity. Indeed, the sufferings of the traveller on these American deserts, is frequently more severe than in the wastes of Africa or Asia, from being less habituated and prepared to cope with them.

On the banks of this blessed stream the travellers encamped for the night; and so great had been their fatigue, and so sound and sweet was their sleep, that it was a late hour the next morning before they awoke. They now recognized the little river to be the Umatalla, the same on the banks of which Mr. Hunt and his followers had arrived after their painful struggle through the Blue mountains, and experienced such a kind relief in the friendly camp of the Sciatogas.

That range of Blue mountains now extended in the distance before them; they were the same among which poor Michael Carriere had perished. They form the southeast boundary of the great plains along the Columbia, dividing the waters of its main stream from those of Lewis river. They are, in fact, a part of a long chain, which stretches over a great extent of country, and includes in its links the Snake river mountains.

The day was somewhat advanced before the travellers left the shady banks of the Umatalla. Their route gradually took them among the Blue mountains, which assumed the most rugged aspect on a near approach. They were shagged with dense and gloomy forests, and cut up by deep and precipitous ravines, extremely toilsome to the horses. Sometimes the travellers had to follow the course of some brawling stream, with a broken, rocky bed, which the shouldering cliffs and promontories on either side, obliged them frequently to cross and recross. For some miles they struggled forward through these savage and darkly wooded defiles, when all at once the whole landscape changed, as if by magic. The rude mountains and rugged ravines softened into beautiful hills, and intervening meadows, with rivulets winding through fresh herbage, and sparkling and murmuring over gravelly beds, the whole forming a verdant and pastoral scene, which derived additional charms from being locked up in the bosom of such a hard-hearted region.

Emerging from the chain of Blue mountains, they descended upon a vast plain, almost a dead level, sixty miles in circumference, of excellent soil, with fine streams meandering through it in every direction, their courses marked out in the wide landscape, by serpentine lines of cotton-wood trees, and willows, which fringed their banks, and afforded sustenance to great numbers of beavers and otters.

Emerging from the chain of Blue mountains, they descended upon a great pool of water, three hundred yards in circumference, fed by a sulphur spring, about ten feet in diameter, boiling up in one corner. The vapor from this pool was extremely noisome, and tainted the air for a considerable distance. The place was much frequented by elk, which were found in considerable numbers in the adjacent mountains, and their horns, shed in the spring time, were strewed in every direction around the pond.

On the 20th of August, they reached the main body of Woodpile creek, the same stream which Mr. Hunt had ascended in the preceding year, shortly after his separation from Mr. Crooks.

On the banks of this stream they saw a herd of nineteen antelopes; a sight so unusual in that part of the country, that at first they doubted the evidence of their senses. They tried by every means to get within shot of them, but they were too shy and fleet, and after alternately bounding to a distance, and then stopping to gaze with capricious curiosity at the hunter, they at length scampered out of sight.

On the 12th of August, the travellers arrived on the banks of Snake river, the scene of so many trials and mishaps to all of the present party excepting Mr. Stuart. They struck the river just above the place where it entered the mountains, through which Messrs. Stuart and Crooks had vainly endeavored to find a passage. The river was here a rapid stream four hundred yards in width, with high sandy banks, and here and there a scanty growth of willow. Up the southern side of the river they now bent their course, intending to visit the caches made by Mr. Hunt at the Caldron Linn.

On the second evening, a solitary Snake Indian visited their camp, at a late hour, and informed them that there was a white man residing at one of the encampments of his tribe, about a day's journey higher up the river. It was immediately concluded, that he must be one of the poor fellows of Mr. Hunt's party, who had given out, exhausted by hunger and fatigue, in the wretched journey of the preceding winter. All present, who had borne a part in the sufferings of that journey, were eager now to press forward, and bring relief to a lost comrade. Early the next morning, therefore, they pushed forward with unusual alacrity. For two days, however, did they travel without being able to find any trace of such a straggler.

On the evening of the second day, they arrived at a place where a large river came in from the east, which was renowned among all the wandering hordes of the Snake nation, for its salmon fishery, that fish being taken in incredible quantities in this neighborhood. Here, therefore, during the fishing season, the Snake Indians resort from far and near, to lay in their stock of salmon, which, with esculent roots, forms the principal food of the inhabitants of these barren regions.

On the bank of a small stream emptying into Snake river at this place, Mr. Stuart found an encampment of Shoshonies. He made the usual inquiry of them concerning the white man of whom he had received intelligence. No such person was dwelling among them, but they said there were white men residing with some of their nation on the opposite side of the river. This was still more animating information. Mr. Crooks now hoped that these might be the men of his party, who, disheartened by perils and hardships, had preferred to remain among the Indians. Others thought they might be Mr. Miller and the hunters who had left the main body at Henry's fort, to trap among the mountain streams. Mr. Stuart halted, therefore, in the neighborhood of the Shoshonie lodges, and sent an Indian across the river to seek out the white men in question, and bring them to his camp.

The travellers passed a restless, miserable night. The place swarmed with myriads of musquitoes, which, with their stings and their music, set all sleep at defiance. The morning dawn, found them in a feverish, irritable mood, and their spleen was completely aroused by the return of the Indian, without any intelligence of the white men. They now considered themselves the dupes of Indian falsehoods and resolved to put no more confidence in Snakes. They soon, however, forgot this resolution. In the course of the morning, an Indian came gallopping after them; Mr. Stuart waited to receive him; no sooner had he come up, than, dismounting and throwing his arms round the neck of Mr. Stuart's horse, he began to kiss and caress the animal, who, on his part, seemed by no means surprised or displeased with his salutation. Mr. Stuart, who valued his horse highly, was somewhat annoyed by these transports; the cause of them was soon explained. The Snake said the horse had belonged to him, and been the best in his possession, and that it had been stolen by the Wallah-Wallahs. Mr. Stuart was by no means pleased with this recognition of his steed, nor disposed to admit any claim on the part of its ancient owner. In fact, it was a noble animal, admirably shaped, of free and generous spirit, graceful in every movement, and fleet as an antelope. It was his intention, if possible, to take the horse to New York, and present him to Mr. Astor.

In the meantime, some of the party came up, and immediately recognized in the Snake an old friend and ally. He was, in fact, one of the two guides who had conducted Mr. Hunt's party, in the preced-

ing autumn, across Mad river mountain, to fort Henry, and who subsequently departed with Mr. Miller and his fellow trappers, to conduct them to a good trapping ground. The reader may recollect that
these two trusty Snakes were engaged by Mr. Hunt to return and take
charge of the horses which the party intended to leave at fort Henry,
when they should embark in canoes.

The party now crowded round the Snake, and began to question
him with eagerness. His replies were somewhat vague, and but partially understood. He told a long story about the horses, from which
it appeared that they had been stolen by various wandering bands,
and scattered in different directions. The cache, too, had been plundered, and the saddles and other equipments carried off. His information concerning Mr. Miller and his comrades, was not more satisfactory. They had trapped for some time about the upper streams,
but had fallen into the hands of a marauding party of Crows, who
had robbed them of horses, weapons, and every thing.

Further questioning brought forth further intelligence, but all of
a disastrous kind. About ten days previously, he had met with three
other white men, in very miserable plight, having one horse each, and
but one rifle among them. They also had been plundered and maltreated by the Crows, those universal freebooters. The Snake endeavored to pronounce the names of these three men, and as far as
his imperfect sounds could be understood, they were supposed to be
three of the party of four hunters, viz. Carson, St. Michael, Detayé
and Delannay, who were detached from Mr. Hunt's party on the 28th
of September, to trap beaver on the head waters of the Columbia.

In the course of conversation, the Indian informed them that the
route by which Mr. Hunt had crossed the Rocky mountains, was very
bad and circuitous, and that he knew one much shorter and easier.
Mr. Stuart urged him to accompany them as guide, promising to reward him with a pistol with powder and ball, a knife, an awl, some
blue beads, a blanket, and a looking-glass. Such a catalogue of riches
was too tempting to be resisted; beside, the poor Snake languished
after the prairies; he was tired, he said, of salmon, and longed for
buffalo meat, and to have a grand buffalo hunt beyond the mountains.

He departed, therefore, with all speed, to get his arms and equipments for the journey, promising to rejoin the party the next day. He kept his word, and, as he no longer said any thing to Mr. Stuart on the subject of the pet horse, they journeyed very harmoniously together; though now and then, the Snake would regard his quondam steed with a wistful eye.

They had not travelled many miles, when they came to a great bend of the river. Here the Snake informed them that, by cutting across the hills they would save many miles of distance. The route across, however, would be a good day's journey. He advised them, therefore, to encamp here for the night, and set off early in the morning. They took his advice, though they had come but nine miles that day.

On the following morning they rose, bright and early, to ascend the hills. On mustering their little party, the guide was missing. They supposed him to be somewhere in the neighborhood, and proceeded to collect the horses. The vaunted steed of Mr. Stuart was not to be found. A suspicion flashed upon his mind. Search for the horse of the Snake!—He likewise was gone—the tracks of two horses, one after the other, were found, making off from the camp. They appeared as if one horse had been mounted, and the other led. They were traced for a few miles above the camp, until they both crossed the river. It was plain the Snake had taken an Indian mode of recovering his horse, having quietly decamped with him in the night.

New vows were made never more to trust in Snakes, or any other Indians. It was determined, also, to maintain, hereafter, the strictest vigilance over their horses, dividing the night into three watches, and one person mounting guard at a time. They resolved, also, to keep along the river, instead of taking the short cut recommended by the fugitive Snake, whom they now set down for a thorough deceiver. The heat of the weather was oppressive, and their horses were, at times, rendered almost frantic by the stings of the prairie flies. The nights were suffocating, and it was almost impossible to sleep, from the swarms of musquitoes.

On the 20th of August they resumed their march, keeping along the prairie parallel to Snake river. The day was sultry, and some of the party, being parched with thirst, left the line of march, and scrambled down the bank of the river to drink. The bank was over-hung with willows, beneath which, to their surprise, they beheld a man fishing. No sooner did he see them, than he uttered an exclamation of joy. It proved to be John Hoback, one of their lost comrades. They had scarcely exchanged greetings, when three other men came out from among the willows. They were Joseph Miller, Jacob Rezner, and Robinson, the scalped Kentuckian, the veteran of the Bloody ground.

The reader will perhaps recollect the abrupt and wilful manner in which Mr. Miller threw up his interest as a partner of the company, and departed from Fort Henry, in company with these three trappers, and a fourth, named Cass. He may likewise recognise in Robinson, Rezner, and Hoback, the trio of Kentucky hunters, who had originally been in the service of Mr. Henry, and whom Mr. Hunt found floating down the Missouri, on their way homeward; and pre-vailed upon, once more, to cross the mountains. The haggard looks and naked condition of these men proved how much they had suf-fered. After leaving Mr. Hunt's party, they had made their way about two hundred miles to the southward, where they trapped beaver on a river which, according to their account, discharged itself into the ocean to the south of the Columbia, but which we apprehend to be Bear river, a stream emptying itself into lake Bonneville, an immense body of salt water, west of the Rocky mountains.

Having collected a considerable quantity of beaver skins, they made them into packs, loaded their horses, and steered two hundred miles due east. Here they came upon an encampment of sixty lodges of Arapahays, an outlawed band of the Arapahoes, and notorious rob-bers. These fell upon the poor trappers; robbed them of their peltries, most of their clothing, and several of their horses. They were glad to escape with their lives, and without being entirely stripped, and after proceeding about fifty miles further, made their halt for the winter.

Early in the spring they resumed their wayfaring, but were unluck-ily overtaken by the same ruffian horde, who levied still further contributions, and carried off the remainder of their horses, excepting two. With these they continued on, suffering the greatest hardships. They still retained rifles and ammunition, but were in a desert country, where neither bird nor beast was to be found. Their only chance was to keep along the rivers and subsist by fishing; but at times, no fish were to be taken, and then their sufferings were horrible. One of their horses was stolen among the mountains by the Snake Indians; the other, they said, was carried off by Cass, who, according to their account, "villainously left them in their extremities." Certain dark doubts and surmises were afterwards circulated concerning the fate of that poor fellow, which, if true, showed to what a desperate state of famine his comrades had been reduced.

Being now completely unhorsed, Mr. Miller and his three companions, wandered on foot for several hundred miles, enduring hunger, thirst, and fatigue, while traversing the barren wastes which abound beyond the Rocky mountains. At the time they were discovered by Mr. Stuart's party, they were almost famished, and were fishing for a precarious meal. Had Mr. Stuart made the short cut across the hills, avoiding this bend of the river, or had not some of his party accidentally gone down to the margin of the stream to drink, these poor wanderers might have remained undiscovered, and have perished in the wilderness. Nothing could exceed their joy on thus meeting with their old comrades, or the heartiness with which they were welcomed. All hands immediately encamped; and the slender stores of the party were ransacked to furnish out a suitable regale.

The next morning they all set out together; Mr. Miller and his comrades being resolved to give up the life of a trapper, and accompany Mr. Stuart back to St. Louis.

For several days they kept along the course of Snake river, occasionally making short cuts across hills and promontories, where there were bends in the stream. In their way they passed several camps of Shoshonies, from some of whom they procured salmon, but in general they were too wretchedly poor to furnish any thing. It was the wish of Mr. Stuart to purchase horses for the recent recruits to his party; but the Indians could not be prevailed upon to part with any, alleging that they had not enough for their own use.

On the 25th of August they reached a great fishing place, to which they gave the name of the Salmon Falls. Here there is a perpendicular fall of twenty feet on the north side of the river, while on the south side there is a succession of rapids. The salmon are taken here in incredible quantities, as they attempt to shoot the falls. It was now a favorable season, and there where about one hundred lodges of Shoshonies busily engaged killing and drying fish. The salmon begin to leap, shortly after sunrise. At this time the Indians swim to the centre of the falls, where some station themselves on rocks, and others stand to their waists in the water, all armed with spears, with which they assail the salmon as they attempt to leap, or fall back exhausted. It is an incessant slaughter, so great is the throng of the fish.

The construction of the spears thus used is peculiar. The head is a straight piece of elk horn, about seven inches long; on the point of which an artificial barb is made fast, with twine well gummed. The head is stuck on the end of the shaft, a very long pole of willow, to which it is likewise connected, by a strong cord a few inches in length. When the spearsman makes a sure blow, he often strikes the head of the spear through the body of the fish. It comes off easily, and leaves the salmon struggling with the string through its body, while the pole is still held by the spearsman. Were it not for the precaution of the string, the willow shaft would be snapped by the struggles and the weight of the fish. Mr. Miller, in the course of his wanderings, had been at these falls, and had seen several thousand salmon taken in the course of one afternoon. He declared that he had seen a salmon leap a distance of about thirty feet, from the commencement of the foam at the foot of the fall, completely to the top.

Having purchased a good supply of salmon from the fishermen, the party resumed their journey, and on the twenty-ninth, arrived at the Caldron Linn; the eventful scene of the preceding autumn. Here, the first thing that met their eyes, was a memento of the perplexities of that period: the wreck of a canoe, lodged between two ledges of rocks. They endeavored to get down to it, but the river banks were too high and precipitous.

They now proceeded to that part of the neighborhood where Mr. Hunt and his party had made the caches, intending to take from them such articles as belonged to Mr. Crooks, M'Lellan, and the Canadians. On reaching the spot, they found, to their astonishment, six of the caches open and rifled of their contents, excepting a few books which lay scattered about the vicinity. They had the appearance of having been plundered in the course of the summer. There were tracks of wolves in every direction, to and from the holes, from which Mr. Stuart concluded that these animals had first been attracted to the place by the smell of the skins contained in the caches, which they had probably torn up, and that their tracks had betrayed the secret to the Indians.

The three remaining caches, had not been molested: they contained a few dry goods, some ammunition, and a number of beaver traps. From these, Mr. Stuart took whatever was requisite for his party; he then deposited within them all his superfluous baggage, and all the books and papers scattered around; the holes were then carefully closed up, and all traces of them effaced. And here we have to record another instance of the indomitable spirit of the western trappers. No sooner did the trio of Kentucky hunters, Robinson, Rezner, and Hoback, find that they could once more be fitted out for a campaign of beaver trapping, than they forgot all that they had suffered, and determined upon another trial of their fortunes; preferring to take their chance in the wilderness, rather than return home ragged and penniless. As to Mr. Miller, he declared his curiosity and his desire of travelling through the Indian countries, fully satisfied; he adhered to his determination, therefore, to keep on with the party to St. Louis, and to return to the bosom of civilized society.

The three hunters, therefore, Robinson, Rezner, and Hoback, were furnished, as far as the caches and the means of Mr. Stuart's party afforded, with the requisite munitions and equipments for a "two years' hunt"; but as their fitting out was yet incomplete, they resolved to wait in this neighborhood until Mr. Reed should arrive; whose arrival might soon be expected, as he was to set out for the caches about twenty days after Mr. Stuart parted with him at the Wallah-Wallah river.

Mr. Stuart gave in charge to Robinson a letter to Mr. Reed, reporting his safe journey thus far, and the state in which he had found the caches. A duplicate of this letter he elevated on a pole, and set it up near the place of deposit.

All things being thus arranged, Mr. Stuart and his little band, now seven in number, took leave of the three hardy trappers, wishing them all possible success in their lonely and perilous sojourn in the wilderness; and we, in like manner, shall leave them to their fortunes, promising to take them up again at some future page, and to close the story of their persevering and ill-fated enterprise.

CHAPTER XLV

On the 1st of September, Mr. Stuart and his companions resumed their journey, bending their course eastward, along the course of Snake river. As they advanced, the country opened. The hills which had hemmed in the river receded on either hand, and great sandy and dusty plains extended before them. Occasionally, there were intervals of pasturage, and the banks of the river were fringed with willows and cotton wood, so that its course might be traced from the hill tops, winding under an umbrageous covert, through a wide sunburnt landscape. The soil, however, was generally poor; there was, in some places a miserable growth of wormwood, and of a plant called slatweed, resembling pennyroyal; but the summer heat had parched the plains, and left but little pasturage. The game too had disappeared. The hunter looked in vain over the lifeless landscape; now and then a few antelope might be seen, but not within reach of the rifle. We forbear to follow the travellers in a week's wandering over these barren wastes, where they suffered much from hunger; having to depend upon a few fish from the streams, and now and then a little dried salmon, or a dog, procured from some forlorn lodge of Shoshonies.

Tired of these cheerless wastes, they left the banks of Snake river on the 7th of September, under guidance of Mr. Miller, who, having acquired some knowledge of the country during his trapping campaign, undertook to conduct them across the mountains by a better route than that by Fort Henry, and one more out of the range of the Blackfeet. He proved, however, but an indifferent guide, and they soon became bewildered among rugged hills and unknown streams, and burnt and barren prairies.

At length they came to a river on which Mr. Miller had trapped, and to which they gave his name; though, as before observed, we presume it to be the same called Bear river, which empties itself into lake Bonneville. Up this river and its branches they kept for two or three days, supporting themselves precariously upon fish. They soon found that they were in a dangerous neighborhood. On the 12th of September, having encamped early, they sallied forth with their rods to angle for their supper. On returning, they beheld a number of Indians prowling about their camp, whom, to their infinite disquiet, they soon perceived to be Upsarokas, or Crows. Their chief came forward with a confident air. He was a dark herculean fellow, full six feet four inches in height, with a mingled air of the ruffian and the rogue. He conducted himself peaceably, however, and despatched some of his people to their camp, which was somewhere in the neighborhood, from whence they returned with a most acceptable supply of buffalo meat. He now signified to Mr. Stuart that he was going to trade with the Snakes, who reside on the west base of the mountains, below Henry's fort. Here they cultivate a delicate kind of tobacco, much esteemed and sought after by the mountain tribes. There was something sinister, however, in the look of this Indian, that inspired distrust. By degrees, the number of his people increased, until, by midnight, there were twenty-one of them about the camp, who began to be impudent and troublesome. The greatest uneasiness was now felt for the safety of the horses and effects, and every one kept vigilant watch throughout the night.

The morning dawned, however, without any unpleasant occurrence, and Mr. Stuart, having purchased all the buffalo meat that the Crows had to spare, prepared to depart. His Indian acquaintance, however, were disposed for further dealings; and, above all, anxious for a supply of gunpowder, for which they offered horses in exchange. Mr. Stuart declined to furnish them with the dangerous commodity. They became more importunate in their solicitations, until they met with a flat refusal.

The gigantic chief now stepped forward, assumed a swelling air, and, slapping himself upon the breast, gave Mr. Crooks to understand that he was a chief of great power and importance. He signified, further, that it was customary for great chiefs when they met, to make each other presents. He requested, therefore, that Mr. Stuart would alight, and give him the horse upon which he was mounted. This was a noble animal, of one of the wild races of the prairies, on which Mr. Stuart set great value; he, of course, shook his head at the request of the Crow dignitary. Upon this the latter strode up to him, and taking hold of him, moved him backwards and forwards in his saddle, as if to make him feel that he was a mere child within his grasp. Mr. Stuart preserved his calmness, and still shook his head. The chief then seized the bridle, and gave it a jerk that startled the horse, and nearly brought the rider to the ground. Mr. Stuart instantly drew forth a pistol, and presented it at the head of the bully-ruffian. In a twinkling, his swaggering was at an end, and he dodged behind his horse to escape the expected shot. As his subject Crows gazed on the affray from a little distance, Mr. Stuart ordered his men to level their rifles at them, but not to fire. The whole crew scampered among the bushes, and throwing themselves upon the ground, vanished from sight.

The chieftain thus left alone, was confounded for an instant; but, recovering himself, with true Indian shrewdness, burst into a loud laugh, and affected to turn off the whole matter as a piece of pleasantry. Mr. Stuart by no means relished such equivocal joking, but it was not his policy to get into a quarrel; so he joined, with the best grace he could assume, in the merriment of the jocular giant; and, to console the latter for the refusal of the horse, made him a present of twenty charges of powder. They parted, according to all outward professions, the best friends in the world; it was evident, however, that nothing but the smallness of his own force, and the martial array and alertness of the white men, had prevented the Crow chief from proceeding to open outrage. As it was, his worthy followers, in the course of their brief interview, had contrived to purloin a bag containing almost all the culinary utensils of the party.

The travellers kept on their way due east, over a chain of hills. The recent rencontre showed them that they were now in a land of danger, subject to the wide roamings of a predacious tribe; nor, in fact, had they gone many miles, before they beheld sights calculated to inspire anxiety and alarm. From the summits of some of the loftiest mountains, in different directions, columns of smoke began to rise. These they concluded to be signals made by the runners of the Crow chieftain, to summon the stragglers of his band, so as to pursue them with greater force. Signals of this kind, made by outrunners from one central point, will rouse a wide circuit of the mountains in a wonderfully short space of time; and bring the straggling hunters and warriors to the standard of their chieftain.

To keep as much as possible out of the way of these freebooters, Mr. Stuart altered his course to the north, and, quitting the main stream of Miller's river, kept up a large branch that came in from the mountains. Here they encamped, after a fatiguing march of twenty-five miles. As the night drew on, the horses were hobbled, or fettered, and tethered close to the camp; a vigilant watch was maintained until morning, and every one slept with his rifle on his arm.

At sunrise, they were again on the march, still keeping to the north. They soon began to ascend the mountains, and occasionally had wide prospects over the surrounding country. Not a sign of a Crow was to be seen; but this did not assure them of their security, well knowing the perseverance of these savages in dogging any party they intend to rob, and the stealthy way in which they can conceal their movements, keeping along ravines and defiles. After a mountain scramble of twenty-one miles, they encamped on the margin of a stream running to the north.

In the evening there was an alarm of Indians, and every one was instantly on the alert. They proved to be three miserable Snakes, who were no sooner informed that a band of Crows was prowling in the neighborhood, than they made off with great signs of consternation.

A couple more of weary days and watchful nights brought them to a strong and rapid stream, running due north, which they concluded to be one of the upper branches of Snake river. It was probably the same since called Salt river. They determined to bend their course down this river, as it would take them still further out of the dangerous neighborhood of the Crows. They then would strike upon Mr. Hunt's track of the preceding autumn, and retrace it across the mountains. The attempt to find a better route under guidance of Mr. Miller had cost them a large bend to the south; in resuming Mr. Hunt's track, they would at least be sure of their road. They accordingly turned down along the course of this stream, and at the end of three days' journey, came to where it was joined by a larger river, and assumed a more impetuous character, raging and roaring among rocks and precipices. It proved, in fact, to be Mad river, already noted in the expedition of Mr Hunt. On the banks of this river, they encamped on the 18th of September, at an early hour.

Six days had now elapsed since their interview with the Crows, during that time they had come nearly a hundred and fifty miles to the north and west, without seeing any signs of those marauders. They considered themselves, therefore, beyond the reach of molestation, and began to relax in their vigilance, lingering occasionally for part of a day, where there was good pasturage. The poor horses needed repose. They had been urged on, by forced marches, over rugged heights, among rocks and fallen timber, or over low swampy valleys, inundated by the labors of the beaver. These industrious animals abounded in all the mountain streams and water courses, wherever there were willows for their subsistence. Many of them they had so completely dammed up as to inundate the low grounds, making shallow pools or lakes, and extensive quagmires: by which the route of the travellers was often impeded.

On the 19th of September, they rose at early dawn; some began to prepare breakfast, and others to arrange the packs preparatory to a march. The horses had been hobbled, but left at large to graze about the adjacent pastures. Mr. Stuart was on the bank of the river, at a short distance from the camp, when he heard the alarm cry—"Indians! Indians!—to arms! to arms!"

A mounted Crow galloped past the camp, bearing a red flag. He reined his steed on the summit of a neighboring knoll, and waved his flaring banner. A diabolical yell now broke forth on the opposite side of the camp, beyond where the horses were grazing, and a small troop of savages came galloping up, whooping and making a terrific clamor. The horses took fright, and dashed across the camp in the direction of the standard bearer, attracted by his waving flag. He instantly put spurs to his steed, and scoured off, followed by the panic stricken herd, their fright being increased by the yells of the savages in their rear.

At the first alarm, Mr. Stuart and his comrades had seized their rifles, and attempted to cut off the Indians, who were pursuing the horses. Their attention was instantly distracted by whoops and yells in an opposite direction. They now apprehended that a reserve party was about to carry off their baggage. They ran to secure it. The reserve party, however, galloped by, whooping and yelling in triumph and derision. The last of them proved to be their commander, the identical giant joker already mentioned. He was not cast in the stern poetical mould of fashionable Indian heroism, but on the contrary, was grievously given to vulgar jocularity. As he passed Mr. Stuart and his companions, he checked his horse, raised himself in the saddle, and clapping his hand on the most insulting part of his body, uttered some jeering words, which, fortunately for their delicacy, they could not understand. The rifle of Ben Jones was levelled in an instant, and he was on the point of whizzing a bullet into the target so tauntingly displayed. "Not for your life! not for your life!" exclaimed Mr. Stuart, "you will bring destruction on us all!"

It was hard to restrain honest Ben, when the mark was so fair and the insult so foul. "Oh, Mr. Stuart," exclaimed he, "only let me have one crack at the infernal rascal, and you may keep all the pay that is due to me."

"By heaven, if you fire," cried Mr. Stuart, "I'll blow your brains out."

By this time, the Indian was far out of reach, and had rejoined his men, and the whole dare-devil band, with the captured horses, scuttled off along the defiles, their red flag flaunting over head, and the rocks echoing to their whoops and yells, and demoniac laughter.

The unhorsed travellers gazed after them in silent mortification and despair; yet Mr. Stuart could not but admire the style and spirit with which the whole exploit had been managed, and pronounced it one of the most daring and intrepid actions he had ever heard of among Indians. The whole number of the Crows did not exceed twenty. In this way, a small gang of lurkers will hurry off the cavalry of a large war party, for when once a drove of horses are seized with a panic, they become frantic, and nothing short of broken necks can stop them.

No one was more annoyed by this unfortunate occurrence than Ben Jones. He declared he would actually have given his whole arrears of pay, amounting to upwards of a year's wages, rather than be balked of such a capital shot. Mr. Stuart, however, represented what might have been the consequence of so rash an act. Life for life is the Indian maxim. The whole tribe would have made common cause in avenging the death of a warrior. The party were but seven dismounted men, with a wide mountain region to traverse, infested by these people, and which might all be roused by signal fires. In fact, the conduct of the band of marauders in question, showed the perseverance of savages when once they have fixed their minds upon a project. These fellows had evidently been silently and secretly dogging the party for a week past, and a distance of a hundred and fifty miles, keeping out of sight by day, lurking about the encampment at night, watching all their movements, and waiting for a favorable moment when they should be off their guard. The menace of Mr. Stuart, in their first interview, to shoot the giant chief with his pistol, and the fright caused among the warriors by presenting the rifles, had probably added the stimulus of pique to their usual horse-stealing propensities, and in this mood of mind they would doubtless have followed the party throughout their whole course over the Rocky mountains, rather than be disappointed in their scheme.

CHAPTER XLVI

F EW reverses in this changeful
world are more complete and disheartening than that of a traveller,
suddenly unhorsed, in the midst of the wilderness. Our unfortunate
travellers, contemplated their situation for a time, in perfect dismay.
A long journey over rugged mountains and immeasurable plains, lay
before them, which they must painfully perform on foot, and every
thing necessary for subsistence or defence, must be carried on their
shoulders. Their dismay, however, was but transient, and they immediately set to work, with that prompt expediency produced by the
exigencies of the wilderness, to fit themselves for the change in their
condition.

Their first attention was to select from their baggage such articles
as were indispensable to their journey; to make them up into convenient packs, and to deposit the residue in caches. The whole day
was consumed in these occupations; at night, they made a scanty meal
of their remaining provisions, and lay down to sleep with heavy hearts.
In the morning, they were up and about at an early hour, and began to
prepare their knapsacks for a march, while Ben Jones repaired to an
old beaver trap which he had set in the river bank at some little distance from the camp. He was rejoiced to find a middle-sized beaver

there, sufficient for a morning's meal to his hungry comrades. On his way back with his prize, he observed two heads peering over the edge of an impending cliff, several hundred feet high, which he supposed to be a couple of wolves. As he continued on, he now and then cast his eye up; the heads were still there, looking down with fixed and watchful gaze. A suspicion now flashed across his mind that they might be Indian scouts; and, had they not been far above the reach of his rifle, he would undoubtedly have regaled them with a shot.

On arriving at the camp, he directed the attention of his comrades to these aerial observers. The same idea was at first entertained, that they were wolves; but their immoveable watchfulness, soon satisfied every one that they were Indians. It was concluded that they were watching the movements of the party, to discover their place of concealment of such articles as they would be compelled to leave behind. There was no likelihood that the caches would escape the search of such keen eyes, and experienced rummagers, and the idea was intolerable, that any more booty should fall into their hands. To disappoint them, therefore, the travellers stripped the caches of the articles deposited there, and collecting together every thing that they could not carry away with them, made a bonfire of all that would burn, and threw the rest into the river. There was a forlorn satisfaction in thus balking the Crows, by the destruction of their own property; and, having thus gratified their pique, they shouldered their packs, about ten o'clock in the morning, and set out on their pedestrian wayfaring.

The route they took was down along the banks of Mad river. This stream makes its way through the defiles of the mountains, into the plain below fort Henry, where it terminates in Snake river. Mr. Stuart was in hopes of meeting with Snake encampments in the plain, where he might procure a couple of horses to transport the baggage. In such case, he intended to resume his eastern course across the mountains, and endeavor to reach the Cheyenne river before winter. Should he fail, however, of obtaining horses, he would probably be compelled to winter on the Pacific side of the mountains, somewhere on the head waters of the Spanish or Colorado river.

With all the care that had been observed in taking nothing with them that was not absolutely necessary, the poor pedestrians were heavily laden, and their burthens added to the fatigues of their rugged road. They suffered much, too, from hunger. The trout they caught, were too poor to yield much nourishment; their main dependance, therefore, was upon an old beaver trap, which they had providentially retained. Whenever they were fortunate enough to entrap a beaver, it was cut up immediately and distributed, that each man might carry his share.

After two days of toilsome travel, during which they made but eighteen miles, they stopped on the 21st, to build two rafts on which to cross to the north side of the river. On these they embarked, on the following morning, four on one raft, and three on the other, and pushed boldly from shore. Finding the rafts sufficiently firm and steady to withstand the rough and rapid water, they changed their minds, and instead of crossing, ventured to float down with the current. The river was, in general, very rapid, and from one to two hundred yards in width, winding in every direction through mountains of hard black rock, covered with pines and cedars. The mountains to the east of the river were spurs of the rocky range, and of great magnitude; those on the west, were little better than hills, bleak and barren, or scantily clothed with stunted grass.

Mad river, though deserving its name from the impetuosity of its current, was free from rapids and cascades, and flowed on in a single channel between gravel banks, often fringed with cotton wood and dwarf willows in abundance. These gave sustenance to immense quantities of beaver, so that the voyageurs found no difficulty in procuring food. Ben Jones, also, killed a fallow deer, and a wolverine, and as they were enable to carry the carcasses on their rafts, their larder was well supplied. Indeed, they might have occasionally shot beavers that were swimming in the river as they floated by, but they humanely spared their lives, being in no want of meat at the time. In this way, they kept down the river for three days, drifting with the current and encamping on land at night, when they drew up their rafts on shore. Towards the evening of the third day, they came to a little island on which they descried a gang of elk. Ben Jones landed, and was fortunate enough to wound one, which immediately took to the water, but, being unable to stem the current, drifted above a mile, when it was over- taken and drawn to shore. As a storm was gathering, they now en- camped on the margin of the river, where they remained all the next day, sheltering themselves as well as they could from rain, and hail, and snow, a sharp foretaste of the impending winter. During their encampment, they employed themselves in jerking a part of the elk for future supply. In cutting up the carcass, they found that the animal had been wounded by hunters, about a week previously, an arrow head and a musket ball remaining in the wounds. In the wilderness, every trivial circumstance is a matter of anxious speculation. The Snake In- dians have no guns; the elk, therfore, could not have been wounded by one of them. They were on the borders of the country infested by the Blackfeet, who carry fire-arms. It was concluded, therefore, that the elk had been hunted by some of that wandering and hostile tribe who, of course, must be in the neighborhood. The idea put an end to the transient solace they had enjoyed in the comparative repose and abundance of the river.

For three days longer they continued to navigate with their rafts. The recent storm had rendered the weather extremely cold. They had now floated down the river about ninety-one miles, when, finding the mountains on the right, diminished to moderate sized hills, they landed, and prepared to resume their journey on foot. Accordingly, having spent a day in preparations, making moccasins, and parcelling out their jerked meat in packs of twenty pounds to each man, they turned their backs upon the river on the 29th of September and struck off to the north-east; keeping along the southern skirt of the moun- tain on which Henry's fort was situated.

Their march was slow and toilsome; part of the time through an al- luvial bottom, thickly grown with cotton wood, hawthorn and willows, and part of the time over rough hills. Three antelopes came within shot, but they dared not fire at them, lest the report of their rifles should betray them to the Blackfeet. In the course of the day, they came upon a large horse track apparently about three weeks old, and in the evening encamped on the banks of a small stream, on a spot which had been the camping place of this same band.

On the following morning they still observed the Indian track, but after a time they came to where it separated in every direction, and was lost. This shewed that the band had dispersed in various hunting parties, and was, in all probability, still in the neighborhood; it was necessary, therefore, to proceed with the utmost caution. They kept a vigilant eye as they marched, upon every height where a scout might be posted, and scanned the solitary landscape and the distant ravines, to observe any column of smoke; but nothing of the kind was to be seen; all was indiscribably stern and lifeless.

Towards evening they came to where there were several hot springs, strongly impregnated with iron and sulphur, and sending up a volume of vapor that tainted the surrounding atmosphere, and might be seen at the distance of a couple of miles.

Near to these they encamped, in a deep gulley, which afforded some concealment. To their great concern, Mr. Crooks, who had been indisposed for the two preceding days, had a violent fever in the night.

Shortly after daybreak they resumed their march. On emerging from the glen, a consultation was held as to their course. Should they continue round the skirt of the mountain, they would be in danger of falling in with the scattered parties of Blackfeet, who were probably hunting in the plain. It was thought most advisable, therefore, to strike directly across the mountain, since the route, though rugged and difficult, would be most secure. This counsel was indignantly derided by M'Lellan as pusillanimous. Hot-headed and impatient at all times, he had been rendered irascible by the fatigues of the journey, and the condition of his feet, which were chafed and sore. He could not endure the idea of encountering the difficulties of the mountain, and swore he would rather face all the Blackfeet in the country. He was overruled, however, and the party began to ascend the mountain, striving, with the ardor and emulation of young men, who should be first up. M'Lellan, who was double the age of some of his companions, soon began to lose breath, and fall in the rear. In the distribution of burthens, it was his turn to carry the old beaver trap. Piqued and irritated, he suddenly came to a halt, swore he would carry it no further, and

jirked it half way down the hill. He was offered in place of it a package
of dried meat, but this he scornfully threw upon the ground. They
might carry it, he said, who needed it, for his part, he could provide
his daily food with his rifle. He concluded by flinging off from the
party, and keeping along the skirts of the mountain, leaving those, he
said, to climb rocks, who were afraid to face Indians. It was in vain that
Mr. Stuart represented to him the rashness of his conduct, and the
dangers to which he exposed himself: he rejected such counsel as
craven. It was equally useless to represent the dangers to which he
subjected his companions; as he could be discovered at a great distance
on those naked plains, and the Indians, seeing him, would know that
there must be other white men within reach. M'Lellan turned a
deaf ear to every remonstrance, and kept on his wilful way.

It seems a strange instance of perverseness in this man thus to fling
himself off alone, in a savage region, where solitude itself was dismal,
but every encounter with his fellow man full of peril. Such, however,
is the hardness of spirit, and the insensibility to danger, that grow
upon men in the wilderness. M'Lellan, moreover, was a man of peculiar temperament, ungovernable in his will, of a courage that absolutely knew not fear, and somewhat of a braggart spirit, that took a
pride in doing desperate and hairbrained things.

Mr. Stuart and his party found the passages of the mountain somewhat difficult, on account of the snow, which in many places was of
considerable depth, though it was now but the 1st of October. They
crossed the summit early in the afternoon, and beheld below them a
plain about twenty miles wide, bounded on the opposite side by their
old acquaintances, the Pilot Knobs, those towering mountains which
had served Mr. Hunt as landmarks in part of his route of the preceding
year. Through the intermediate plain wandered a river about fifty
yards wide, sometimes gleaming in open day, but oftener running
through willowed banks, which marked its serpentine course.

Those of the party who had been across these mountains, pointed
out much of the bearings of the country to Mr. Stuart. They shewed
him in what direction must lie the deserted post called Henry's fort,
where they had abandoned their horses and embarked in canoes, and

they informed him that the stream which wandered through the plain below them, fell into Henry river, half way between the fort and the mouth of Mad or Snake river. The character of all this mountain region was decidedly volcanic; and to the north-west, between Henry's fort and the source of the Missouri, Mr. Stuart observed several very high peaks covered with snow, from two of which smoke ascended in considerable volumes, apparently from craters, in a state of eruption.

On their way down the mountain, when they had reached the skirts, they descried M'Lellan at a distance, in the advance, traversing the plain. Whether he saw them or not, he showed no disposition to rejoin them, but pursued his sullen and solitary way.

After descending into the plain, they kept on about six miles, until they reached the little river, which was here about knee deep, and richly fringed with willow. Here they encamped for the night. At this encampment the fever of Mr. Crooks increased to such a degree that it was impossible for him to travel. Some of the men were strenuous for Mr. Stuart to proceed without him, urging the imminent danger they were exposed to by delay in that unknown and barren region, infested by the most treacherous and inveterate of foes. They represented that the season was rapidly advancing; the weather for some days had been extremely cold; the mountains were already almost impassable from snow, and would soon present effectual barriers. Their provisions were exhausted; there was no game to be seen, and they did not dare to use their rifles, through fear of drawing upon them the Blackfeet.

The picture thus presented, was too true to be contradicted, and made a deep impression on the mind of Mr. Stuart; but the idea of abandoning a fellow being, and a comrade, in such a forlorn situation, was too repugnant to his feelings to be admitted for an instant. He represented to the men that the malady of Mr. Crooks could not be of long duration, and that in all probability, he would be able to travel in the course of a few days. It was with great difficulty, however, that he prevailed upon them to abide the event.

CHAPTER XLVII

As the travellers were now in a
dangerous neighborhood, where the report of a rifle might bring the
savages upon them, they had to depend upon their old beaver trap for
subsistence. The little river on which they were encamped gave many
"beaver signs," and Ben Jones set off at daybreak, along the willowed
banks, to find a proper trapping place. As he was making his
way among the thickets, with his trap on his shoulder and his rifle in
his hand, he heard a crashing sound, and turning, beheld a huge grizzly
bear advancing upon him, with terrific growl. The sturdy Kentuckian
was not to be intimidated by man or monster. Levelling his rifle, he
pulled trigger. The bear was wounded, but not mortally: instead, however, of rushing upon his assailant, as is generally the case with this
kind of bear, he retreated into the bushes. Jones followed him for some
distance, but with suitable caution, and Bruin effected his escape.

As there was every prospect of a detention of some days in this
place, and as the supplies of the beaver trap were too precarious to be
depended upon, it became absolutely necessary to run some risk of
discovery by hunting in the neighborhood. Ben Jones, therefore, obtained permission to range with his rifle some distance from the camp,
and set off to beat up the river banks, in defiance of bear or Blackfeet.

He returned in great spirits in the course of a few hours, having come upon a gang of elk about six miles off, and killed five. This was joyful news, and the party immediately moved forward to the place where he had left the carcases. They were obliged to support Mr. Crooks the whole distance, for he was unable to walk. Here they remained for two or three days, feasting heartily on elk meat, and drying as much as they would be able to carry away with them.

By the 5th of October, some simple prescriptions, together with an "Indian sweat," had so far benefited Mr. Crooks, that he was enabled to move about; they, therefore, set forward slowly, dividing his pack and accoutrements among them, and made a creeping day's progress of eight miles south. Their route for the most part lay through swamps, caused by the industrious labors of the beaver; for this little animal had dammed up numerous small streams, issuing from the Pilot Knob mountains, so that the low grounds on their borders, were completely inundated. In the course of their march they killed a grizzly bear, with fat on its flanks upwards of three inches in thickness. This was an acceptable addition to their stock of elk meat. The next day, Mr. Crooks was sufficiently recruited in strength to be able to carry his rifle and pistols, and they made a march of seventeen miles along the borders of the plain.

Their journey daily became more toilsome, and their sufferings more severe, as they advanced. Keeping up the channel of a river, they traversed the rugged summit of the Pilot Knob mountain, covered with snow nine inches deep. For several days they continued, bending their course as much as possible to the east, over a succession of rocky heights, deep valleys, and rapid streams. Sometimes their dizzy path lay along the margin of perpendicular precipices, several hundred feet in height, where a single false step might precipitate them into the rocky bed of a torrent which roared below. Not the least part of their weary task was the fording of the numerous windings and branchings of the mountain rivers, all boisterous in their currents, and icy cold.

Hunger was added to their other sufferings, and soon became the keenest. The small supply of bear and elk meat which they had been able to carry, in addition to their previous burthens, served but for a very short time. In their anxiety to struggle forward, they had but little time to hunt, and scarce any game came in their path. For three days they had nothing to eat but a small duck, and a few poor trout. They occasionally saw numbers of antelopes, and tried every art to get within shot; but the timid animals were more than commonly wild, and after tantalizing the hungry hunters for a time, bounded away beyond all chance of pursuit. At length they were fortunate enough to kill one: it was extremely meagre, and yielded but a scanty supply; but on this they subsisted for several days.

On the 11th, they encamped on a small stream, near the foot of the Spanish river mountain. Here they met with traces of that wayward and solitary being, M'Lellan, who was still keeping on ahead of them through these lonely mountains. He had encamped the night before on this stream; they found the embers of the fire by which he had slept, and the remains of a miserable wolf on which he had supped. It was evident he had suffered, like themselves, the pangs of hunger, though he had fared better at this encampment; for they had not a mouthful to eat.

The next day, they rose hungry and alert, and set out with the dawn to climb the mountain, which was steep and difficult. Traces of volcanic operations were to be seen in various directions. There was a species of clay also to be met with, out of which the Indians manufacture pots and jars and dishes. It is very fine and light, of an agreeable smell, and of a brown color spotted with yellow, and dissolves readily in the mouth. Vessels manufactured of it, are said to impart a pleasant smell and flavor to any liquids. These mountains abound also with mineral earths, or chalks of various colors; especially two kinds of ochre, one a pale, the other a bright red, like vermilion; much used by the Indians, in painting their bodies.

About noon, the travellers reached the "drains" and brooks that formed the head waters of the river, and later in the day, descended to where the main body, a shallow stream, about a hundred and sixty yards wide, poured through its mountain valley.

Here the poor famishing wanderers had expected to find buffalo in abundance, and had fed their hungry hopes during their scrambling toil, with the thoughts of roasted ribs, juicy humps, and broiled marrow bones. To their great disappointment, the river banks were deserted; a few old tracks, showed where a herd of bulls had some time before passed along, but not a horn nor hump was to be seen in the sterile landscape. A few antelopes looked down upon them from the brow of a crag, but flitted away out of sight at the least approach of the hunter.

In the most starving mood they kept for several miles further, along the bank of the river, seeking for "beaver signs." Finding some, they encamped in the vicinity, and Ben Jones immediately proceeded to set the trap. They had scarce come to a halt, when they perceived a large smoke at some distance to the southwest. The sight was hailed with joy, for they trusted it might rise from some Indian camp, where they could procure something to eat, and the dread of starvation had now overcome even the terror of the Blackfeet. Le Clerc, one of the Canadians, was instantly despatched by Mr. Stuart, to reconnoitre; and the travellers sat up till a late hour, watching and listening for his return, hoping he might bring them food. Midnight arrived, but Le Clerc did not make his appearance, and they laid down once more supperless to sleep, comforting themselves with the hopes that their old beaver trap might furnish them with a breakfast.

At daybreak they hastened with famished eagerness to the trap—they found in it the fore paw of a beaver; the sight of which tantalized their hunger, and added to their dejection. They resumed their journey with flagging spirits, but had not gone far when they perceived Le Clerc approaching at a distance. They hastened to meet him, in hopes of tidings of good cheer. He had none such to give them; but news of that strange wanderer, M'Lellan. The smoke had risen from his encampment, which took fire while he was at a little distance from it fishing. Le Clerc found him in forlorn condition. His fishing had been unsuccessful. During twelve days that he had been wandering alone through these savage mountains, he had found scarce any thing to eat. He had been ill, wayworn, sick at heart, still he had kept forward; but now his strength and his stubbornness were exhausted. He expressed his satisfaction at hearing that Mr. Stuart and his party were near, and said he would wait at his camp for their arrival, in hopes they would give him something to eat, for without food he declared he should not be able to proceed much further.

When the party reached the place, they found the poor fellow lying on a parcel of withered grass, wasted to a perfect skeleton, and so feeble that he could scarce raise his head or speak. The presence of his old comrades seemed to revive him; but they had no food to give him, for they themselves were almost starving. They urged him to rise and accompany them, but he shook his head. It was all in vain, he said; there was no prospect of their getting speedy relief, and without it he should perish by the way: he might as well, therefore, stay and die where he was. At length, after much persuasion, they got him upon his legs; his rifle and other effects were shared among them, and he was cheered and aided forward. In this way they proceeded for seventeen miles, over a level plain of sand, until, seeing a few antelopes in the distance, they encamped on the margin of a small stream. All now that were capable of the exertion, turned out to hunt for a meal. Their efforts were fruitless, and after dark they returned to their camp, famished almost to desperation.

As they were preparing for the third time to lay down to sleep without a mouthful to eat, Le Clerc, one of the Canadians, gaunt and wild with hunger, approached Mr. Stuart with his gun in his hand. "It was all in vain," he said, "to attempt to proceed any further without food. They had a barren plain before them, three or four days' journey in extent, on which nothing was to be procured. They must all perish before they could get to the end of it. It was better, therefore, that one should die to save the rest." He proposed, therefore, that they should cast lots; adding, as an inducement for Mr. Stuart to assent to the proposition, that he, as leader of the party, should be exempted.

Mr. Stuart shuddered at the horrible proposition, and endeavored to reason with the man, but his words were unavailing. At length, snatching up his rifle, he threatened to shoot him on the spot if he persisted. The famished wretch dropped on his knees, begged pardon in the most abject terms, and promised never again to offend him with such a suggestion.

Quiet being restored to the forlorn encampment, each one sought repose. Mr. Stuart, however, was so exhausted by the agitation of the past scene, acting upon his emaciated frame, that he could scarce crawl to his miserable couch; where, notwithstanding his fatigues, he passed a sleepless night, revolving upon their dreary situation, and the desperate prospect before them.

Before daylight the next morning, they were up and on their way; they had nothing to detain them; no breakfast to prepare, and to linger was to perish. They proceeded, however, but slowly, for all were faint and weak. Here and there they passed the sculls and bones of buffaloes, which showed that those animals must have been hunted here during the past season; the sight of these bones served only to mock their misery. After travelling about nine miles along the plain, they ascended a range of hills, and had scarcely gone two miles further, when, to their great joy, they discovered "an old run-down buffalo bull;" the laggard probably of some herd that had been hunted and harassed through the mountains. They now all stretched themselves out to encompass and make sure of this solitary animal, for their lives depended upon their success. After considerable trouble and infinite anxiety, they at length succeeded in killing him. He was instantly flayed and cut up, and so ravenous was their hunger, that they devoured some of the flesh raw. The residue they carried to a brook near by, where they encamped, lit a fire, and began to cook.

Mr. Stuart was fearful that in their famished state they would eat to excess and injure themselves. He caused a soup to be made of some of the meat, and that each should take a quantity of it as a prelude to his supper. This may have had a beneficial effect, for though they sat up the greater part of the night, cooking and cramming, no one suffered any inconvenience.

The next morning the feasting was resumed, and about midday, feeling somewhat recruited and refreshed, they set out on their journey with renovated spirits, shaping their course towards a mountain, the summit of which they saw towering in the east, and near to which they expected to find the head waters of the Missouri.

As they proceeded, they continued to see the skeletons of buffaloes scattered about the plain in every direction, which showed that there had been much hunting here by the Indians in the recent season. Further on they crossed a large Indian trail, forming a deep path, about fifteen days old, which went in a north direction. They concluded it to have been made by some numerous band of Crows, who had hunted in this country for the greater part of the summer.

On the following day they forded a stream of considerable magnitude, with banks clothed with pine trees. Among these they found the traces of a large Indian camp, which had evidently been the head quarters of a hunting expedition, from the great quantities of buffalo bones strewed about the neighborhood. The camp had apparently been abandoned about a month.

In the centre was a singular lodge one hundred and fifty feet in circumference, supported by the trunks of twenty trees, about twelve inches in diameter, and forty-four feet long. Across these were laid branches of pine and willow trees, so as to yield a tolerable shade. At the west end, immediately opposite to the door, three bodies lay interred with their feet towards the east. At the head of each grave was a branch of red cedar firmly planted in the ground. At the foot was a large buffalo's scull, painted black. Savage ornaments were suspended in various parts of the edifice, and a great number of children's moccasins. From the magnitude of this building, and the time and labor that must have been expended in erecting it, the bodies which it contained were probably those of noted warriors and hunters.

The next day, October 17th, they passed two large tributary streams of the Spanish river. They took their rise in the Wind river mountains, which ranged along to the east, stupendously high and rugged, composed of vast masses of black rock, almost destitute of wood, and covered in many places with snow. This day they saw a few buffalo bulls, and some antelopes, but could not kill any; and their stock of provisions began to grow scanty as well as poor.

On the 18th, after crossing a mountain ridge, and traversing a plain, they waded one of the branches of Spanish river, and on ascending its bank, met with about a hundred and thirty Snake Indians. They were friendly in their demeanor, and conducted them to their encampment,

which was about three miles distant. It consisted of about forty wig-
wams, constructed principally of pine branches. The Snakes, like most
of their nation, were very poor; the marauding Crows, in their late
excursion through the country, had picked this unlucky band to the
very bone, carrying off their horses, several of their squaws, and most
of their effects. In spite of their poverty, they were hospitable in the
extreme, and made the hungry strangers welcome to their cabins. A
few trinkets procured from them a supply of buffalo meat, and of
leather for moccasins, of which the party were greatly in need. The
most valuable prize obtained from them, however, was a horse: it
was a sorry old animal in truth, but it was the only one that remained
to the poor fellows, after the fell swoop of the Crows; yet this they
were prevailed upon to part with to their guests for a pistol, an axe, a
knife, and a few other trifling articles.

They had doleful stories to tell of the Crows, who were encamped
on a river at no great distance to the east, and were in such force that
they dared not venture to seek any satisfaction for their outrages, or
to get back a horse or squaw. They endeavored to excite the indignation of their visiters by accounts of robberies and murders committed
on lonely white hunters and trappers by Crows and Blackfeet. Some of
these were exaggerations of the outrages already mentioned, sustained
by some of the scattered members of Mr. Hunt's expedition; others
were in all probability sheer fabrications, to which the Snakes seem to
have been a little prone. Mr. Stuart assured them that the day was not
far distant when the whites would make their power to be felt throughout that country, and take signal vengeance on the perpetrators of
these misdeeds. The Snakes expressed great joy at the intelligence,
and offered their services to aid the righteous cause, brightening at the
thoughts of taking the field with such potent allies, and doubtless
anticipating their turn at stealing horses and abducting squaws. Their
offers of course were accepted; the calumet of peace was produced, and
the two forlorn powers smoked eternal friendship between themselves,
and vengeance upon their common spoilers, the Crows.

CHAPTER XLVIII

By sunrise on the following morning, (October 19th,) the travellers had loaded their old horse with buffalo meat, sufficient for five day's provisions, and, taking leave of their new allies, the poor, but hospitable Snakes, set forth in somewhat better spirits, though the increasing cold of the weather, and the sight of the snowy mountains, which they had yet to traverse, were enough to chill their very hearts. The country along this branch of the Spanish river, as far as they could see, was perfectly level, bounded by ranges of lofty mountains, both to the east and west. They proceeded about three miles to the south, where they came again upon the large trail of Crow Indians, which they had crossed four day's previously, made, no doubt, by the same marauding band that had plundered the Snakes; and which, according to the account of the latter, was now encamped on a stream to the eastward. The trail kept on to the south-east, and was so well beaten by horse and foot, that they supposed at least a hundred lodges had passed along it. As it formed, therefore, a convenient highway, and ran in a proper direction, they turned into it, and determined to keep along it as far as safety would permit; as the Crow encampment must be some distance off, and it

was not likely those savages would return upon their steps. They travelled forward, therefore, all that day, in the track of their dangerous
predecessors, which led them across mountain streams, and along
ridges, and through narrow valleys, all tending generally towards the
south-east. The wind blew coldly from the north-east, with occasional
flurries of snow, which made them encamp early, on the sheltered
banks of a brook. The two Canadians, Vallée and Le Clerc, killed a
young buffalo bull in the evening, which was in good condition, and
afforded them a plentiful supply of fresh beef. They loaded their spits,
therefore, and crammed their camp kettle with meat, and while the
wind whistled, and the snow whirled around them, huddled round a
rousing fire, basked in its warmth, and comforted both soul and body
with a hearty and invigorating meal. No enjoyments have greater zest
than these, snatched in the very midst of difficulty and danger; and it is
probable the poor way-worn and weather-beaten travellers relished
these creature comforts the more highly, from the surrounding desolation, and the dangerous proximity of the Crows.

The snow which had fallen in the night made it late in the morning
before the party loaded their solitary pack-horse, and resumed their
march. They had not gone far before the Crow trace which they were
following, changed its direction, and bore to the north of east. They
had already begun to feel themselves on dangerous ground, in keeping along it, as they might be descried by some scouts and spies of that
race of Ishmaelites, whose predatory life required them to be constantly on the alert. On seeing the trace turn so much to the north,
therefore, they abandoned it, and kept on their course to the south-
east, for eighteen miles, through a beautifully undulating country,
having the main chain of mountains on the left, and a considerably
elevated ridge on the right. Here the mountain ridge which divides
Wind river from the head waters of the Columbia and Spanish rivers,
ends abruptly, and winding to the north of east, becomes the dividing
barrier between a branch of the Bighorn and Cheyenne rivers, and
those head waters which flow into the Missouri, below the Sioux country.

The ridge which lay on the right of the travellers having now become very low, they passed over it, and came into a level plain, about ten miles in circumference, and encrusted to the depth of a foot or eighteen inches with salt as white as snow. This is furnished by numerous salt springs of limpid water, which are continually welling up, overflowing their borders, and forming beautiful crystallizations. The Indian tribes of the interior are excessively fond of this salt, and repair to the valley to collect it, but it is held in distaste by the tribes of the sea coast, who will eat nothing that has been cured or seasoned by it.

This evening they encamped on the banks of a small stream, in the open prairie. The north-east wind was keen and cutting; they had nothing wherewith to make a fire, but a scanty growth of sage, or wormwood, and were fain to wrap themselves up in their blankets, and huddle themselves in their "nests," at an early hour. In the course of the evening, Mr. M'Lellan, who had now regained his strength, killed a buffalo, but it was some distance from the camp, and they postponed supplying themselves from the carcass until the following morning.

The next day, (October 21st,) the cold continued, accompanied by snow. They set forward on their bleak and toilsome way, keeping to the east north-east, towards the lofty summit of a mountain, which it was necessary for them to cross. Before they reached its base they passed another large trail, steering a little to the right of the point of the mountain. This they presumed to have been made by another band of Crows, who had probably been hunting lower down on the Spanish river.

The severity of the weather compelled them to encamp at the end of fifteen miles, on the skirts of the mountain, where they found sufficient dry aspen trees to supply them with fire, but they sought in vain about the neighborhood for a spring or rill of water.

At daybreak they were up and on the march, scrambling up the mountain side for the distance of eight painful miles. From the casual hints given in the travelling memoranda of Mr. Stuart, this mountain would seem to offer a rich field of speculation for the geologist. Here was a plain three miles in diameter, strewed with pumice stones and other volcanic reliques, with a lake in the centre, occupying what had probably been the crater. Here were also, in some places, deposites of marine shells, indicating that this mountain crest had at some remote period been below the waves.

After pausing to repose, and to enjoy these grand but savage and awful scenes, they began to descend the eastern side of the mountain. The descent was rugged and romantic, along deep ravines and defiles, overhung with crags and cliffs, among which they beheld numbers of the ahsahta or bighorn, skipping fearlessly from rock to rock. Two of them they succeeded in bringing down with their rifles, as they peered fearlessly from the brow of their airy precipices.

Arrived at the foot of the mountain, the travellers found a rill of water oozing out of the earth, and resembling in look and taste, the water of the Missouri. Here they encamped for the night, and supped sumptuously upon their mountain mutton, which they found in good condition, and extremely well tasted.

The morning was bright, and intensely cold. Early in the day they came upon a stream running to the east, between low hills of bluish earth, strongly impregnated with copperas. Mr. Stuart supposed this to be one of the head waters of the Missouri, and determined to follow its banks. After a march of twenty-six miles, however, he arrived at the summit of a hill, the prospect of which induced him to alter his intention. He beheld, in every direction south of east, a vast plain, bounded only by the horizon, through which wandered the stream in question, in a south, south-east direction. It could not, therefore, be a branch of the Missouri. He now gave up all idea of taking the stream for his guide, and shaped his course towards a range of mountains in the east, about sixty miles distant, near which he hoped to find another stream.

The weather was now so severe, and the hardships of travelling so great, that he resolved to halt for the winter, at the first eligible place. That night they had to encamp on the open prairie, near a scanty pool of water, and without any wood to make a fire. The north-east wind blew keenly across the naked waste, and they were fain to decamp from their inhospitable bivouac before the dawn.

For two days they kept on in an eastward direction, against wintry blasts and occasional snow storms. They suffered, also, from scarcity of water, having occasionally to use melted snow; this, with the want of pasturage, reduced their old pack horse sadly. They saw many tracks of buffalo, and some few bulls, which, however, got the wind of them, and scampered off.

On the 26th of October, they steered east-north-east, for a wooded ravine, in a mountain at a small distance from the base of which, to their great joy, they discovered an abundant stream, running between willowed banks. Here they halted for the night, and Ben Jones having luckily trapped a beaver, and killed two buffalo bulls, they remained all the next day encamped, feasting and reposing, and allowing their jaded horse to rest from his labors.

The little stream on which they were encamped, was one of the head waters of the Platte river, which flows into the Missouri; it was in fact, the northern fork, or branch of that river, though this the travellers did not discover until long afterwards. Pursuing the course of this stream for about twenty miles, they came to where it forced a passage through a range of high hills, covered with cedars, into an extensive low country, affording excellent pasture to numerous herds of buffalo. Here they killed three cows, which were the first they had been able to get, having hitherto had to content themselves with bull beef, which at this season of the year is very poor. The hump meat afforded them a repast fit for an epicure.

Late on the afternoon of the 30th, they came to where the stream, now increased to a considerable size, poured along in a ravine between precipices of red stone, two hundred feet in height. For some distance it dashed along, over huge masses of rock, with foaming violence, as if exasperated by being compressed into so narrow a channel, and at length leaped down a chasm that looked dark and frightful in the gathering twilight.

For a part of the next day, the wild river, in its capricious wanderings, led them through a variety of striking scenes. At one time they were upon high plains, like platforms among the mountains, with herds of buffaloes roaming about them; at another, among rude rocky defiles, broken into cliffs and precipices, where the black-tailed deer bounded off among the crags, and the bighorn basked in the sunny brow of the precipice.

In the after part of the day, they came to another scene, surpassing in savage grandeur those already described. They had been travelling for some distance through a pass of the mountains, keeping parallel with the river, as it roared along, out of sight, through a deep ravine. Sometimes their devious path approached the margin of cliffs below which the river foamed, and boiled and whirled among the masses of rock that had fallen into its channel. As they crept cautiously on, leading their solitary pack horse along these giddy heights, they all at once came to where the river thundered down a succession of precipices, throwing up clouds of spray, and making a prodigious din and uproar. The travellers remained, for a time, gazing with mingled awe and delight, at this furious cataract, to which Mr. Stuart gave, from the color of the impending rocks, the name of "the Fiery Narrows."

CHAPTER XLIX

THE travellers encamped for the
night on the banks of the river, below the cataract. The night
was cold, with partial showers of rain and sleet. The morning dawned
gloomily, the skies were sullen and overcast, and threatened further
storms; but the little band resumed their journey, in defiance of the
weather. The increasing rigor of the season, however, which makes itself felt early in these mountainous regions, and on these naked and
elevated plains, brought them to a pause, and a serious deliberation,
after they had descended about thirty miles further along the course
of the river.

All were convinced that it was vain to attempt to accomplish their
journey on foot, at this inclement season. They had still many hundred
miles to traverse before they should reach the main course of the Missouri, and their route would lay over immense prairies, naked and
bleak, and destitute of fuel. The question then was, where to choose
their wintering place, and whether or not to proceed further down
the river. They had at first imagined it to be one of the head waters,

or tributary streams, of the Missouri. Afterwards they had believed it to be Rapid, or Quicourt river, in which opinion they had not come nearer to the truth; they now, however, were persuaded, with equal fallacy, by its inclining somewhat to the north of east, that it was the Cheyenne. If so, by continuing down it much further they must arrive among the Indians, from whom the river takes its name. Among these they would be sure to meet some of the Sioux tribe. These would apprize their relatives, the piratical Sioux of the Missouri, of the approach of a band of white traders; so that, in the spring time, they would be likely to be waylaid and robbed on their way down the river, by some party in ambush upon its banks.

Even should this prove to be the Quicourt or Rapid river, it would not be prudent to winter much further down upon its banks, as though they might be out of the range of the Sioux, they would be in the neighborhood of the Poncas, a tribe nearly as dangerous. It was resolved, therefore, since they must winter somewhere on this side of the Missouri, to descend no lower, but to keep up in these solitary regions, where they would be in no danger of molestation.

They were brought the more promptly and unanimously to this decision, by coming upon an excellent wintering place, that promised every thing requisite for their comfort. It was on a fine bend of the river, just below where it issued out from among a ridge of mountains, and bent towards the north-east. Here was a beautiful low point of land, covered by cottonwood, and surrounded by a thick growth of willow, so as to yield both shelter and fuel, as well as materials for building. The river swept by in a strong current, about a hundred and fifty yards wide. To the south-east were mountains of moderate height, the nearest about two miles off, but the whole chain ranging to the east, south, and south-west, as far as the eye could reach. Their summits were crowned with extensive tracts of pitch pine, chequered with small patches of the quivering aspen. Lower down were thick forests of firs and red cedars, growing out in many places from the very fissures of the rocks. The mountains were broken and precipitous, with huge bluffs protruding from among the forests. Their rocky recesses, and beetling cliffs, afforded retreats to innumerable flocks of

the bighorn, while their woody summits and ravines abounded with
bears, and black-tailed deer. These, with the numerous herds of buffalo
that ranged the lower grounds along the river, promised the travellers
abundant cheer in their winter quarters.

On the 2d of November, therefore, they pitched their camp for
the winter, on the woody point, and their first thought was, to obtain
a supply of provisions. Ben Jones and the two Canadians accordingly
sallied forth, accompanied by two others of the party, leaving but one
to watch the camp, Their hunting was uncommonly successful. In the
course of two days, they killed thirty-two buffaloes, and collected their
meat on the margin of a small brook, about a mile distant. Fortunately, a severe frost froze the river, so that the meat was easily transported to the encampment. On a succeeding day, a herd of buffalo
came trampling through the woody bottom on the river banks, and
fifteen more were killed.

It was soon discovered, however, that there was game of a more
dangerous nature in the neighborhood. On one occasion, Mr. Crooks
had wandered about a mile from the camp, and had ascended a small
hill commanding a view of the river. He was without his rifle, a rare
circumstance, for in these wild regions, where one may put up a wild
animal, or a wild Indian, at every turn, it is customary never to stir
from the camp-fire unarmed. The hill where he stood overlooked the
place where the massacre of the buffalo had taken place. As he was
looking around on the prospect, his eye was caught by an object below, moving directly towards him. To his dismay, he discovered it to be
a grizzly bear, with two cubs. There was no tree at hand into which he
could climb; to run, would only be to provoke pursuit, and he should
soon be overtaken. He threw himself on the ground, therefore, and lay
motionless, watching the movements of the animal with intense anxiety. It continued to advance until at the foot of the hill, where it
turned, and made into the woods, having probably gorged itself with
buffalo flesh. Mr. Crooks made all haste back to the camp, rejoicing at
his escape, and determining never to stir out again without his rifle. A
few days after this circumstance, a grizzly bear was shot in the neighborhood, by Mr. Miller.

As the slaughter of so many buffaloes had provided the party with beef for the winter, in case they met with no further supply, they now set to work, heart and hand, to build a comfortable wigwam. In a little while the woody promontory rang with the unwonted sound of the axe. Some of its lofty trees were laid low, and by the second evening the cabin was complete. It was eight feet wide, and eighteen feet long. The walls were six feet high, and the whole was covered with buffalo skins. The fire-place was in the centre, and the smoke found its way out by a hole in the roof.

The hunters were next sent out to procure deer-skins for garments, moccasins, and other purposes. They made the mountains echo with their rifles, and, in the course of two day's hunting, killed twenty-eight bighorns and black-tailed deer.

The party now revelled in abundance. After all that they had suffered from hunger, cold, fatigue and watchfulness; after all their perils from treacherous and savage men, they exulted in the snugness and security of their isolated cabin, hidden, as they thought, even from the prying eyes of Indian scouts, and stored with creature comforts; and they looked forward to a winter of peace and quietness; of roasting, and boiling, and broiling, and feasting upon venison, and mountain mutton, and bear's meat, and marrow bones, and buffalo humps, and other hunter's dainties, and of dosing and reposing round their fire, and gossipping over past dangers and adventures, and telling long hunting stories, until spring should return; when they would make canoes of buffalo skins, and float themselves down the river.

From such halcyon dreams, they were startled one morning, at daybreak, by a savage yelp. They started up and seized their rifles. The yelp was repeated by two or three voices. Cautiously peeping out, they beheld, to their dismay, several Indian warriors among the trees, all armed and painted in warlike style; being evidently bent on some hostile purpose.

Miller changed countenance as he regarded them. "We are in trouble," said he, "these are some of the rascally Arapahays that robbed me last year." Not a word was uttered by the rest of the party, but they silently slung their powder horns and ball pouches, and prepared for battle. M'Lellan, who had taken his gun to pieces the evening before, put it together in all haste. He proposed that they should break out the clay from between the logs, so as to be able to fire upon the enemy.

"Not yet," replied Stuart; "it will not do to show fear or distrust; we must first hold a parley. Some one must go out and meet them as a friend."

Who was to undertake the task! it was full of peril, as the envoy might be shot down at the threshold.

"The leader of a party," said Miller, "always takes the advance."

"Good!" replied Stuart; "I am ready." He immediately went forth; one of the Canadians followed him; the rest of the party remained in garrison, to keep the savages in check.

Stuart advanced holding his rifle in one hand, and extending the other to the savage that appeared to be the chief. The latter stepped forward and took it; his men followed his example, and all shook hands with Stuart, in token of friendship. They now explained their errand. They were a war party of Arapahay braves. Their village lay on a stream several day's journey to the eastward. It had been attacked and ravaged during their absence, by a band of Crows, who had carried off several of their women, and most of their horses. They were in quest of vengeance. For sixteen days they had been tracking the Crows about the mountains, but had not yet come upon them. In the mean time they had met with scarcely any game, and were half famished. About two days previously, they had heard the report of fire-arms among the mountains, and on searching in the direction of the sound, had come to a place where a deer had been killed. They had immediately put themselves upon the track of the hunters, and by following it up, had arrived at the cabin.

Mr. Stuart now invited the chief and another, who appeared to be his lieutenant, into the hut, but made signs that no one else was to enter. The rest halted at the door; others came straggling up, until the whole party, to the number of twenty-three, were gathered before the hut. They were armed with bows and arrows, tomahawks and scalping knives, and some few with guns. All were painted and dressed for war, and had a wild and fierce appearance. Mr. Miller recognised among them some of the very fellows who had robbed him in the preceding year; and put his comrades upon their guard. Every man stood ready to resist the first act of hostility; the savages, however, conducted themselves peaceably, and showed none of that swaggering arrogance which a war party is apt to assume.

On entering the hut the chief and his lieutenant cast a wilful look at the rafters, laden with venison and buffalo meat. Mr. Stuart made a merit of necessity, and invited them to help themselves. They did not wait to be pressed. The rafters were soon eased of their burthen; venison and beef were passed out to the crew before the door, and a scene of gormandizing commenced, of which few can have an idea, who have not witnessed the gastronomic powers of an Indian, after an interval of fasting. This was kept up throughout the day; they paused now and then, it is true, for a brief interval, but only to return to the charge with renewed ardor. The chief and the lieutenant surpassed all the rest in the vigor and perseverance of their attacks; as if, from their station they were bound to signalize themselves in all onslaughts. Mr. Stuart kept them well supplied with choice bits, for it was his policy to over-feed them, and keep them from leaving the hut, where they served as hostages for the good conduct of their followers. Once, only, in the course of the day, did the chief sally forth. Mr. Stuart and one of the men accompanied him, armed with their rifles, but without betraying any distrust. The chieftain soon returned, and renewed his attack upon the larder. In a word, he and his worthy coadjutor, the lieutenant, ate until they were both stupified.

Towards evening the Indians made their preparations for the night according to the practice of war parties. Those outside of the hut threw up two breast works, into which they retired at a tolerably early hour, and slept like over-fed hounds. As to the chief and his lieutenant, they passed the night in the hut, in the course of which, they, two or three times, got up to eat. The travellers took turns, one at a time, to mount guard until the morning.

Scarce had the day dawned, when the gormandizing was renewed by the whole band, and carried on with surprising vigor until ten o'clock, when all prepared to depart. They had six day's journey yet to make, they said, before they should come up with the Crows, who they understood were encamped on a river to the northward. Their way lay through a hungry country where there was no game; they would moreover, have but little time to hunt; they, therefore, craved a small supply of provisions for the journey. Mr. Stuart again invited them to help themselves. They did so with keen forethought, loading themselves with the choicest parts of the meat, and leaving the late plenteous larder far gone in a consumption. Their next request was for a supply of amunition, having guns, but no powder and ball. They promised to pay magnificently out of the spoils of their foray. "We are poor now," said they, "and are obliged to go on foot, but we shall soon come back laden with booty, and all mounted on horseback, with scalps hanging at our bridles. We will then give each of you a horse to keep you from being tired on your journey."

"Well," said Mr. Stuart, "when you bring the horses, you shall have the ammunition, but not before." The Indians saw by his determined tone, that all further entreaty would be unavailing, so they desisted, with a good humored laugh, and went off exceedingly well freighted, both within and without, promising to be back again in the course of a fortnight.

No sooner were they out of hearing, than the luckless travellers held another council. The security of their cabin was at an end, and with it all their dreams of a quiet and cosey winter. They were between two fires. On one side were their old enemies, the Crows; on the other side, the Arapahays, no less dangerous freebooters. As to the moderation of this war party, they considered it assumed, to put them off their guard against some more favorable opportunity for a surprisal. It was determined, therefore, not to await their return, but to abandon, with all speed, this dangerous neighborhood. From the accounts of their recent visitors, they were led to believe, though erroneously, that they were upon the Quicourt, or Rapid river. They proposed now to keep along it, to its confluence with the Missouri; but, should they be prevented by the rigors of the season, from proceeding so far, at least to reach a part of the river where they might be able to construct canoes of greater strength and durability than those of buffalo skins.

Accordingly, on the 13th of December, they bade adieu, with many a regret, to their comfortable quarters, where, for five weeks, they had been indulging the sweets of repose, of plenty, and of fancied security. They were still accompanied by their veteran pack horse, which the Arapahays had omitted to steal, either because they intended to steal him on their return, or because they thought him not worth stealing.

CHAPTER L

———

THE interval of comfort and repose which the party had enjoyed in their wigwam, rendered the renewal of their fatigues intolerable for the first two or three days. The snow lay deep, and was slightly frozen on the surface, but not sufficiently to bear their weight. Their feet became sore by breaking through the crust, and their limbs weary by floundering on without firm foothold. So exhausted and dispirited were they, that they began to think it would be better to remain and run the risk of being killed by the Indians, than to drag on thus painfully, with the probability of perishing by the way. Their miserable horse fared no better than themselves, having for the first day or two no other fodder than the ends of willow twigs, and the bark of the cotton-wood tree.

They all, however, appeared to gain patience and hardihood as they proceeded, and for fourteen days kept steadily on, making a distance of about three hundred and thirty miles. For some days, the range of mountains which had been near to their wigwam, kept parallel to the river at no great distance, but at length subsided into hills. Sometimes they found the river bordered with alluvial bottoms, and groves with cotton-wood and willows; sometimes the adjacent country was naked and barren. In one place it ran for a considerable distance between rocky hills and promontories covered with cedar and pitch pines, and peopled with the bighorn and the mountain deer; at other places it wandered through prairies well stocked with buffaloes and antelopes. As they descended the course of the river, they began to perceive the ash and white oak here and there among the cotton-wood and willow; and at length caught a sight of some wild horses on the distant prairies.

The weather was various; at one time the snow lay deep; then they had a genial day or two, with the mildness and serenity of autumn; then again, the frost was so severe that the river was sufficiently frozen to bear them upon the ice.

During the last three days of their fortnight's travel, however, the face of the country changed. The timber gradually diminished, until they could scarcely find fuel sufficient for culinary purposes. The game grew more and more scanty, and finally, none were to be seen but a few miserable broken down buffalo bulls, not worth killing. The snow lay fifteen inches deep, and made the travelling grievously painful and toilsome. At length they came to an immense plain, where no vestige of timber was to be seen; nor a single quadruped to enliven the desolate landscape. Here, then, their hearts failed them, and they held another consultation. The width of the river, which was upwards of a mile, its extreme shallowness, the frequency of quicksands, and various other characteristics, had at length made them sensible of their errors with respect to it, and they now came to the correct conclusion, that they were on the banks of the Platte or Shallow river. What were they to do? Pursue its course to the Missouri? To go on at this season of the year seemed dangerous in the extreme. There was no prospect of obtaining either food or firing. The country was destitute of trees, and though there might be drift wood along the river, it lay too deep beneath the snow for them to find it.

The weather was threatening a change, and a snow storm on these boundless wastes, might prove as fatal as a whirlwind of sand on an Arabian desert. After much dreary deliberation, it was at length determined to retrace their three last days' journey, of seventy-seven miles, to a place which they had remarked; where there was a sheltering growth of forest trees, and a country abundant in game. Here they would once more set up their winter quarters, and await the opening of the navigation to launch themselves in canoes.

Accordingly, on the 27th of December they faced about, retraced their steps, and on the 30th, regained the part of the river in question. Here the alluvial bottom was from one to two miles wide, and thickly covered with the forest of cotton-wood trees; while herds of buffalo were scattered about the neighboring prairie, several of which soon fell beneath their rifles.

They encamped on the margin of the river, in a grove where there were trees large enough for canoes. Here they put up a shed for immediate shelter, and immediately proceeded to erect a hut. New-year's day dawned when, as yet, but one wall of their cabin was completed; the genial and jovial day, however, was not permitted to pass uncelebrated, even by this weather beaten crew of wanderers. All work was suspended, except that of roasting and boiling. The choicest of the buffalo meat, with tongues, and humps, and marrow bones, were devoured in quantities that would astonish any one that has not lived among hunters or Indians; and as an extra regale, having no tobacco left, they cut up an old tobacco pouch, still redolent with the potent herb, and smoked it in honor of the day. Thus for a time, in present revelry, however uncouth, they forgot all past troubles and all anxieties about the future, and their forlorn wigwam echoed to the sound of gayety.

The next day they resumed their labors, and by the 6th of the month it was complete. They soon killed abundance of buffalo, and again laid in a stock of winter provisions.

The party were more fortunate in this their second cantonment. The winter passed away without any Indian visiters: and the game continued to be plenty in the neighborhood. They felled two large trees, and shaped them into canoes; and, as the spring opened, and a thaw of several days continuance melted the ice in the river, they made every preparation for embarking. On the 8th of March they launched forth in their canoes, but soon found that the river had not depth sufficient even for such slender barks. It expanded into a wide, but extremely shallow stream, with many sand bars, and occasionally various channels. They got one of their canoes a few miles down it, with extreme difficulty, sometimes wading, and dragging it over the shoals; at length they had to abandon the attempt, and to resume their journey on foot, aided by their faithful old pack horse, who had recruited strength during the repose of the winter.

The weather delayed them for a few days, having suddenly become more rigorous than it had been at any time during the winter; but on the 20th of March they were again on their journey.

In two days they arrived at the vast naked prairie, the wintry aspect of which had caused them, in December, to pause and turn back. It was now clothed in the early verdure of spring, and plentifully stocked with game. Still, when obliged to bivouac on its bare surface, without any shelter, and by a scanty fire of dry buffalo dung, they found the night blasts piercing cold. On one occasion, a herd of buffalo, straying near their evening camp, they killed three of them merely for their hides, wherewith to make a shelter for the night.

They continued on for upwards of a hundred miles; with vast prairies extending before them as they advanced; sometimes diversified by undulating hills, but destitute of trees. In one place they saw a gang of sixty-five wild horses, but as to the buffaloes, they seemed absolutely to cover the country. Wild geese abounded, and they passed extensive swamps that were alive with innumerable flocks of waterfowl, among which were a few swans, but an endless variety of ducks.

The river continued a winding course to the east-northeast, nearly a mile in width, but too shallow to float even an empty canoe. The country spread out into a vast level plain, bounded by the horizon alone, excepting to the north, where a line of hills seemed like a long promontory stretching into the bosom of the ocean. The dreary sameness of the prairie wastes began to grow extremely irksome. The travellers longed for the sight of a forest, or grove, or single tree, to break the level uniformity, and began to notice every object that gave reason to hope they were drawing towards the end of this weary wilderness.

Thus the occurrence of a particular kind of grass was hailed as a proof that they could not be far from the bottoms of the Missouri; and they were rejoiced at putting up several prairie hens, a kind of grouse seldom found far in the interior. In picking up drift wood for fuel, also, they found on some pieces the mark of an axe, which caused much speculation as to the time when and the persons by whom the trees had been felled. Thus they went on, like sailors at sea, who perceive in every floating weed and wandering bird, harbingers of the wished-for land.

By the close of the month the weather became very mild, and, heavily burthened as they were, they found the noontide temperature uncomfortably warm. On the 30th, they came to three deserted hunting camps, either of Pawnees or Ottoes, about which were buffalo sculls in all directions; and the frames on which the hides had been stretched and cured. They had apparently been occupied the preceding autumn.

For several days they kept patiently on, watching every sign that might give them an idea as to where they were, and how near to the banks of the Missouri.

Though there were numerous traces of hunting parties and encampments, they were not of recent date. The country seemed deserted. The only human beings they met with were three Pawnee squaws, in a hut in the midst of a deserted camp. Their people had all gone to the south, in pursuit of the buffalo, and had left these poor women behind, being too sick and infirm to travel.

It is a common practice with the Pawnees, and probably with other roving tribes, when departing on a distant expedition, which will not admit of incumbrance or delay, to leave their aged and infirm with a supply of provisions sufficient for temporary subsistence. When this is exhausted they must perish, though sometimes their sufferings are abridged by hostile prowlers who may visit the deserted camp.

The poor squaws in question expected some such fate at the hands of the white strangers, and though the latter accosted them in the kindest manner, and made them presents of dried buffalo meat, it was impossible to soothe their alarm, or get any information from them.

The first landmark by which the travellers were enabled to conjecture their position with any degree of confidence, was an island about seventy miles in length, which they presumed to be Brand isle. If so, they were within one hundred and forty miles of the Missouri. They kept on, therefore, with renewed spirit, and at the end of three days met with an Otto Indian, by whom they were confirmed in their conjecture. They learnt at the same time another piece of information, of an uncomfortable nature. According to his account, there was war between the United States and England, and in fact it had existed for a whole year, during which time they had been beyond the reach of all knowledge of the affairs of the civilized world.

The Otto conducted the travellers to his village, situated a short distance from the banks of the Platte. Here they were delighted to meet with two white men, Messrs. Dornin and Roi, Indian traders recently from St. Louis. Of these they had a thousand inquiries to make concerning all affairs, foreign and domestic, during their year of sepulture in the wilderness; and especially about the events of the existing war.

They now prepared to abandon their weary travel by land, and to embark upon the water. A bargain was made with Mr. Dornin, who engaged to furnish them with a canoe and provisions for the voyage, in exchange for their venerable and well-tried fellow traveller, the old Snake horse.

Accordingly, in a couple of days, the Indians employed by that gentleman, constructed for them a canoe twenty feet long, four feet wide, and eighteen inches deep. The frame was of poles and willow twigs, on which were stretched five elk and buffalo hides, sewed together with sinews, and the seams payed with unctuous mud. In this they embarked at an early hour on the 16th of April, and drifted down ten miles with the stream, when the wind being high they encamped, and set to work to make oars, which they had not been able to procure at the Indian village.

Once more afloat, they went merrily down the stream, and after making thirty-five miles, emerged into the broad turbid current of the Missouri. Here they were borne along briskly by the rapid stream, though, by the time their fragile bark had floated a couple of hundred miles, its frame began to show the effects of the voyage. Luckily they came to the deserted wintering place of some hunting party, where they found two old wooden canoes. Taking possession of the largest, they again committed themselves to the current, and after dropping down fifty-five miles further, arrived safely at fort Osage.

Here they found Lieutenant Brownson still in command; the officer who had given the expedition a hospitable reception on its way up the river, eighteen months previously. He received this remnant of the party with a cordial welcome, and endeavored in every way to promote their comfort and enjoyment during their sojourn at the fort. The greatest luxury they met with on their return to the abode of civilized man, was bread, not having tasted any for nearly a year.

Their stay at fort Osage was but short. On re-embarking they were furnished with an ample supply of provisions by the kindness of Lieutenant Brownson, and performed the rest of their voyage without adverse circumstance. On the 30th of April they arrived in perfect health and fine spirits at St. Louis, having been ten months performing this perilous expedition from Astoria. Their return caused quite a sensation at the place, bringing the first intelligence of the fortune of Mr. Hunt and his party, in their adventurous route across the Rocky mountains, and of the new establishment on the shores of the Pacific.

CHAPTER LI

IT is now necessary, in linking to-
gether the parts of this excursive narrative, that we notice the proceedings of Mr. Astor, in support of his great undertaking. His project
with respect to the Russian establishments along the north-west coast,
had been diligently prosecuted. The agent sent by him to St. Petersburgh, to negotiate in his name as president of the American Fur
Company, had, under sanction of the Russian government, made a
provisional agreement with the Russian company.

By this agreement, which was ratified by Mr. Astor in 1813, the
two companies bound themselves not to interfere with each other's
trading and hunting grounds, nor to furnish arms and ammunition to
the Indians. They were to act in concert, also, against all interlopers,
and to succor each other in case of danger. The American company
was to have the exclusive right of supplying the Russian posts with
goods and necessaries, receiving peltries in payment at stated prices.
They were, also, if so requested by the Russian governor, to convey the
furs of the Russian company to Canton, sell them on commission,
and bring back the proceeds, at such fright as might be agreed on
at the time. This agreement was to continue in operation four years,
and to be renewable for a similar term, unless some unforeseen contingency should render a modification necessary.

It was calculated to be of great service to the infant establishment at Astoria; dispelling the fears of hostile rivalry on the part of the foreign companies in its neighborhood, and giving a formidable blow to the irregular trade along the coast. It was also the intention of Mr. Astor to have coasting vessels of his own, at Astoria, of small tonnage and draft of water, fitted for coasting service. These, having a place of shelter and deposit, could ply about the coast in short voyages, in favorable weather, and would have vast advantage over chance ships, which must make long voyages, maintain numerous crews, and could only approach the coast at certain seasons of the year. He hoped, therefore, gradually to make Astoria the great emporium of the American fur trade in the Pacific, and the nucleus of a powerful American state. Unfortunately for these sanguine anticipations, before Mr. Astor had ratified the agreement, as above stated, war broke out between the United States and Great Britain. He perceived at once, the peril of the case. The harbor of New York would doubtless be blockaded, and the departure of the annual supply ship in the autumn prevented; or if she should succeed in getting out to sea, she might be captured on her voyage.

In this emergency, he wrote to Captain Sowle, commander of the Beaver. The letter, which was addressed to him at Canton, directed him to proceed to the factory at the mouth of the Columbia, with such articles as the establishment might need; and to remain there, subject to the orders of Mr. Hunt, should that gentleman be in command there.

The war continued. No tidings had yet been received from Astoria; the despatches having been delayed by the misadventure of Mr. Reed at the falls of the Columbia, and the unhorsing of Mr. Stuart, by the Crows among the mountains. A painful uncertainty, also, prevailed about Mr. Hunt and his party. Nothing had been heard of them since their departure from the Arickara village; Lisa, who parted from them there, had predicted their destruction; and some of the traders of the North-west Company, had actually spread a rumor of their having been cut off by the Indians.

It was a hard trial of the courage and means of an individual, to have to fit out another costly expedition, where so much had already been expended, so much uncertainty prevailed, and where the risk of loss was so greatly enhanced, that no insurance could be effected.

In spite of all these discouragements, Mr. Astor determined to send another ship to the relief of the settlement. He selected for this purpose, a vessel called the Lark, remarkable for her fast sailing. The disordered state of the times, however, caused such delay, that February arrived, while the vessel was yet lingering in port.

At this juncture, Mr. Astor learnt that the North-west Company were preparing to send out an armed ship of twenty guns, called the Isaac Todd, to form an establishment at the mouth of the Columbia. These tidings gave him great uneasiness. A considerable proportion of the persons in his employ were Scotchmen and Canadians, and several of them had been in the service of the North-west Company. Should Mr. Hunt have failed to arrive at Astoria, the whole establishment would be under the control of Mr. M'Dougal, of whose fidelity he had received very disparaging accounts from Captain Thorn. The British government, also, might deem it worth while to send a force against the establishment, having been urged to do so some time previously, by the North-west Company.

Under all these circumstances, Mr. Astor wrote to Mr. Monroe, then secretary of state, requesting protection from the government of the United States. He represented the importance of his settlement, in a commercial point of view, and the shelter it might afford to the American vessels in those seas. All he asked was, that the American government would throw forty or fifty men into the fort at his establishment, which would be sufficient for its defence, until he could send reinforcements over land.

He waited in vain for a reply to this letter, the government, no doubt, being engrossed at the time, by an overwhelming crowd of affairs. The month of March arrived, and the Lark was ordered by Mr. Astor, to put to sea. The officer who was to command her, shrunk from his engagement, and in the exigency of the moment, she was given in charge to Mr. Northrop, the mate. Mr. Nicholas G. Ogden, a gentleman on whose talents and integrity the highest reliance could be

placed, sailed as supercargo. The Lark put to sea in the beginning of
March, 1813.

By this opportunity, Mr. Astor wrote to Mr. Hunt, as head of the
establishment at the mouth of the Columbia, for he would not allow
himself to doubt of his welfare. "I always think you are well," said he,
"and that I shall see you again, which heaven, I hope, will grant."

He warned him to be on his guard against any attempts to surprise
the post; suggesting the probability of armed hostility on the part of
the North-west Company, and expressing his indignation at the un-
grateful returns made by that association for his frank and open conduct, and advantageous overtures. "Were I on the spot," said he, "and
had the management of affairs, I would defy them all; but as it is, every
thing depends upon you and your friends about you. *Our enterprise
is grand, and deserves success, and I hope in God it will meet it.* If
my object was merely gain of money, I should say, think whether it is
best to save what we can, and abandon the place; *but the very idea is
like a dagger to my heart.*" This extract is sufficient to show the spirit
and the views which actuated Mr. Astor in this great undertaking.

Week after week, and month after month elapsed, without any thing
to dispel the painful incertitude that hung over every part of this enterprize. Though a man of resolute spirit, and not easily cast down, the
dangers impending over this darling scheme of his ambition, had a
gradual effect upon the spirits of Mr. Astor. He was sitting one gloomy
evening by his window revolving over the loss of the Tonquin, and the
fate of her unfortunate crew, and fearing that some equally tragical
calamity might have befallen the adventurers across the mountains,
when the evening newspaper was brought to him. The first paragraph
that caught his eye, announced the arrival of Mr. Stuart and his party
at St. Louis, with intelligence that Mr. Hunt and his companions had
effected their perilous expedition to the mouth of the Columbia. This
was a gleam of sunshine that for a time dispelled every cloud, and he
now looked forward with sanguine hope to the accomplishment of all
his plans.

CHAPTER LII

THE course of our narrative now takes us back to the regions beyond the mountains, to dispose of the parties that set out from Astoria, in company with Mr. Robert Stuart, and whom he left on the banks of the Wallah-Wallah. Those parties, likewise separated from each other shortly after his departure, proceeding to their respective destinations, but agreeing to meet at the mouth of the Wallah-Wallah, about the beginning of June in the following year, with such peltries as they should have collected in the interior, so as to convoy each other through the dangerous passes of the Columbia.

Mr. David Stuart, one of the parties, proceeded with his men to the post already established by him at the mouth of the Oakinagan; having furnished this with goods and ammunition, he proceeded three hundred miles up that river, where he established another post in a good trading neighborhood.

Mr. Clarke, another partner, conducted his little band up Lewis river to the mouth of a small stream coming in from the north, to

which the Canadians gave the name of the Pavion. Here he found a
village or encampment of forty huts or tents, covered with mats, and
inhabited by *Nez perces*, or Pierced-nose Indians, as they are called by
the traders; but Chipunnish, as they are called by themselves. They are
a hardy, laborious, and somewhat knavish race, who lead a precarious
life, fishing, and digging roots during the summer and autumn, hunting the deer on snow shoes during the winter, and traversing the
Rocky mountains in the spring, to trade for buffalo skins with the
hunting tribes of the Missouri. In these migrations they are liable to
be waylaid and attacked by the Blackfeet, and other warlike and predatory tribes, and driven back across the mountains with the loss of
their horses, and of many of their comrades.

A life of this unsettled and precarious kind is apt to render men
selfish, and such Mr. Clarke found the inhabitants of this village, who
were deficient in the usual hospitality of Indians; parting with every
thing with extreme reluctance, and showing no sensibility to any act
of kindness. At the time of his arrival, they were all occupied in catching and curing salmon. The men were stout, robust, active, and good
looking, and the women handsomer than those of the tribes nearer to
the coast.

It was the plan of Mr. Clarke to lay up his boats here, and proceed
by land to his place of destination, which was among the Spokan
tribe of Indians, about a hundred and fifty miles distant. He accordingly endeavored to purchase horses for the journey, but in this he
had to contend with the sordid disposition of these people. They
asked high prices for their horses, and were so difficult to deal with,
that Mr. Clarke was detained seven days among them, before he could
procure a sufficient number. During that time he was annoyed by
repeated pilferings, for which he could get no redress. The chief
promised to recover the stolen articles; but failed to do so, alleging
that the thieves belonged to a distant tribe, and had made off with
their booty. With this excuse Mr. Clarke was fain to content himself,
though he laid up in his heart a bitter grudge against the whole
pierced-nose race, which it will be found he took occasion subsequently to gratify in a signal manner.

Having made arrangements for his departure, Mr. Clarke laid up his barge and canoes in a sheltered place, on the banks of a small bay, overgrown with shrubs and willows, confiding them to the care of the Nezpercé chief, who on being promised an ample compensation, engaged to have a guardian eye upon them; then mounting his steed, and putting himself at the head of his little caravan, he shook the dust off of his feet as he turned his back upon this village of rogues and hard dealers. We shall not follow him minutely in his journey; which lay at times over steep and rocky hills, and among crags and precipices; at other times over vast naked and sunburnt plains, abounding with rattlesnakes, in traversing which, both men and horses suffered intolerably from heat and thirst. The place on which he fixed for a trading post was a fine point of land at the junction of the Pointed Heart and Spokan rivers. His establishment was intended to compete with a trading post of the North-west Company, situated at no great distance, and to rival it in the trade with the Spokan Indians; as well as with the Cootonais and Flatheads. In this neighborhood we shall leave him for the present.

Mr. M'Kenzie, who conducted the third party from the Wallah-Wallah, navigated for several days up the south branch of the Columbia, named the Camōenum by the natives, but commonly called Lewis river, in honor of the first explorer. Wandering bands of various tribes were seen along this river, travelling in various directions; for the Indians generally are restless roving beings, continually intent on enterprises of war, traffic, and hunting. Some of these people were driving large gangs of horses, as if to a distant market. Having arrived at the mouth of the Shahaptan, he ascended some distance up that river, and established his trading post upon its banks. This appeared to be a great thoroughfare for the tribes from the neighborhood of the falls of the Columbia, in their expeditions to make war upon the tribes of the Rocky mountains; to hunt buffalo on the plains beyond, or to traffic for roots and buffalo robes. It was the season of migration, and the Indians from various distant parts were passing and repassing in great numbers.

Mr. M'Kenzie now detached a small band, under the conduct of

Mr. John Reed, to visit the caches made by Mr. Hunt at the Caldron Linn, and to bring the contents to his post; as he depended, in some measure, on them for his supplies of goods and ammunition. They had not been gone a week, when two Indians arrived of the Pallatapalla tribe, who live upon a river of the same name. These communicated the unwelcome intelligence that the caches had been robbed. They said that some of their tribe had, in the course of the preceding spring, been across the mountains, which separated them from Snake river, and had traded horses with the Snakes in exchange for blankets, robes, and goods of various descriptions. These articles the Snakes had procured from caches to which they were guided by some white men who resided among them, and who afterwards accompanied them across the Rocky mountains. This intelligence was extremely perplexing to Mr. M'Kenzie, but the truth of part of it was confirmed by the two Indians, who brought them an English saddle and bridle, which was recognised as having belonged to Mr. Crooks. The perfidy of the white men who revealed the secret of the caches, was, however, perfectly inexplicable. We shall presently account for it, in narrating the expedition of Mr. Reed.

That worthy Hibernian proceeded on his mission with his usual alacrity. His forlorn travels of the preceding winter had made him acquainted with the topography of the country, and he reached Snake river without any material difficulty. Here, in an encampment of the natives, he met with six white men, wanderers from the main expedition of Mr. Hunt, who, after having had their respective shares of adventures and mishaps, had fortunately come together at this place. Three of these men were Turcotte, La Chapelle, and Francis Landry; the three Canadian voyageurs who, it may be recollected, had left Mr. Crooks in February, in the neighborhood of Snake river, being dismayed by the increasing hardships of the journey, and fearful of perishing of hunger. They had returned to a Snake encampment, where they passed the residue of the winter.

Early in the spring, being utterly destitute, and in great extremity, and having worn out the hospitality of the Snakes, they determined to avail themselves of the buried treasures within their knowledge.

They accordingly informed the Snake chieftains that they knew where a great quantity of goods had been left in cache, enough to enrich the whole tribe; and offered to conduct them to the place, on condition of being rewarded with horses and provisions. The chieftains pledged their faith and honor as great men and Snakes, and the three Canadians conducted them to the place of deposit at the Caldron Linn. This is the way that the savages got knowledge of the caches, and not by following the tracks of wolves, as Mr. Stuart had supposed. Never did money diggers turn up a miser's hoard with more eager delight, than did the savages lay open the treasures of the caches. Blankets and robes; brass trinkets and blue beads were drawn forth with chuckling exultation, and long strips of scarlet cloth, produced yells of exstacy.

The rifling of the caches effected a change in the fortunes and deportment of the whole party. The Snakes were better clad and equipped than ever were Snakes before, and the three Canadians, suddenly finding themselves with horse to ride and weapon to wear, were, like beggars on horseback, ready to ride on any wild scamper. An opportunity soon presented. The Snakes determined on a hunting match on the buffalo prairies, to lay in a supply of beef, that they might live in plenty, as became men of their improved condition. The three newly mounted cavaliers must fain accompany them. They all traversed the Rocky mountains in safety, descended to the head waters of the Missouri, and made great havoc among the buffaloes.

Their hunting camp was full of meat; they were gorging themselves, like true Indians, with present plenty, and drying and jerking great quantities for a winter's supply. In the midst of their revelry and good cheer, the camp was surprised by the Blackfeet. Several of the Snakes were slain on the spot; the residue, with their three Canadian allies, fled to the mountains, stripped of horses, buffalo meat, every thing; and made their way back to the old encampment on Snake river, poorer than ever, but esteeming themselves fortunate in having escaped with their lives. They had not been long there when the Canadians were cheered by the sight of a companion in misfortune, Dubreuil, the poor voyageur who had left Mr. Crooks in March, being too much exhausted to keep on with him. Not long afterwards, three other straggling members of the main expedition made their appearance. These were Carson, St. Michael, and Pierre Delaunay, three of the trappers who, in company with Pierre Detayé, had been left among the mountains by Mr. Hunt, to trap beaver, in the preceding month of September. They had departed from the main body well armed and provided, with horses to ride, and horses to carry the peltries they were to collect. They came wandering into the Snake camp as ragged and destitute as their predecessors. It appears that they had finished their trapping, and were making their way in the spring to the Missouri, when they were met and attacked by a powerful band of the all-pervading Crows. They made a desperate resistance, and killed seven of the savages, but were overpowered by numbers. Pierre Detayé was slain, the rest were robbed of horses and effects, and obliged to turn back, when they fell in with their old companions, as already mentioned.

We should observe, that at the heels of Pierre Delaunay came draggling an Indian wife, whom he had picked up in his wanderings; having grown weary of celibacy among the savages.

The whole seven of this forlorn fraternity of adventurers, thus accidentally congregated on the banks of Snake river, were making arrangements once more to cross the mountains, when some Indian scouts brought word of the approach of the little band headed by John Reed.

The latter, having heard the several stories of these wanderers, took them all into his party, and set out for the Caldron Linn, to clear out two or three of the caches which had not been revealed to the Indians.

At that place he met with Robinson, the Kentucky veteran, who, with his two comrades, Rezner and Hoback, had remained there when Mr. Stuart went on. This adventurous trio had been trapping higher up the river, but Robinson had come down in a canoe, to await the expected arrival of the party, and obtain horses and equipments. He told Reed the story of the robbery of his party by the Arapahays, but it differed, in some particulars, from the account given by him to

Mr. Stuart. In that, he had represented Cass as having shamefully deserted his companions in their extremity, carrying off with him a horse: in the one now given, he spoke of him as having been killed in the affray with the Arapahays. This discrepancy, of which, of course, Reed could have had no knowledge at the time, concurred with other circumstances, to occasion afterwards some mysterious speculations and dark surmises, as to the real fate of Cass; but as no substantial grounds were ever adduced for them, we forbear to throw any deeper shades into this story of sufferings in the wilderness.

Mr. Reed having gathered the remainder of the goods from the caches, put himself at the head of his party, now augmented by the seven men thus casually picked up, and the squaw of Pierre Delaunay, and made his way successfully to M'Kenzie's post, on the waters of the Shahaptan.

CHAPTER LIII

AFTER the departure of the differ-
ent detachments, or *brigades,* as they are called by the fur traders,
the Beaver prepared for her voyage along the coast, and her visit to
the Russian establishment, at New Archangel, where she was to carry
supplies. It had been determined in the council of partners at Astoria,
that Mr. Hunt should embark in this vessel, for the purpose of ac-
quainting himself with the coasting trade, and of making arrangements
with the commander of the Russian post, and that he should be re-
landed in October, at Astoria, by the Beaver, on her way to the Sandwich islands, and Canton.

The Beaver put to sea in the month of August. Her departure, and
that of the various brigades, left the little fortress of Astoria but
slightly garrisoned. This was soon perceived by some of the Indian
tribes, and the consequence was, increased insolence of deportment,
and a disposition to hostility. It was now the fishing season, when the
tribes from the northern coast drew into the neighborhood of the

Columbia. These were warlike and perfidious, in their dispositions; and noted for their attempts to surprize trading ships. Among them were numbers of the Neweetees, the ferocious tribe that massacred the crew of the Tonquin.

Great precautions, therefore, were taken at the factory, to guard against surprise while these dangerous intruders were in the vicinity. Galleries were constructed inside of the palisades; the bastions were heightened, and sentinels were posted day and night. Fortunately, the Chinooks and other tribes resident in the vicinity manifested the most pacific disposition. Old Comcomly, who held sway over them, was a shrewd calculator. He was aware of the advantages of having the whites as neighbors, and allies, and of the consequence derived to himself and his people from acting as intermediate traders between them and the distant tribes. He had, therefore, by this time, become a firm friend of the Astorians, and formed a kind of barrier between them and the hostile intruders from the north.

The summer of 1812 passed away without any of the hostilities that had been apprehended; the Neweetees, and other dangerous visiters to the neighborhood, finished their fishing and returned home, and the inmates of the factory once more felt secure from attack.

It now became necessary to guard against other evils. The season of scarcity arrived, which commences in October, and lasts until the end of January. To provide for the support of the garrison, the shallop was employed to forage about the shores of the river. A number of the men, also, under the command of some of the clerks, were sent to quarter themselves on the banks of the Wollamut, (the Multnomah of Lewis and Clark), a fine river which disembogues itself into the Columbia, about sixty miles above Astoria. The country bordering on the river is finely diversified with prairies and hills, and forests of oak, ash, maple and cedar. It abounded at that time, with elk and deer, and the streams were well stocked with beaver. Here the party, after supplying their own wants, were enabled to pack up quantities of dried meat, and send it by canoes, to Astoria.

The month of October elapsed without the return of the Beaver. November, December, January, passed away, and still nothing was

seen or heard of her. Gloomy apprehensions now began to be entertained: she might have been wrecked in the course of her coasting
voyage, or surprised, like the Tonquin, by some of the treacherous
tribes of the north.

No one indulged more in these apprehensions that M'Dougal, who
had now the charge of the establishment. He no longer evinced the
bustling confidence and buoyancy which once characterized him.
Command seemed to have lost its charms for him; or rather, he gave
way to the most abject despondency, decrying the whole enterprize,
magnifying every untoward circumstance, and foreboding nothing but
evil.

While in this moody state, he was surprised, on the 16th of January,
by the sudden appearance of M'Kenzie, way-worn and weather-beaten
by a long wintry journey from his post on the Shahaptan, and with a
face the very frontispiece for a volume of misfortune. M'Kenzie had
been heartily disgusted and disappointed at his post. It was in the
midst of the Tushepaws, a powerful and warlike nation, divided into
many tribes, under different chiefs, who possessed innumerable horses,
but, not having turned their attention to beaver trapping, had no furs
to offer. According to M'Kenzie, they were but a "rascally tribe;" from
which we may infer that they were prone to consult their own interests, more than comported with the interests of a greedy Indian trader.

Game being scarce, he was obliged to rely for the most part, on
horse flesh for subsistence, and the Indians discovering his necessities,
adopted a policy usual in civilized trade, and raised the price of horses
to an exorbitant rate, knowing that he and his men must eat or die.
In this way, the goods he had brought to trade for beaver skins, were
likely to be bartered for horse flesh, and all the proceeds devoured
upon the spot.

He had despatched trappers in various directions, but the country
around did not offer more beaver than his own station. In this emergency he began to think of abandoning his unprofitable post, sending
his goods to the posts of Clarke and David Stuart, who could make a
better use of them, as they were in a good beaver country, and returning with his party to Astoria, to seek some better destination. With

this view he repaired to the post of Mr. Clarke, to hold a consultation. While the two partners were in conference in Mr. Clarke's wigwam, an unexpected visiter came bustling in upon them.

This was Mr. John George M'Tavish, a partner of the North-west Company who had charge of the rival trading posts established in that neighborhood. Mr. M'Tavish was the delighted messenger of bad news. He had been to lake Winnipeg, where he received an express from Canada, containing the declaration of war, and President Madison's proclamation, which he handed with the most officious complaisance to Messrs Clarke and M'Kenzie. He moreover told them, that he had received a fresh supply of goods from the north-west posts on the other side of the Rocky mountains, and was prepared for vigorous opposition to the establishments of the American company. He capped the climax of this obliging, but belligerent intelligence, by informing them that the armed ship, Isaac Todd, was to be at the mouth of the Columbia about the beginning of March, to get possession of the trade of the river, and that he was ordered to join her there at that time.

The receipt of this news determined M'Kenzie. He immediately returned to the Shahaptan, broke up his establishment, deposited his goods in *cache*, and hastened, with all his people, to Astoria.

The intelligence thus brought, completed the dismay of M'Dougal, and seemed to produce a complete confusion of mind. He held council of war with M'Kenzie, at which some of the clerks were present, but of course had no votes. They gave up all hope of maintaining their post at Astoria. The Beaver had probably been lost; they could receive no aid from the United States, as all the ports would be blockaded. From England nothing could be expected but hostility. It was determined, therefore, to abandon the establishment in the course of the following spring, and return across the Rocky mountains.

In pursuance of the resolution, they suspended all trade with the natives, except for provisions, having already more peltries than they could carry away, and having need of all the goods for the clothing and subsistence of their people, during the remainder of their sojourn, and on their journey across the mountains. This intention of abandoning Astoria was, however, kept secret from the men, lest they should at once give up all labor, and become restless and insubordinate.

In the mean time, M'Kenzie set off for his post at the Shahaptan, to get his goods from the caches, and buy horses and provisions with them for the caravan, across the mountains. He was charged with despatches from M'Dougal to Messrs. Stuart and Clarke, apprising them of the intended migration, that they might make timely preparations.

M'Kenzie was accompanied by two of the clerks, Mr. John Reed, the Irishman, and Mr. Alfred Seton of New York. They embarked in two canoes, manned by seventeen men, and ascended the river without any incident of importance, until they arrived in the eventful neighborhood of the rapids. They made the portage of the narrows and the falls early in the afternoon, and, having partaken of a scanty meal, had now a long evening on the their hands.

On the opposite side of the river lay the village of Wish-ram, of freebooting renown. Here lived the savages who had robbed and maltreated Reed, when bearing his tin box of despatches. It was known that the rifle of which he was despoiled, was retained as a trophy at the village. M'Kenzie offered to cross the river, and demand the rifle, if any one would accompany him. It was a hair-brained project, for these villages were noted for the ruffian character of their inhabitants; yet two volunteers promptly stepped forward; Alfred Seton, the clerk, and Joe de la Pierre, the cook. The trio soon reached the opposite side of the river. On landing, they freshly primed their rifles and pistols. A path winding for about a hundred yards among rocks and crags, led to the village. No notice seemed to be taken of their approach. Not a solitary being, man woman or child, greeted them. The very dogs, those noisy pests of an Indian town, kept silence. On entering the village, a boy made his appearance, and pointed to a house of larger dimensions than the rest. They had to stoop to enter it; as soon as they had passed the threshold, the narrow passage behind them was filled up by a sudden rush of Indians, who had before kept out of sight.

M'Kenzie and his companions found themselves in a rude chamber of about twenty-five feet long, and twenty wide. A bright fire was blazing at one end, near which sat the chief, about sixty years' old. A large number of Indians, wrapped in buffalo robes, were squatted in rows, three deep, forming a semicircle round three sides of the room. A single glance around sufficed to show them the grim and dangerous assemblage into which they had intruded, and that all retreat was cut off by the mass which blocked up the entrance.

The chief pointed to the vacant side of the room opposite to the door, and motioned for them to take their seats. They complied. A dead pause ensued. The grim warriors around sat like statues; each muffled in his robe with his fierce eyes bent on the intruders. The latter felt they were in a perilous predicament.

"Keep your eyes on the chief, while I am addressing him," said M'Kenzie to his companions. "Should he give any sign to his band, shoot him, and make for the door."

M'Kenzie advanced, and offered the pipe of peace to the chief, but it was refused. He then made a regular speech, explaining the object of their visit, and proposing to give in exchange for the rifle, two blankets, an axe, some beads and tobacco.

When he had done, the chief rose, began to address him in a low voice, but soon became loud and violent, and ended by working himself up into a furious passion. He upbraided the white men for their sordid conduct in passing and repassing through their neighborhood, without giving them a blanket or any other article of goods, merely because they had no furs to barter in exchange; and he alluded with menaces of vengeance, to the death of the Indian killed by the whites in the skirmish at the falls.

Matters were verging to a crisis. It was evident the surrounding savages were only waiting a signal from the chief to spring upon their prey. M'Kenzie and his companions had gradually risen on their feet during the speech, and had brought their rifles to a horizontal position, the barrels resting in their left hands; the muzzle of M'Kenzie's piece was within three feet of the speaker's heart. They cocked their rifles; the click of the locks for a moment suffused the dark cheek of the savage, and there was a pause. They cooly, but promptly, advanced to the door; the Indians fell back in awe, and suffered them to pass. The sun was just setting, as they emerged from this dangerous den. They took the precaution to keep along the tops of the rocks as much as possible on their way back to the canoe, and reached their camp in safety, congratulating themselves on their escape, and feeling no desire to make a second visit to the grim warriors of Wish-ram.

M'Kenzie and his party resumed their journey the next morning. At some distance above the falls of the Columbia, they observed two bark canoes, filled with white men, coming down the river, to the full chant of a set of Canadian voyageurs. A parley ensued. It was a detachment of northwesters, under the command of Mr. John George M'Tavish, bound, full of song and spirit, to the mouth of the Columbia, to await the arrival of the Isaac Todd.

M'Kenzie and M'Tavish came to a halt, and landing, encamped together for the night. The voyageurs of either party hailed each other as brothers, and old "comrades," and they mingled together as if united by one common interest, instead of belonging to rival companies, and trading under hostile flags.

In the morning they proceeded on their different ways, in style corresponding to their different fortunes: the one toiling painfully against the stream, the other sweeping down gaily with the current.

M'Kenzie arrived safely at his deserted post on the Shahaptan, but found, to his chagrin, that his caches had been discovered and rifled by the Indians. Here was a dilemma, for, on the stolen goods he had depended to purchase horses of the Indians. He sent out men in all directions to endeavor to discover the thieves, and despatched Mr. Reed to the posts of Messrs. Clarke and David Stuart, with the letters of Mr. M'Dougal.

The resolution announced in these letters, to break up and depart from Astoria, was condemned by both Clarke and Stuart. These two gentlemen had been very successful at their posts, and considered it rash and pusilanimous to abandon, on the first difficulty, an enterprise of such great cost and ample promise. They made no arrangements, therefore, for leaving the country, but acted with a view to the maintenance of their new and prosperous establishments.

The regular time approached, when the partners of the interior posts were to rendezvous at the mouth of the Wallah-Wallah, on their way to Astoria, with the peltries they had collected. Mr. Clarke accordingly packed all his furs on twenty-eight horses, and, leaving a clerk and four men to take charge of the post, departed on the 25th of May with the residue of his force.

On the 30th, he arrived at the confluence of the Pavion and Lewis rivers, where he had left his barge and canoes, in the guardianship of the old Pierced-nose chieftain. That dignitary had acquitted himself more faithfully of his charge than Mr. Clarke had expected, and the canoes were found in very tolerable order. Some repairs were necessary, and, while they were making, the party encamped close by the village. Having had repeated and vexatious proofs of the pilfering propensities of this tribe during his former visit, Mr. Clarke ordered that a wary eye should be kept upon them.

He was a tall, good-looking man, and somewhat given to pomp and circumstance, which made him an object of note in the eyes of the wondering savages. He was stately, too, in his appointments, and had a silver goblet or drinking cup, out of which he would drink with a magnificent air, and then lock it up in a large *garde vin*, which accompanied him in his travels, and stood in his tent. This goblet had originally been sent as a present from Mr. Astor to Mr. M'Kay, the partner who had unfortunately been blown up in the Tonquin. As it reached Astoria after the departure of that gentleman, it had remained in the possession of Mr. Clarke.

A silver goblet was too glittering a prize not to catch the eye of a Pierced-nose. It was like the shining tin case of John Reed. Such a wonder had never been seen in the land before. The Indians talked about it to one another. They marked the care with which it was deposited in the *garde vin*, like a relic in its shrine, and concluded that it must be a "great medicine." That night Mr. Clarke neglected to lock up his treasure; in the morning the sacred casket was open—the precious relic gone!

Clarke was now outrageous. All the past vexations that he had suffered from this pilfering community rose to mind, and he threatened, that, unless the goblet were promptly returned, he would hang the thief should he eventually discover him. The day passed away, however, without the restoration of the cup. At night, sentinels were secretly posted about the camp. With all their vigilance, a Pierced-nose contrived to get into the camp unperceived, and to load himself with booty; it was only on his retreat that he was discovered and taken.

At daybreak, the culprit was brought to trial, and promptly convicted. He stood responsible for all the spoliations of the camp, the precious goblet among the number, and Mr. Clarke passed sentence of death upon him.

A gibbet was accordingly constructed of oars: the chief of the village and his people were assembled, and the culprit was produced, with his legs and arms pinioned. Clarke then made a harangue. He reminded the tribe of the benefits he had bestowed upon them during his former visit, and the many thefts and other misdeeds which he had overlooked. The prisoner, especially, had always been peculiarly well treated by the white men, but had repeatedly been guilty of pilfering. He was to be punished for his own misdeeds, and as a warning to his tribe.

The Indians now gathered round Mr. Clarke, and interceded for the culprit. They were willing he should be punished severely, but implored that his life might be spared. The companions, too, of Mr. Clarke considered the sentence too severe, and advised him to mitigate it; but he was inexorable. He was not naturally a stern or cruel man; but from his boyhood he had lived in the Indian country among Indian traders, and held the life of a savage extremely cheap. He was, moreover, a firm believer in the doctrine of intimidation.

Farnham, a clerk, a tall "Green-mountain boy" from Vermont, who had been robbed of a pistol, acted as executioner. The signal was given, and the poor Pierced-nose, resisting, struggling, and screaming, in the most frightful manner, was launched into eternity. The Indians stood round gazing in silence and mute awe, but made no attempt to oppose the execution, nor testified any emotion when it was over. They locked up their feelings within their bosoms until an opportunity should arrive to gratify them with a bloody act of vengeance.

To say nothing of the needless severity of this act, its impolicy was glaringly obvious. Mr. M'Lennan and three men were to return to the post with the horses, their loads having been transferred to the canoes. They would have to pass through a tract of country infested by this tribe, who were all horsemen and hard riders, and might pursue them to take vengeance for the death of their comrade. M'Lennan, however, was a resolute fellow, and made light of all dangers. He and his three men were present at the execution, and set off as soon as life was extinct in the victim; but, to use the words of one of their comrades, "they did not let the grass grow under the heels of their horses, as they clattered out of the Pierced-nose country," and were glad to find themselves in safety at the post.

Mr. Clarke and his party embarked about the same time in their canoes, and early on the following day reached the mouth of the Wallah-Wallah, where they found Messrs. Stuart and M'Kenzie awaiting them; the latter having recovered part of the goods stolen from his cache. Clarke informed them of the signal punishment he had inflicted on the Pierced-nose, evidently expecting to excite their admiration by such a hardy act of justice, performed in the very midst of the Indian country, but was mortified at finding it strongly censured as inhuman, unnecessary, and likely to provoke hostilities.

The parties thus united formed a squadron of two boats and six canoes, with which they performed their voyage in safety down the river, and arrived at Astoria on the 12th of June, bringing with them a valuable stock of peltries.

About ten days previously, the brigade which had been quartered on the banks of the Wollamut, had arrived with numerous packs of beaver, the result of a few months' sojourn on that river. These were the first fruits of the enterprise, gathered by men as yet mere strangers in the land; but they were such as to give substantial grounds for sanguine anticipations of profit, when the country should be more completely explored, and the trade established.

CHAPTER LIV

THE partners found Mr. M'Dougal
in all the bustle of preparation; having about nine days previously announced at the factory, his intention of breaking up the establishment, and fixed upon the 1st of July for the time of departure.
Messrs. Stuart and Clarke felt highly displeased at his taking so precipitate a step, without waiting for their concurrence, when he must
have known that their arrival could not be far distant.

Indeed, the whole conduct of Mr. M'Dougal was such as to awaken
strong doubts of his loyal devotion to the cause. His old sympathies
with the North-west Company seemed to have revived. He had received M'Tavish and his party with uncalled-for hospitality, as though
they were friends and allies, instead of being a party of observation,
come to reconnoitre the state of affairs at Astoria, and to await the
arrival of a hostile ship. Had they been left to themselves, they would
have been starved off for want of provisions, or driven away by the
Chinooks, who only wanted a signal from the factory to treat them as
intruders and enemies. M'Dougal, on the contrary, had supplied them
from the stores of the garrison, and had gained them the favor of the
Indians, by treating them as friends.

Having set his mind fixedly on the project of breaking up the establishment at Astoria, in the current year, M'Dougal was sorely disappointed at finding that Messrs. Stuart and Clarke had omitted to comply with his request to purchase horses and provisions for the caravan, across the mountains. It was now too late to make the necessary preparations in time for traversing the mountains before winter, and the project had to be postponed.

In the mean time, the non arrival of the annual ship, and the apprehensions entertained of the loss of the Beaver and of Mr. Hunt, had their effect upon the minds of Messrs. Stuart and Clarke. They began to listen to the desponding representations of M'Dougal, seconded by M'Kenzie, who inveighed against their situation as desperate and forlorn; left to shift for themselves, or perish upon a barbarous coast; neglected by those who sent them there, and threatened with dangers of every kind. In this way they were brought to consent to the plan of abandoning the country in the ensuing year.

About this time, M'Tavish applied at the factory to purchase a small supply of goods wherewith to trade his way back to his post on the upper waters of the Columbia, having waited in vain for the arrival of the Isaac Todd. His request brought on a consultation among the partners. M'Dougal urged that it should be complied with. He furthermore proposed, that they should give up to M'Tavish, for a proper consideration, the post on the Spokan, and all its dependencies, as they had not sufficient goods on hand to supply that post themselves, and to keep up a competition with the North-west Company, in the trade with the neighboring Indians. This last representation has since been proved incorrect. By inventories, it appears, that that their stock in hand for the supply of the interior posts, was superior to that of the North-west Company; so that they had nothing to fear from competition.

Through the influence of Messrs. M'Dougal and M'Kenzie, this proposition was adopted, and was promptly accepted by M'Tavish. The merchandize sold to him, amounted to eight hundred and fifty-eight dollars, to be paid for, in the following spring, in horses, or in any other manner most acceptable to the partners at that period.

This agreement being concluded, the partners formed their plans for the year that they would yet have to pass in the country. Their objects were, chiefly, present subsistence, and the purchase of horses for the contemplated journey, though they were likewise to collect as much peltries as their diminished means would command. Accordingly, it was arranged, that David Stuart should return to his former post on the Oakinagan, and Mr. Clarke should make his sojourn among the Flatheads. John Reed, the sturdy Hibernian, was to undertake the Snake river country, accompanied by Pierre Dorion and Pierre Delaunay, as hunters, and Francis Landry, Jean Baptiste Turcotte, André la Chapelle, and Gilles le Clerc, Canadian voyageurs.

Astoria, however, was the post about which they felt the greatest solicitude, and on which they all more or less depended. The maintenance of this in safety throughout the coming year, was, therefore, their grand consideration. Mr. M'Dougal was to continue in command of it, with a party of forty men. They would have to depend chiefly upon the neighboring savages for their subsistence. These, at present, were friendly, but it was to be feared that, when they should discover the exigencies of the post, and its real weakness, they might proceed to hostilities; or, at any rate, might cease to furnish their usual supplies. It was important, therefore, to render the place as independent as possible, of the surrounding tribes for its support; and it was accordingly resolved that M'Kenzie, with four hunters, and eight common men should winter in the abundant country of the Wollamut, from whence they might be enabled to furnish a constant supply of provisions to Astoria.

As there was too great a proportion of clerks for the number of privates in the service, the engagements of three of them, Ross Cox, Ross, and M'Lennan, were surrendered to them, and they immediately enrolled themselves in the service of the North-west Company; glad, no doubt, to escape from what they considered a sinking ship.

Having made all these arrangements, the four partners, on the first of July, signed a formal manifesto, stating the alarming state of their affairs, from the non-arrival of the annual ship, and the absence and apprehended loss of the Beaver, their want of goods, their despair of receiving any further supply, their ignorance of the coast, and their disappointment as to the interior trade, which they pronounced unequal to the expenses incurred, and incompetent to stand against the powerful opposition of the North-west Company. And as by the 16th article of the company's agreement, they were authorized to abandon this undertaking, and dissolve the concern, if before the period of five years, it should be found unprofitable; they now formally announced their intention to do so on the 1st day of June, of the ensuing year, unless in the interim, they should receive the necessary support and supplies from Mr. Astor, or the stockholders, with orders to continue.

This instrument, accompanied by private letters of similar import, was delivered to Mr. M'Tavish, who departed on the 5th of July. He engaged to forward the despatches to Mr. Astor, by the usual winter express sent over land by the North-west Company.

The manifesto was signed with great reluctance by Messrs. Clarke and D. Stuart, whose experience by no means justified the discouraging account given in it, of the internal trade, and who considered the main difficulties of exploring an unknown and savage country, and of ascertaining the best trading and trapping grounds, in a great measure overcome. They were overruled, however, by the urgent instances of M'Dougal and M'Kenzie, who, having resolved upon abandoning the enterprise, were desirous of making as strong a case as possible to excuse their conduct to Mr. Astor and to the world.

CHAPTER LV

WHILE difficulties and disasters had been gathering about the infant settlement of Astoria, the mind of its projector at New York, was a prey to great anxiety. The ship Lark, despatched by him with supplies for the establishment, sailed on the 6th of March, 1813. Within a fortnight afterwards, he received intelligence which justified all his apprehensions of hostility on the part of the British. The North-west Company had made a second memorial to that government, representing Astoria as an American establishment, stating the vast scope of its contemplated operations, magnifying the strength of its fortifications, and expressing their fears that, unless crushed in the bud, it would effect the downfall of their trade.

Influenced by these representations, the British government ordered the frigate Phoebe to be detached as a convoy for the armed ship, Isaac Todd, which was ready to sail with men and munitions for forming a new establishment. They were to proceed together to the mouth of the Columbia, capture or destroy whatever American fortress they should find there, and plant the British flag on its ruins.

Informed of these movements, Mr. Astor lost no time in addressing a second letter to the secretary of state, communicating this intelligence, and requesting it might be laid before the president; as no notice, however, had been taken of his previous letter, he contented himself with this simple communication, and made no further application for aid.

Awakened now to the danger that menaced the establishment at Astoria, and aware of the importance of protecting this foothold of American commerce and empire on the shores of the Pacific, the government determined to send the frigate Adams, Captain Crane, upon this service. On hearing of this determination, Mr. Astor immediately proceeded to fit out a ship called the Enterprise, to sail in company with the Adams, freighted with additional supplies and reinforcements for Astoria.

About the middle of June, while in the midst of these preparations, Mr. Astor received a letter from Mr. R. Stuart dated St. Louis, May 1st, confirming the intelligence already received through the public newspapers, of his safe return, and of the arrival of Mr. Hunt and his party at Astoria, and giving the most flattering accounts of the prosperity of the enterprise.

So deep had been the anxiety of Mr. Astor, for the success of this great object of his ambition, that this gleam of good news was almost overpowering. "I felt ready," said he, "to fall upon my knees in a transport of gratitude."

At the same time he heard that the Beaver had made good her voyage from New York to the Columbia. This was additional ground of hope for the welfare of the little colony. The post being thus relieved and strengthened with an American at its head, and a ship of war about to sail for its protection, the prospect for the future seemed full of encouragement, and Mr. Astor proceeded with fresh vigor, to fit out his merchant ship.

Unfortunately for Astoria, this bright gleam of sunshine was soon overclouded. Just as the Adams had received her compliment of men, and the two vessels were ready for sea, news came from Commodore Chauncey, commanding on lake Ontario, that a reinforcement of seamen was wanted in that quarter. The demand was urgent, the crew of the Adams was immediately transferred to that service, and the ship was laid up.

This was a most ill-timed and discouraging blow, but Mr. Astor
would not yet allow himself to pause in his undertaking. He determined to send the Enterprise to sea alone, and let her take the chance
of making her unprotected way across the ocean. Just at this time,
however, a British force made its appearance off the Hook; and the
port of New York was effectually blockaded. To send a ship to sea
under these circumstances, would be to expose her to almost certain
capture. The Enterprise was, therefore, unloaded and dismantled,
and Mr. Astor was obliged to comfort himself with the hope that the
Lark might reach Astoria in safety, and that aided by her supplies,
and by the good management of Mr. Hunt and his associates, the little colony might be able to maintain itself until the return of peace.

CHAPTER LVI

WE have hitherto had so much to
relate of a gloomy and disastrous nature, that it is with a feeling of
momentary relief we turn to something of a more pleasing complex-
ion, and record the first, and indeed only nuptials in high life that
took place in the infant settlement of Astoria.

M'Dougal, who appears to have been a man of a thousand projects,
and of great, though somewhat irregular ambition, suddenly conceived
the idea of seeking the hand of one of the native princesses, a daughter of the one-eyed potentate Comcomly, who held sway over the fishing tribe of the Chinooks, and had long supplied the factory with
smelts and sturgeons.

Some accounts give rather a romantic origin to this affair, tracing
it to the stormy night, when M'Dougal, in the course of an exploring
expedition, was driven by stress of weather, to seek shelter in the royal
abode of Comcomly. Then and there he was first struck with the
charms of this piscatory princess, as she exerted herself to entertain
her father's guest.

The "journal of Astoria," however, which was kept under his own
eye, records this union as a high state alliance, and great stroke of
policy. The factory had to depend, in a great measure, on the Chi-

nooks for provisions. They were at present friendly, but it was to be feared they would prove otherwise, should they discover the weakness and the exigencies of the post, and the intention to leave the country. This alliance, therefore, would infallibly rivet Comcomly to the interests of the Astorians, and with him the powerful tribe of the Chinooks. Be this as it may, and it is hard to fathom the real policy of governors and princes, M'Dougal despatched two of the clerks as ambassadors extraordinary, to wait upon the one-eyed chieftain, and make overtures for the hand of his daughter.

The Chinooks, though not a very refined nation, have notions of matrimonial arrangements that would not disgrace the most refined sticklers for settlements and pin money. The suitor repairs not to the bower of his mistress, but to her father's lodge, and throws down a present at his feet. His wishes are then disclosed by some discreet friend employed by him for the purpose. If the suitor and his present find favor in the eyes of the father, he breaks the matter to his daughter, and inquires into the state of her inclinations. Should her answer be favorable, the suit is accepted, and the lover has to make further presents to the father, of horses, canoes, and other valuables, according to the beauty and merits of the bride; looking forward to a return in kind whenever they shall go to house-keeping.

We have more than once had occasion to speak of the shrewdness of Comcomly; but never was it exerted more adroitly than on this occasion. He was a great friend of M'Dougal, and pleased with the idea of having so distinguished a son-in-law; but so favorable an opportunity of benefiting his own fortune, was not likely to occur a second time, and he determined to make the most of it. Accordingly, the negotiation was protracted with true diplomatic skill. Conference after conference was held with the two ambassadors: Comcomly was extravagant in his terms; rating the charms of his daughter at the highest price, and indeed she is represented as having one of the flattest and most aristocratical heads in the tribe. At length the preliminaries were all happily adjusted. On the 20th of July, early in the afternoon, a squadron of canoes crossed from the village of the Chinooks, bearing the royal family of Comcomly, and all his court.

That worthy sachem landed in princely state, arrayed in a bright blue blanket and red breech clout, with an extra quantity of paint and feathers, attended by a train of half-naked warriors and nobles. A horse was in waiting to receive the princess, who was mounted behind one of the clerks, and thus conveyed, coy but compliant, to the fortress. Here she was received with devout, though decent joy, by her expecting bridegroom.

Her bridal adornments, it is true, at first caused some little dismay, having painted and anointed herself for the occasion according to the Chinook toilet; by dint, however, of copious ablutions, she was freed from all adventitious tint and fragrance, and entered into the nuptial state, the cleanest princess that had ever been known, of the somewhat unctuous tribe of the Chinooks.

From that time forward, Comcomly was a daily visiter at the fort, and was admitted into the most intimate councils of his son-in-law. He took an interest in everything that was going forward, but was particularly frequent in his visits to the blacksmith's shop; tasking the labors of the artificer in iron for every kind of weapon and implement suited to the savage state, insomuch that the necessary business of the factory was often postponed to attend to his requisitions.

The honey moon had scarce passed away, and M'Dougal was seated with his bride in the fortress of Astoria, when, about noon of the 20th of August, Gassacop, the son of Comcomly, hurried into his presence with great agitation, and announced a ship at the mouth of the river. The news produced a vast sensation. Was it a ship of peace or war? Was it American or British? Was it the Beaver or the Isaac Todd? M'Dougal hurried to the water side, threw himself into a boat, and ordered the hands to pull with all speed for the mouth of the harbor. Those in the fort remained watching the entrance of the river, anxious to know whether they were to prepare for greeting a friend or fighting an enemy. At length the ship was descried crossing the bar, and bending her course towards Astoria. Every gaze was fixed upon her in silent scrutiny, until the American flag was recognised. A general shout was the first expression of joy, and next a salutation was thundered from the cannon of the fort.

The vessel came to anchor on the opposite side of the river, and returned the salute. The boat of Mr. M'Dougal went on board, and was seen returning late in the afternoon. The Astorians watched her with straining eyes, to discover who were on board, but the sun went down, and the evening closed in, before she was sufficiently near. At length she reached the land, and Mr. Hunt stepped on shore. He was hailed as one risen from the dead, and his return was a signal for merriment almost equal to that which prevailed at the nuptials of M'Dougal.

We must now explain the cause of this gentleman's long absence, which had given rise to such gloomy and dispiriting surmises.

CHAPTER LVII

I<small>T</small> will be recollected, that the destination of the Beaver, when she sailed from Astoria on the 4th of August in 1812, was to proceed northwardly along the coast to Sheetka, or New Archangel, there to dispose of that part of her cargo intended for the supply of the Russian establishment at that place, and then to return to Astoria, where it was expected, she would arrive in October.

New Archangel is situated in Norfolk Sound, lat. 57° 2' N., long. 135° 50' W. It was the head quarters of the different colonies of the Russian Fur Company, and the common rendezvous of the American vessels trading along the coast.

The Beaver met with nothing worthy of particular mention in her voyage, and arrived at New Archangel on the 19th of August. The place at that time was the residence of Count Baranoff, the governor of the different colonies: a rough, rugged, hospitable, hard drinking old Russian; somewhat of a soldier, somewhat of a trader; above all, a boon companion of the old roystering school, with a strong cross of the bear.

Mr. Hunt found this hyperborean veteran ensconced in a fort

which crested the whole of a high rocky promontory. It mounted one hundred guns, large and small, and was impregnable to Indian attack, unaided by artillery. Here the old governor lorded it over sixty Russians, who formed the corps of the trading establishment, beside an indefinite number of Indian hunters of the Kodiak tribe, who were continually coming and going, or lounging and loitering about the fort like so many hounds round a sportsman's hunting quarters. Though a loose liver among his guests, the governor was a strict disciplinarian among his men; keeping them in perfect subjection, and having seven on guard night and day.

Beside those immediate serfs and dependants just mentioned, the old Russian potentate exerted a considerable sway over a numerous and irregular class of maritime traders, who looked to him for aid and munitions, and through whom he may be said to have, in some degree, extended his power along the whole north-west coast. These were American captains of vessels engaged in a particular department of trade. One of these captains would come, in a manner, empty handed to New Archangel. Here his ship would be furnished with about fifty canoes and a hundred Kodiak hunters, and fitted out with provisions, and every thing necessary for hunting the sea otter on the coast of California, where the Russians have another establishment. The ship would ply along the Californian coast from place to place, dropping parties of otter hunters in their canoes, furnishing them only with water, and leaving them to depend upon their own dexterity for a maintenance. When a sufficient cargo was collected, she would gather up her canoes and hunters, and return with them to Archangel; where the captain would render in the returns of his voyage, and receive one half of the skins for his share.

Over these coasting captains, as we have hinted, the verteran governor exerted some sort of sway, but it was of a peculiar and characteristic kind; it was the tyranny of the table. They were obliged to join him in his "prosnics" or carousals, and to drink "potations pottle deep." His carousals, too, were not of the most quiet kind, nor were his potations as mild as nectar. "He is continually," said Mr. Hunt, "giving entertainments by way of parade, and if you do not drink raw rum, and boiling punch as strong as sulphur, he will insult you as soon as he gets drunk, which is very shortly after setting down to table."

As to any "temperance captain" who stood fast to his faith, and refused to give up his sobriety, he might go elsewhere for a market, for he stood no chance with the governor. Rarely, however, did any cold water caitiff of the kind darken the door of old Baranhoff; the coasting captains knew too well his humor and their own interests; they joined in his revels, they drank, and sang, and whooped, and hiccuped, until they all got "half seas over," and then affairs went on swimmingly.

An awful warning to all "flinchers" occurred shortly before Mr. Hunt's arrival. A young naval officer had recently been sent out by the emperor to take command of one of the company's vessels. The governor, as usual, had him at his "prosnics," and plied him with fiery potations. The young man stood on the defensive until the old count's ire was completely kindled; he carried his point, and made the greenhorn tipsy, willy nilly. In proportion as they grew fuddled they grew noisy, they quarrelled in their cups; the youngster paid old Baranhoff in his own coin by rating him soundly; in reward for which, when sober, he was taken the rounds of four pickets, and received seventy-nine lashes, taled out with Russian punctuality of punishment.

Such was the old grizzled bear with whom Mr. Hunt had to do his business. How he managed to cope with his humor; whether he pledged him in raw rum and blazing punch, and "clinked the can" with him as they made their bargains, does not appear upon record; we must infer, however, from his general observations on the absolute sway of this hard-drinking potentate, that he had to conform to the customs of his court, and that their business transactions presented a maudlin mixture of punch and peltry.

The greatest annoyance to Mr. Hunt, however, was the delay to which he was subjected, in disposing of the cargo of the ship, and getting the requisite returns. With all the governor's devotions to the bottle, he never obfuscated his faculties sufficiently to lose sight of his interest, and is represented by Mr. Hunt as keen, not to say crafty,

at a bargain, as the most arrant water drinker. A long time was expended negotiating with him, and by the time the bargain was concluded, the month of October had arrived. To add to the delay he
was to be paid for his cargo in seal skins. Now it so happened that
there was none of this kind of peltry at the fort of old Baranhoff. It
was necessary, therefore, for Mr. Hunt to proceed to a seal catching
establishment, which the Russian company had at the island of St.
Paul, in the sea of Kamschatka. He accordingly set sail on the 4th of
October, after having spent forty-five days at New Archangel, boosing
and bargaining with its roystering commander, and right glad was he
to escape from the clutches of this "old man of the sea."

The Beaver arrived at St. Paul's on the 31st of October; by which
time, according to arrangement, he ought to have been back at Astoria. The island of St. Paul's is in latitude 57° N., longitude 170° or
171° W. Its shores, in certain places, and at certain seasons, are covered with seals, while others are playing about in the water. Of these,
the Russians take only the small ones, from seven to ten months old,
and carefully select the males, giving the females their freedom, that
the breed may not be diminished. The islanders, however, kill the
large ones for provisions, and for skins wherewith to cover their canoes. They drive them from the shore over the rocks, until within a
short distance of their habitations, where they kill them. By this
means, they save themselves the trouble of carrying the skins, and
have the flesh at hand. This is thrown in heaps, and when the season
for skinning is over, they take out the entrails, and make one heap of
the blubber. This, with drift wood, serves for fuel, for the island is
entirely destitute of trees. They make another heap of the flesh,
which, with the eggs of sea fowls, preserved in oil, an occasional sea
lion, a few ducks in winter, and some wild roots, composes their food.

Mr. Hunt found seven Russians at the island, and one hundred
hunters, natives of Oonalaska, with their families. They lived in cabins that looked like canoes; being, for the most part formed of the jaw
bone of a whale, put up as rafters, across which were laid pieces of
drift wood covered over with long grass, the skins of large sea animals,
and earth; so as to be quite comfortable, in despite of the rigors of

the climate; though we are told they had as ancient and fish-like an odor, "as had the quarters of Jonah, when lodged within the whale."

In one of these odoriferous mansions, Mr. Hunt occasionally took up his abode, that he might be at hand to hasten the loading of the ship. The operation, however, was somewhat slow, for it was necessary to overhaul and inspect every pack, to prevent imposition, and the peltries had then to be conveyed in large boats, made of skins, to the ship, which was some little distance from the shore, standing off and on.

One night, while Mr. Hunt was on shore, with some others of the crew, there rose a terrible gale. When the day broke, the ship was not to be seen. He watched for her with anxious eyes until night, but in vain. Day after day of boisterous storms, and howling wintry weather, were passed in watchfulness and solicitude. Nothing was to be seen but a dark and angry sea, and a scowling northern sky; and at night he retired within the jaws of the whale, and nestled disconsolately among seal skins.

At length, on the 13th of November, the Beaver made her appearance; much the worse for the stormy conflicts, she had sustained in those hyperborean seas. She had been obliged to carry a press of sail in heavy gales, to be able to hold her ground, and had consequently sustained great damage in her canvass and rigging. Mr. Hunt lost no time in hurrying the residue of the cargo on board of her; then, bidding adieu to his seal fishing friends, and his whale-bone habitation, he put forth once more to sea.

He was now for making the best of his way to Astoria, and fortunate would it have been for the interests of that place, and the interests of Mr. Astor, had he done so; but, unluckily, a perplexing question rose in his mind. The sails and rigging of the Beaver had been much rent and shattered in the late storm; would she be able to stand the hard gales to be expected in making Columbia river at this season? Was it prudent, also, at this boisterous time of the year, to risk the valuable cargo which she now had on board, by crossing and recrossing the dangerous bar of that river? These doubts were probably suggested or enforced by Captain Sowle, who, it has already been seen, was an over-cautious, or rather, a timid seaman, and they may have had some weight with Mr. Hunt; but there were other considerations, which more strongly swayed his mind. The lateness of the season, and the unforeseen delays the ship had encountered at New Archangel, and by being obliged to proceed to St. Paul's, had put her so much back in her calculated time, that there was a risk of her arriving so late at Canton, as to come to a bad market, both for the sale of her peltries, and the purchase of a return cargo. He considered it to the interest of the company, therefore, that he should proceed at once to the Sandwich islands; there wait the arrival of the annual vessel from New York, take passage in her to Astoria, and suffer the Beaver to continue on to Canton.

On the other hand, he was urged to the other course by his engagements; by the plan of the voyage marked out for the Beaver, by Mr. Astor; by his inclination, and the possibility that the establishment might need his presence, and by the recollection that there must already be a large amount of peltries collected at Astoria, and waiting for the return of the Beaver, to convey them to market.

These conflicting questions perplexed and agitated his mind, and gave rise to much anxious reflection, for he was a conscientious man that seems ever to have aimed at a faithful discharge of his duties, and to have had the interests of his employers earnestly at heart. His decision in the present instance was injudicious, and proved unfortunate. It was, to bear away for the Sandwich islands. He persuaded himself that it was matter of necessity, and that the distressed condition of the ship left him no other alternative; but we rather suspect he was so persuaded by the representations of the timid captain. They accordingly stood for the Sandwich islands, arrived at Woahoo, where the ship underwent the necessary repairs, and again put to sea on the 1st of January, 1813; leaving Mr. Hunt on the island.

We will follow the Beaver to Canton, as her fortunes, in some measure, exemplify the evil of commanders of ships acting contrary to orders; and as they form a part of the tissue of cross purposes that marred the great commercial enterprise, we have undertaken to record.

The Beaver arrived safe at Canton, where Captain Sowle found the letter of Mr. Astor, giving him information of the war, and directing him to convey the intelligence to Astoria. He wrote a reply, dictated either by timidity or obstinacy, in which he declined complying with the orders of Mr. Astor, but said he would wait for the return of peace, and then come home. The other proceedings of Captain Sowle were equally wrong headed and unlucky. He was offered one hundred and fifty thousand dollars for the fur he had taken on board at St. Paul's. The goods for which it had been procured, cost but twenty-five thousand dollars in New York. Had he accepted this offer, and re-invested the amount in nankeens, which at that time, in consequence of the interruption to commerce by the war, were at two thirds of their usual price, the whole would have brought three hundred thousand dollars in New York. It is true, the war would have rendered it unsafe to attempt the homeward voyage, but he might have put the goods in store at Canton, until after the peace, and have sailed without risk of capture to Astoria; bringing to the partners at that place tidings of the great profits realized on the outward cargo, and the still greater to be expected from the returns. The news of such a brilliant commencement to their undertaking would have counterbalanced the gloomy tidings of the war; it would have infused new spirit into them all, and given them courage and constancy to persevere in the enterprise. Captain Sowle, however, refused the offer of one hundred and fifty thousand dollars, and stood wavering and chaffering for higher terms. The furs began to fall in value; this only increased his irresolution; they sunk so much that he feared to sell at all; he borrowed money on Mr. Astor's account at an interest of eighteen per cent. and laid up his ship to await the return of peace.

In the meanwhile, Mr. Hunt soon saw reason to repent the resolution he had adopted in altering the destination of the ship. His stay at the Sandwich islands was prolonged far beyond all expectation. He looked in vain for the annual ship in the spring. Month after month passed by, and still she did not make her appearance. He, too, proved the danger of departing from orders. Had he returned from St. Paul's to Astoria, all the anxiety and despondency about his fate, and about the whole course of the undertaking, would have been obviated. The Beaver would have received the furs collected at the factory, and taken them to Canton, and great gains, instead of great losses, would have been the result. The greatest blunder, however, was that committed by Captain Sowle.

At length, about the 20th of June, the ship Albatross, Captain Smith, arrived from China, and brought the first tidings of the war to the Sandwich islands. Mr. Hunt was no longer in doubt and perplexity as to the reason of the non-appearance of the annual ship. His first thoughts were for the welfare of Astoria, and, concluding that the inhabitants would probably be in want of provisions, he chartered the Albatross for two thousand dollars, to land him, with some supplies, at the mouth of the Columbia, where he arrived, as we have seen, on the 20th of August, after a year's sea-faring that might have furnished a chapter in the wanderings of Sinbad.

CHAPTER LVIII

MR. HUNT was overwhelmed with
surprise when he learnt the resolution taken by the partners to abandon Astoria. He soon found, however, that matters had gone too
far, and the minds of his colleagues had become too firmly bent upon
the measure, to render any opposition of avail. He was beset, too,
with the same disparaging accounts of the interior trade, and of the
whole concerns and prospects of the company that had been rendered
to Mr. Astor. His own experience had been full of perplexities and discouragements. He had a conscientious anxiety for the interests of
Mr. Astor, and, not comprehending the extended views of that gentleman, and his habit of operating with great amounts, he had from
the first been daunted by the enormous expenses required, and had
become disheartened by the subsequent losses sustained, which appeared to him to be ruinous in their magnitude. By degrees, therefore,
he was brought to acquiesce in the step taken by his colleagues, as
perhaps advisable in the exigencies of the case; his only care was to
wind up the business with as little further loss as possible to Mr.
Astor.

A large stock of valuable furs was collected at the factory, which it was necessary to get to a market. There were twenty-five Sandwich islanders also in the employ of the company, whom they were bound by express agreement to restore to their native country. For these purposes a ship was necessary.

The Albatross was bound to the Marquesas, and thence to the Sandwich islands. It was resolved that Mr. Hunt should sail in her in quest of a vessel, and should return, if possible, by the 1st of January, bringing with him a supply of provisions. Should any thing occur, however, to prevent his return, an arrangement was to be proposed to Mr. M'Tavish, to transfer such of the men as were so disposed, from the service of the American Fur Company into that of the North-west, the latter becoming responsible for the wages due them, on receiving an equivalent in goods from the storehouse of the factory. As a means of facilitating the despatch of business, Mr. M'Dougal proposed, that in case Mr. Hunt should not return, the whole arrangement with Mr. M'Tavish should be left solely to him. This was assented to; the contingency being considered possible, but not probable.

It is proper to note, that, on the first announcement by Mr. M'Dougal of his intention to break up the establishment, three of the clerks, British subjects, had, with his consent, passed into the service of the North-west Company, and departed with Mr. M'Tavish for his post in the interior.

Having arranged all these matters during a sojourn of six days at Astoria, Mr. Hunt set sail in the Albatross on the 26th of August, and arrived, without accident at the Marquesas. He had not been there long, when Porter arrived in the frigate Essex, bringing in a number of stout London whalers as prizes, having made a sweeping cruize in the Pacific. From Commodore Porter, he received the alarming intelligence that the British frigate Phoebe, with a storeship, mounted with battering pieces, calculated to attack forts, had arrived at Rio Janeiro, where she had been joined by the sloops of war Cherub and Racoon, and that they had all sailed in company on the 6th of July for the Pacific, bound, as it was supposed, to Columbia river.

Here, then, was the death-warrant of unfortunate Astoria! The anxious mind of Mr. Hunt was in greater perplexity than ever. He had

been eager to extricate the property of Mr. Astor from a failing concern with as little loss as possible; there was now danger that the
whole would be swallowed up. How was it to be snatched from the
gulf? It was impossible to charter a ship for the purpose, now that a
British squadron was on its way to the river. He applied to purchase
one of the whale ships brought in by Commodore Porter. The commodore demanded twenty-five thousand dollars for her. The price
appeared exorbitant, and no bargain could be made. Mr. Hunt then
urged the commodore to fit out one of his prizes, and send her to
Astoria, to bring off the property and part of the people, but he declined, "from want of authority." He assured Mr. Hunt, however, that
he would endeavor to fall in with the enemy, or, should he hear of
their having certainly gone to the Columbia, he would either follow
or anticipate them, should his circumstances warrant such a step.

In this tantalizing state of suspense, Mr. Hunt was detained at the
Marquesas until November 23d, when he proceeded in the Albatross
to the Sandwich islands. He still cherished a faint hope that, notwithstanding the war, and all other discouraging circumstances, the
annual ship might have been sent by Mr. Astor, and might have
touched at the islands, and proceeded to the Columbia. He knew
the pride and interest taken by that gentleman in his great enterprise, and that he would not be deterred by dangers and difficulties
from prosecuting it; much less would he leave the infant establishment without succor and support in the time of trouble. In this, we
have seen, he did but justice to Mr. Astor; and we must now turn to
notice the cause of the non-arrival of the vessel which he had despatched with reinforcements and supplies. Her voyage forms another
chapter of accidents in this eventful story.

The Lark sailed from New York on the 6th of March, 1813, and
proceeded prosperously on her voyage, until within a few degrees of
the Sandwich islands. Here a gale sprang up that soon blew with tremendous violence. The Lark was a stanch and noble ship, and for a
time buffeted bravely with the storm. Unluckily, however, she
"broached to," and was struck by a heavy sea, that hove her on her
beam ends. The helm, too, was knocked to leeward, all command of

the vessel was lost, and another mountain wave completely overset her. Orders were given to cut away the masts. In the hurry and con-fusion, the boats also were unfortunately cut adrift. The wreck then righted, but was a mere hulk, full of water, with a heavy sea washing over it, and all the hatches off. On mustering the crew, one man was missing, who was discovered below in the forecastle, drowned.

In cutting away the masts, it had been utterly impossible to ob-serve the necessary precaution of commencing with the lee rigging, that being, from the position of the ship, completely under water. The masts and spars, therefore, being linked to the wreck by the shrouds and rigging, remained alongside for four days. During all this time, the ship lay rolling in the trough of the sea, the heavy surges breaking over her, and the spars heaving and banging to and fro, bruis-ing the half-drowned sailors that clung to the bowsprit and the stumps of the masts. The sufferings of these poor fellows were intolerable. They stood to their waists in water, in imminent peril of being washed off by every surge. In this position they dared not sleep, lest they should let go their hold and be swept away. The only dry place on the wreck was the bowsprit. Here they took turns to be tied on, for half an hour at a time, and in this way gained short snatches of sleep.

On the 14th, the first mate died at his post, and was swept off by the surges. On the 17th, two seamen, faint and exhausted, were washed overboard. The next wave threw their bodies back upon the deck, where they remained, swashing backward and forward, ghastly objects to the almost perishing survivors. Mr. Ogden, the supercargo, who was at the bowsprit, called to the men nearest to the bodies, to fasten them to the wreck; as a last horrible resource in case of being driven to extremity by famine!

On the 17th, the gale gradually subsided, and the sea became calm. The sailors now crawled feebly about the wreck, and began to relieve it from the main incumbrances. The spars were cleared away, the anchors and guns heaved overboard; the spritsail yard was rigged for a jurymast, and a mizen topsail set upon it. A sort of stage was made of a few broken spars, on which the crew were raised above the surface of the water, so as to be enabled to keep themselves dry, and to sleep comfortably. Still their sufferings from hunger and thirst were great; but there was a Sandwich islander on board, an expert swimmer, who found his way into the cabin, and occasionally brought up a few bottles of wine and porter, and at length got into the run, and secured a quarter cask of wine. A little raw pork was likewise procured, and dealt out with a sparing hand. The horrors of their situation were increased by the sight of numerous sharks prowling about the wreck, as if waiting for their prey. On the 24th, the cook, a black man, died and was cast into the sea, when he was instantly seized on by these ravenous monsters.

They had been several days making slow headway under their scanty sail, when, on the 25th, they came in sight of land. It was about fifteen leagues distant, and they remained two or three days drifting along in sight of it. On the 28th, they descried, to their great transport, a canoe approaching, managed by natives. They came alongside, and brought a most welcome supply of potatoes. They informed them that the land they had made was one of the Sandwich islands. The second mate and one of the seamen went on shore in the canoe for water and provisions, and to procure aid from the islanders in towing the wreck into a harbor.

Neither of the men returned, nor was any assistance sent from shore. The next day, ten or twelve canoes came alongside, but roamed round the wreck like so many sharks, and would render no aid in towing her to land.

The sea continued to break over the vessel with such violence, that it was impossible to stand at the helm without the assistance of lashings. The crew were now so worn down by famine and thirst, that the captain saw it would be impossible for them to withstand the breaking of the sea, when the ship should ground; he deemed the only chance for their lives, therefore, was to get to land in the canoes, and stand ready to receive and protect the wreck when she should drift to shore. Accordingly, they all got safe to land, but had scarcely touched the beach when they were surrounded by the natives, who stripped them almost naked. The name of this inhospitable island was Tahoorowa.

In the course of the night, the wreck came drifting to the strand, with the surf thundering around her, and shortly afterwards bilged. On the following morning, numerous casks of provisions floated on shore. The natives staved them for the sake of the iron hoops, but would not allow the crew to help themselves to the contents, or to go on board of the wreck.

As the crew were in want of every thing, and as it might be a long time before any opportunity occurred for them to get away from these islands, Mr. Ogden, as soon as he could get a chance, made his way to the island of Owyhee, and endeavored to make some arrangement with the king for the relief of his companions in misfortune.

The illustrious Tamaahmaah, as we have shown on a former occasion, was a shrewd bargainer, and in the present instance proved himself an experienced wrecker. His negotiations with M'Dougal, and the other "Eris of the great American Fur Company," had but little effect on present circumstances, and he proceeded to avail himself of their misfortunes. He agreed to furnish the crew with provisions during their stay in his territories, and to return to them all their clothing that could be found, but he stipulated that the wreck should be abandoned to him as a waif cast by fortune on his shores. With these conditions Mr. Ogden was fain to comply. Upon this the great Tamaahmaah deputed his favorite, John Young, the tarpawlin governor of Owyhee, to proceed with a number of the royal guards, and take possession of the wreck on behalf of the crown. This was done accordingly, and the property and crew were removed to Owyhee. The royal bounty appears to have been but scanty in its dispensations. The crew fared but meagerly; though, on reading the journal of the voyage, it is singular to find them, after all the hardships they had suffered, so sensitive about petty inconveniences, as to exclaim against the king as a "savage monster," for refusing them a "pot to cook in," and denying Mr. Ogden the use of a knife and fork which had been saved from the wreck.

Such was the unfortunate catastrophe of the Lark; had she reached her destination in safety, affairs at Astoria might have taken a different course. A strange fatality seems to have attended all the expeditions by sea, nor were those by land much less disastrous.

Captain Northrop was still at the Sandwich islands, on December 20th, when Mr. Hunt arrived. The latter immediately purchased, for ten thousand dollars, a brig called the Pedlar, and put Captain Northrop in command of her. They set sail for Astoria on the 22d January, intending to remove the property from thence as speedily as possible to the Russian settlements on the north-west coast, to prevent it from falling into the hands of the British. Such were the orders of Mr. Astor, sent out by the Lark.

We will now leave Mr. Hunt on his voyage, and return to see what has taken place at Astoria during his absence.

CHAPTER LIX

ON the 2d of October, about five weeks after Mr. Hunt had sailed in the Albatross from Astoria, Mr. M'Kenzie set off with two canoes, and twelve men, for the posts of Messrs. Stuart and Clarke, to apprize them of the new arrangements determined upon in the recent conference of the partners at the factory.

He had not ascended the river a hundred miles, when he met a squadron of ten canoes, sweeping merrily down under British colors, the Canadian oarsmen, as usual, in full song.

It was an armament fitted out by M'Tavish, who had with him Mr. J. Stuart, another partner of the North-west Company, together with some clerks, and sixty eight men—seventy-five souls in all. They had heard of the frigate Phoebe and the Isaac Todd being on the high seas, and were on their way down to await their arrival. In one of the canoes Mr. Clarke came passenger, the alarming intelligence having brought him down from his post on the Spokan. Mr. M'Kenzie immediately determined to return with him to Astoria, and, veering about, the two parties encamped together for the night. The leaders, of course, observed a due decorum; but some of the subalterns could not restrain their chuckling exultation, boasting that they would soon plant the British standard on the walls of Astoria, and drive the Americans out of the country.

In the course of the evening, Mr. M'Kenzie had a secret conference with Mr. Clarke, in which they agreed to set off privately, before daylight, and get down in time to apprize M'Dougal of the approach of these North-westers. The latter, however, were completely on the alert; just as M'Kenzie's canoes were about to push off, they were joined by a couple from the north-west squadron, in which was M'Tavish, with two clerks, and eleven men. With these, he intended to push forward and make arrangements, leaving the rest of the convoy, in which was a large quantity of furs, to await his orders.

The two parties arrived at Astoria on the 7th of October. The North-westers encamped under the guns of the fort, and displayed the British colors. The young men in the fort, natives of the United States, were on the point of hoisting the American flag, but were forbidden by Mr. M'Dougal. They were astonished at such a prohibition, and were exceedingly galled by the tone and manner assumed by the clerks and retainers of the North-west Company, who ruffled about in that swelling and braggart style which grows up among these heroes of the wilderness; they, in fact, considered themselves lords of the ascendant, and regarded the hampered and harassed Astorians as a conquered people.

On the following day M'Dougal convened the clerks, and read to them an extract of a letter from his uncle, Mr. Angus Shaw, one of the principal partners of the North-west Company, announcing the coming of the Phoebe and Isaac Todd, "to take and destroy every thing American on the north-west coast."

This intelligence was received without dismay by such of the clerks as were natives of the United States. They had felt indignant at seeing their national flag struck by a Canadian commander, and the British flag flowed, as it were, in their faces. They had been stung to the quick, also, by the vaunting airs assumed by the North-westers. In this mood of mind, they would willingly have nailed their colors to the staff, and defied the frigate. She could not come within many miles of the fort, they observed, and any boats she might send could be destroyed by their cannon.

There were cooler and more calculating spirits, however, who had the control of affairs, and felt nothing of the patriotic pride and indignation of these youths. The extract of the letter had, apparently, been read by M'Dougal, merely to prepare the way for a preconcerted stroke of management. On that same day Mr. M'Tavish proposed to purchase the whole stock of goods and furs belonging to the company, both at Astoria and in the interior, at cost and charges. Mr. M'Dougal undertook to comply; assuming the whole management of the negotiation in virtue of the power vested in him, in case of the non-arrival of Mr. Hunt. That power, however, was limited and specific, and did not extend to an operation of this nature and extent; no objection, however, was made to his assumption, and he and M'Tavish soon made a preliminary arrangement, perfectly satisfactory to the latter.

Mr. Stuart, and the reserve party of North-westers, arrived shortly afterwards, and encamped with M'Tavish. The former exclaimed loudly against the terms of the arrangement, and insisted upon a reduction of the prices. New negotiations had now to be entered into. The demands of the North-westers were made in a peremptory tone, and they seemed disposed to dictate like conquerors. The Americans looked on with indignation and impatience. They considered M'Dougal as acting, if not a perfidious, certainly a craven part. He was continually repairing to the camp to negotiate, instead of keeping within his walls and receiving overtures in his fortress. His case, they observed, was not so desperate as to excuse such crouching. He might, in fact, hold out for his own terms. The north-west party had lost their ammunition; they had no goods to trade with the natives for provisions; and were so destitute that M'Dougal had absolutely to feed them, while he negotiated with them. He, on the contrary, was well lodged and victualled; had sixty men, with arms, ammunition, boats, and every thing requisite either for defence or retreat. The party, beneath the guns of his fort, were at his mercy; should an enemy appear in the offing, he could pack up the most valuable part of the property and retire to some place of concealment, or make off for the interior.

These considerations, however, had no weight with Mr. M'Dougal, or were overruled by other motives. The terms of sale were lowered by him to the standard fixed by Mr. Stuart, and an agreement executed on the 16th of October, by which the furs and merchandise of all kinds in the country, belonging to Mr. Astor, passed into the possession of the North-west Company at about a third of their real value.* A safe passage through the north-west posts was guaranteed to such as did not choose to enter into the service of that company, and the amount of wages due to them was to be deducted from the price paid for Astoria.

The conduct and motives of Mr. M'Dougal, throughout the whole of this proceeding, have been strongly questioned by the other partners. He has been accused of availing himself of a wrong construction of powers vested in him at his own request, and of sacrificing the interests of Mr. Astor to the North-west Company, under the promise or hope of advantage to himself.

He always insisted, however, that he made the best bargain for Mr. Astor that circumstances would permit; the frigate being hourly expected, in which case the whole property of that gentleman would be liable to capture. That the return of Mr. Hunt was problematical; the

---

* Not quite $40,000 were allowed for furs worth upwards of $100,000. Beaver was valued at two dollars per skin, though worth five dollars. Land otter at fifty cents, though worth five dollars. Sea otter at twelve dollars, worth from forty-five to sixty dollars; and for several kinds of furs nothing was allowed. Moreover, the goods and merchandise for the Indian trade ought to have brought three times the amount for which they were sold.

The following estimate has been made of the articles on hand, and the prices:—

17,705 lbs. beaver parchment,	valued at	$2,00	worth	$5,00
465 old coat beaver, . . .	" "	1,66	"	$3,50
907 land otter, ...	" "	,50	"	$5,00
68 sea otter, ...	" "	12,00	" 45 to	60,00
30 " "	" "	5,00	"	25,00

Nothing was allowed for

179 mink skins,	worth each	. . . .	,40
22 raccoon,	" "	. . . . . .	,40
38 lynx,	" "	. . . .	2,00
18 fox,	" "	. . . . . .	1,00
106 "	" "	. . . .	1,50
71 black bear,	" "	. . . . . .	4,00
16 grizzly bear,	" "	. . . .	10,00

frigate intending to cruise along the coast for two years, and clear it of all American vessels. He moreover averred, and M'Tavish corroborated his averment by certificate, that he proposed an arrangement to that gentleman, by which the furs were to be sent to Canton, and sold there at Mr. Astor's risk, and for his account; but the proposition was not acceded to.

Notwithstanding all his representations, several of the persons present at the transaction, and acquainted with the whole course of the affair, and among the number Mr. M'Kenzie himself, his occasional coadjutor, remained firm in the belief that he had acted a hollow part. Neither did he succeed in exculpating himself to Mr. Astor; that gentleman declaring, in a letter written some time afterwards, to Mr. Hunt, that he considered the property virtually given away. "Had our place and our property," he adds, "been fairly captured, I should have preferred it. I should not feel as if I were disgraced."

All these may be unmerited suspicions; but it certainly is a circumstance strongly corroborative of them, that Mr. M'Dougal, shortly after concluding this agreement, became a member of the North-west Company, and received a share productive of a handsome income.

CHAPTER LX

On the morning of the 30th of
November, a sail was descried doubling Cape Disappointment. It
came to anchor in Baker's bay, and proved to be a ship of war. Of
what nation? was now the anxious inquiry. If English, why did it come
alone? where was the merchant vessel that was to have accompanied
it? If American, what was to become of the newly acquired possession of the North-west Company?

In this dilemma, M'Tavish, in all haste, loaded two barges with
all the packages of furs bearing the mark of the North-west Company,
and made off for Tongue point, three miles up the river. There he was
to await a preconcerted signal from M'Dougal, on ascertaining the
character of the ship. If it should prove American, M'Tavish would
have a fair start, and could bear off his rich cargo to the interior. It is
singular that this prompt mode of conveying valuable, but easily
transportable effects, beyond the reach of a hostile ship, should not
have suggested itself while the property belonged to Mr. Astor.

In the meantime, M'Dougal, who still remained nominal chief at
the fort, launched a canoe, manned by men recently in the employ of
the American Fur Company, and steered for the ship. On the way, he
instructed his men to pass themselves for Americans or Englishmen,

according to the exigencies of the case.

The vessel proved to be the British sloop of war Racoon, of twenty-six guns, and one hundred and twenty men, commanded by Captain Black. According to the account of that officer, the frigate Phoebe, and the two sloops of war Cherub and Racoon, had sailed in convoy of the Isaac Todd from Rio Janeiro. On board of the Phoebe, Mr. John M'Donald, a partner of the North-west Company, embarked as passenger, to profit by the anticipated catastrophe at Astoria. The convoy was separated by stress of weather off Cape Horn. The three ships of war came together again at the island of Juan Fernandez, their appointed rendezvous, but waited in vain for the Isaac Todd.

In the meantime, intelligence was received of the mischief that Commodore Porter was doing among the British whale ships. Commodore Hillyer immediately set sail in quest of him, with the Phoebe and the Cherub, transferring Mr. M'Donald to the Racoon, and ordering that vessel to proceed to the Columbia.

The officers of the Racoon were in high spirits. The agents of the North-west Company, in instigating the expedition, had talked of immense booty to be made by the fortunate captors of Astoria. Mr. M'Donald had kept up the excitement during the voyage, so that not a midshipman but revelled in dreams of ample prize-money, nor a lieutenant that would have sold his chance for a thousand pounds. Their disappointment, therefore, may easily be conceived, when they learned that their warlike attack upon Astoria had been forestalled by a snug commercial arrangement; that their anticipated booty had become British property in the regular course of traffic, and that all this had been effected by the very company which had been instrumental in getting them sent on what they now stigmatized as a fool's errand. They felt as if they had been duped and made tools of, by a set of shrewd men of traffic, who had employed them to crack the nut, while they carried off the kernel. In a word, M'Dougal found himself so ungraciously received by his countrymen on board of the ship, that he was glad to cut short his visit, and return to shore. He was busy at the fort, making preparations for the reception of the captain of the Racoon, when his one-eyed Indian father-in-law made his appearance, with a train of Chinook warriors, all painted and equipped in warlike style.

Old Comcomly had beheld, with dismay, the arrival of a "big war canoe" displaying the British flag. The shrewd old savage had become something of a politician in the course of his daily visits at the fort. He knew of the war existing between the nations, but knew nothing of the arrangement between M'Dougal and M'Tavish. He trembled, therefore, for the power of his white son-in-law, and the new fledged grandeur of his daughter, and assembled his warriors in all haste. "King George," said he, "has sent his great canoe to destroy the fort, and make slaves of all the inhabitants. Shall we suffer it? The Americans are the first white men that have fixed themselves in the land. They have treated us like brothers. Their great chief has taken my daughter to be his squaw: we are, therefore, as one people."

His warriors all determined to stand by the Americans to the last, and to this effect they came painted and armed for battle. Comcomly made a spirited war speech to his son-in-law. He offered to kill every one of King George's men that should attempt to land. It was an easy matter. The ship could not approach within six miles of the fort; the crew could only land in boats. The woods reached to the water's edge; in these, he and his warriors would conceal themselves, and shoot down the enemy as fast as they put foot on shore.

M'Dougal was, doubtless, properly sensible of this parental devotion on the part of his savage father-in-law, and perhaps a little rebuked by the game spirit, so opposite to his own. He assured Comcomly, however, that his solicitude for the safety of himself and the princess was superfluous; as, though the ship belonged to King George, her crew would not injure the Americans, or their Indian allies. He advised him and his warriors, therefore, to lay aside their weapons and war shirts, wash off the paint from their faces and bodies, and appear like clean and civil savages, to receive the strangers courteously.

Comcomly was sorely puzzled at this advice, which accorded so little with his Indian notions of receiving a hostile nation; and it was only after repeated and positive assurances of the amicable intentions of the strangers that he was induced to lower his fighting tone. He said something to his warriors explanatory of this singular posture of affairs, and in vindication, perhaps, of the pacific temper of his son-in-law. They all gave a shrug and an Indian grunt of acquiescence, and went off sulkily to their village, to lay aside their weapons for the present.

The proper arrangements being made for the reception of Captain Black, that officer caused his ship's boats to be manned, and landed with befitting state at Astoria. From the talk that had been made by the North-west Company, of the strength of the place, and the armament they had required to assist in its reduction, he expected to find a fortress of some importance. When he beheld nothing but stockades and bastions, calculated for defence against naked savages, he felt an emotion of indignant surprise, mingled with something of the ludicrous. "Is this the fort," cried he, "about which I have heard so much talking? D—n me, but I'd batter it down in two hours, with a four pounder!"

When he learned, however, the amount of rich furs that had been passed into the hands of the North-westers, he was outrageous, and insisted that an inventory should be taken of all the property purchased of the Americans, "with a view to ulterior measures in England, for the recovery of the value from the North-west Company."

As he grew cool, however, he gave over all idea of preferring such a claim, and reconciled himself, as well as he could, to the idea of having been forestalled by his bargaining coadjutors.

On the 12th of December, the fate of Astoria was consummated by a regular ceremonial. Captain Black, attended by his officers, entered the fort, caused the British standard to be erected, broke a bottle of wine, and declared, in a loud voice, that he took possession of the establishment and of the country, in the name of his Britannic majesty, changing the name of Astoria to that of Fort George.

The Indian warriors, who had offered their services to repel the strangers, were present on this occasion. It was explained to them as being a friendly arrangement and transfer, but they shook their heads grimly, and considered it an act of subjugation of their ancient allies.

They regretted that they had complied with M'Dougal's wishes, in laying aside their arms, and remarked, that, however the Americans might conceal the fact, they were undoubtedly all slaves; nor could they be persuaded of the contrary, until they beheld the Racoon depart without taking away any prisoners.

As to Comcomly, he no longer prided himself upon his white son-in-law, but, whenever he was asked about him, shook his head, and replied, that his daughter had made a mistake, and, instead of getting a great warrior for a husband, had married herself to a squaw.

CHAPTER LXI

HAVING given the catastrophe at the fort of Astoria, it remains now but to gather up a few loose ends of this widely excursive narrative, and conclude. On the 28th of February, the brig Pedlar anchored in Columbia river. It will be recollected that Mr. Hunt had purchased this vessel at the Sandwich islands, to take off the furs collected at the factory, and to restore the Sandwich islanders to their homes. When that gentleman learned, however, the precipitate and summary manner in which the property had been bargained away by Mr. M'Dougal, he expressed his indignation in the strongest terms, and determined to make an effort to get back the furs. As soon as his wishes were known in this respect, M'Dougal came to sound him on behalf of the North-west Company, intimating that he had no doubt the peltries might be repurchased at an advance of fifty per cent. This overture was not calculated to sooth the angry feelings of Mr. Hunt, and his indignation was complete, when he discovered that M'Dougal had become a partner of the North-west Company, and had actually been so since the 23d of December. He had kept his partnership a secret, however; had retained the papers of the Pacific Fur Company in his possession; and had continued to act as Mr. Astor's agent, though two of the partners of the other company, Mr. M'Kenzie and Mr. Clarke, were present. He had, moreover, divulged to his new associates all that he knew as to Mr. Astor's plans and affairs, and had made copies of his business letters for their perusal.

Mr. Hunt now considered the whole conduct of M'Dougal hollow and collusive. His only thought was, therefore, to get all the papers of the concern out of his hands, and bring the business to a close; for the interests of Mr. Astor were yet completely at stake: the drafts of the North-west Company in his favor, for the purchase money, not having yet been obtained. With some difficulty he succeeded in getting possession of the papers. The bills or drafts were delivered without hesitation. The latter he remitted to Mr. Astor by some of his associates, who were about to cross the continent to New York. This done, he embarked on board the Pedlar, on the 3d of April, accompanied by two of the clerks, Mr. Seton and Mr. Halsey, and bade a final adieu to Astoria.

The next day, April 4th, Messrs. Clarke, M'Kenzie, David Stuart, and such of the Astorians as had not entered into the service of the North-west Company, set out to cross the Rocky mountains. It is not our intention to take the reader another journey across those rugged barriers; but we will step forward with the travellers to a distance on their way, merely to relate their interview with a character already noted in this work.

As the party were proceeding up the Columbia, near the mouth of the Wallah-Wallah river, several Indian canoes put off from the shore to overtake them, and a voice called upon them in French, and requested them to stop. They accordingly put to shore, and were joined by those in the canoes. To their surprise, they recognised in the person who had hailed them the Indian wife of Pierre Dorion, accompanied by her two children. She had a story to tell, involving the fate of several of our unfortunate adventurers.

Mr. John Reed, the Hibernian, it will be remembered, had been detached during the summer to the Snake river. His party consisted of four Canadians, Gilles Le Clerc, Francois Landry, Jean Baptiste

Turcot, and Andre La Chapelle, together with two hunters, Pierre Dorion and Pierre Delaunay; Dorion, as usual, being accompanied by his wife and children. The objects of this expedition were twofold: to trap beaver, and to search for the three hunters, Robinson, Hoback, and Rezner.

In the course of the autumn, Reed lost one man, Landry, by death; another one, Pierre Delaunay, who was of a sullen, perverse disposition, left him in a moody fit, and was never heard of afterwards. The number of his party was not, however, reduced by these losses, as the three hunters, Robinson, Hoback, and Rezner, had joined it.

Reed now built a house on the Snake river, for their winter quarters; which being completed, the party set about trapping. Rezner, Le Clerc, and Pierre Dorion, went about five days' journey from the wintering house, to a part of the country well stocked with beaver. Here they put up a hut, and proceeded to trap with great success. While the men were out hunting, Pierre Dorion's wife remained at home to dress the skins and prepare the meals. She was thus employed one evening about the beginning of January, cooking the supper of the hunters, when she heard footsteps, and Le Clerc staggered, pale and bleeding, into the hut. He informed her that a party of savages had surprised them, while at their traps, and had killed Rezner and her husband. He had barely strength left to give this information, when he sank upon the ground.

The poor woman saw that the only chance for life was instant flight, but, in this exigency, showed that presence of mind and force of character for which she had frequently been noted. With great difficulty, she caught two of the horses belonging to the party. Then collecting her clothes, and a small quantity of beaver meat and dried salmon, she packed them upon one of the horses, and helped the wounded man to mount upon it. On the other horse she mounted with her two children, and hurried away from this dangerous neighborhood, directing her flight for Mr. Reed's establishment. On the third day, she descried a number of Indians on horseback proceeding in an easterly direction. She immediately dismounted with her children, and helped Le Clerc likewise to dismount, and all concealed themselves. Fortunately they escaped the sharp eyes of the savages, but had to proceed with the utmost caution. That night, they slept without fire or water; she managed to keep her children warm in her arms; but before morning, poor Le Clerc died.

With the dawn of day, the resolute woman resumed her course, and, on the fourth day, reached the house of Mr. Reed. It was deserted, and all around were marks of blood and signs of a furious massacre. Not doubting that Mr. Reed and his party had all fallen victims, she turned in fresh horror from the spot. For two days she continued hurrying forward, ready to sink for want of food, but more solicitous about her children than herself. At length she reached a range of the Rocky mountains, near the upper part of the Wallah-Wallah river. Here she chose a wild lonely ravine, as her place of winter refuge.

She had fortunately a buffalo robe and three deer skins; of these, and of pine bark and cedar branches, she constructed a rude wigwam, which she pitched beside a mountain spring. Having no other food, she killed the two horses, and smoked their flesh. The skins aided to cover her hut. Here she dragged out the winter, with no other company than her two children. Towards the middle of March, her provisions were nearly exhausted. She therefore packed up the remainder, slung it on her back, and, with her helpless little ones, set out again on her wanderings. Crossing the ridge of mountains, she descended to the banks of the Wallah-Wallah, and kept along them until she arrived where that river throws itself into the Columbia. She was hospitably received and entertained by the Wallah-Wallahs, and had been nearly two weeks among them, when the two canoes passed.

On being interrogated, she could assign no reason for this murderous attack of the savages; it appeared to be perfectly wanton and unprovoked. Some of the Astorians supposed it an act of butchery by a roving band of Blackfeet; others, however, and with greater probability of correctness, have ascribed it to the tribe of Pierced-nose Indians, in revenge for the death of their comrade hanged by order of Mr. Clarke. If so, it shows that these sudden and apparently wanton outbreakings of sanguinary violence on the part of savages, have often some previous, though perhaps remote, provocation.

The narrative of the Indian woman closes the checkered adventures of some of the personages of this motley story; such as the honest Hibernian Reed, and Dorion the hybred interpreter. Turcot and La Chapelle were two of the men who fell off from Mr. Crooks in the course of his wintry journey, and had subsequently such disastrous times among the Indians. We cannot but feel some sympathy with that persevering trio of Kentuckians, Robinson, Rezner, and Hoback; who twice turned back when on their way homeward, and lingered in the wilderness to perish by the hands of savages.

The return parties from Astoria, both by sea and land, experienced on the way as many adventures, vicissitudes, and mishaps, as the far-famed heroes of the Odyssey; they reached their destination at different times, bearing tidings to Mr. Astor of the unfortunate termination of his enterprise.

That gentleman, however, was not disposed, even yet, to give the matter up as lost. On the contrary, his spirit was roused by what he considered ungenerous and unmerited conduct on the part of the North-west Company. "After their treatment of me," said he, in a letter to Mr. Hunt, "I have no idea of remaining quiet and idle." He determined, therefore, as soon as circumstances would permit, to resume his enterprise.

At the return of peace, Astoria, with the adjacent country, reverted to the United States by the treaty of Ghent, on the principle of *status ante bellum,* and Captain Biddle was despatched in the sloop of war Ontario, to take formal repossession.

In the winter of 1815, a law was passed by congress, prohibiting all traffic of British traders within the territories of the United States.

The favorable moment seemed now to Mr. Astor to have arrived for the revival of his favorite enterprise, but new difficulties had grown up to impede it. The North-west Company were now in complete occupation of the Columbia river, and its chief tributary streams, holding the posts which he had established, and carrying on a trade throughout the neighboring region, in defiance of the prohibitory law of congress, which, in effect, was a dead letter beyond the mountains.

To dispossess them, would be an undertaking of almost a belligerant nature; for their agents and retainers were well armed, and skilled in the use of weapons, as is usual with Indian traders. The ferocious and bloody contests which had taken place between the rival trading parties of the North-west and Hudson's Bay Companies, had shown what might be expected from commercial feuds in the lawless depths of the wilderness. Mr. Astor did not think it advisable, therefore, to attempt the matter without the protection of the American flag; under which his people might rally in case of need. He accordingly made an informal overture to the President of the United States, Mr. Madison, through Mr. Gallatin, offering to renew his enterprise, and to re-establish Astoria, provided it would be protected by the American flag, and made a military post; stating that the whole force required would not exceed a lieutenant's command.

The application, approved and recommended by Mr. Gallatin, one of the most enlightened statesmen of our country, was favorably received, but no step was taken in consequence; the president not being disposed, in all probability, to commit himself by any direct countenance or overt act. Discouraged by this supineness on the part of the government, Mr. Astor did not think fit to renew his overtures in a more formal manner, and the favorable moment for the re-occupation of Astoria was suffered to pass unimproved.

The British trading establishments were thus enabled, without molestation, to strike deep their roots, and extend their ramifications, in despite of the prohibition of congress, until they had spread themselves over the rich field of enterprise opened by Mr. Astor. The British government soon began to perceive the importance of this region, and to desire to include it within their territorial domains. A question has consequently risen as to the right to the soil, and has become one of the most perplexing now open between the United States and Great Britain. In the first treaty relative to it, under date of October 20th, 1818, the question was left unsettled, and it was agreed that the country on the north-west coast of America, westward of the Rocky mountains, claimed by either nation, should be open to the inhabitants of both for ten years, for the purposes of trade, with the equal right of navigating all its rivers. When these ten years had expired, a subsequent treaty, in 1828, extended the arrangement to ten additional years. So the matter stands at present.

On casting back our eyes over the series of events we have recorded, we see no reason to attribute the failure of this great commercial undertaking to any fault in the scheme, or omission in the execution of it, on the part of the projector. It was a magnificent enterprise; well concerted and carried on, without regard to difficulties or expense. A succession of adverse circumstances and cross purposes, however, beset it almost from the outset; some of them, in fact, arising from neglect of the orders and instructions of Mr. Astor. The first crippling blow was the loss of the Tonquin, which clearly would not have happened, had Mr. Astor's earnest injunctions with regard to the natives been attended to. Had this ship performed her voyage prosperously, and revisited Astoria in due time, the trade of the establishment would have taken its preconcerted course, and the spirits of all concerned been kept up by a confident prospect of success. Her dismal catastrophe struck a chill into every heart, and prepared the way for subsequent despondency.

Another cause of embarrassment and loss was the departure from the plan of Mr. Astor, as to the voyage of the Beaver, subsequent to her visiting Astoria. The variation from this plan produced a series of cross purposes, disastrous to the establishment, and detained Mr. Hunt absent from his post, when his presence there was of vital importance to the enterprise; so essential is it for an agent, in any great and complicated undertaking, to execute faithfully, and to the letter, the part marked out for him by the master mind which has concerted the whole.

The breaking out of the war between the United States and Great Britain, multiplied the hazards and embarrassments of the enterprise. The disappointment as to convoy, rendered it difficult to keep up reinforcements and supplies; and the loss of the Lark added to the tissue of misadventures.

That Mr. Astor battled resolutely against every difficulty, and pursued his course in defiance of every loss, has been sufficiently shown.

Had he been seconded by suitable agents, and properly protected by government, the ultimate failure of his plan might yet have been averted. It was his great misfortune, that his agents were not imbued with his own spirit. Some had not capacity sufficient to comprehend the real nature and extent of his scheme; others were alien in feeling and interest, and had been brought up in the service of a rival company. Whatever sympathies they might originally have had with him, were impaired, if not destroyed, by the war. They looked upon his cause as desperate, and only considered how they might make interest to regain a situation under their former employers. The absence of Mr. Hunt, the only real representative of Mr. Astor, at the time of the capitulation with the North-west Company, completed the series of cross purposes. Had that gentleman been present, the transfer, in all probability, would not have taken place.

It is painful, at all times, to see a grand and beneficial stroke of genius fail of its aim: but we regret the failure of this enterprise in a national point of view; for, had it been crowned with success, it would have redounded greatly to the advantage and extension of our commerce. The profits drawn from the country in question by the British Fur Company, though of ample amount, form no criterion by which to judge of the advantages that would have arisen had it been entirely in the hands of citizens of the United States. That company, as has been shown, is limited in the nature and scope of its operations, and can make but little use of the maritime facilities held out by an emporium and a harbor on that coast. In our hands, beside the roving bands of trappers and traders, the country would have been explored and settled by industrious husbandmen; and the fertile valleys bordering its rivers, and shut up among its mountains, would have been made to pour forth their agricultural treasures to contribute to the general wealth.

In respect to commerce, we should have had a line of trading posts from the Mississippi and the Missouri across the Rocky mountains, forming a high road from the great regions of the west to the shores of the Pacific. We should have had a fortified post and port at the mouth of the Columbia, commanding the trade of that river and its tributaries, and of a wide extent of country and sea coast; carrying on an active and profitable commerce with the Sandwich islands, and a direct and frequent communication with China. In a word, Astoria might have realized the anticipations of Mr. Astor, so well understood and appreciated by Mr. Jefferson, in gradually becoming a commercial empire beyond the mountains, peopled by "free and independent Americans, and linked with us by ties of blood and interest."

We repeat, therefore, our sincere regret, that our government should have neglected the overture of Mr. Astor, and suffered the moment to pass by, when full possession of this region might have been taken quietly, as a matter of course, and a military post established, without dispute, at Astoria. Our statesmen have become sensible, when too late, of the importance of this measure. Bills have repeatedly been brought into Congress for the purpose, but without success; and our rightful possessions on that coast, as well as our trade on the Pacific, have no rallying point protected by the national flag, and by a military force.

In the meantime, the second period of ten years is fast elapsing. In 1838, the question of title will again come up, and most probably, in the present amicable state of our relations with Great Britain, will be again postponed. Every year, however, the litigated claim is growing in importance. There is no pride so jealous and irritable as the pride of territory. As one wave of emigration after another rolls into the vast regions of the west, and our settlements stretch towards the Rocky mountains, the eager eyes of our pioneers will pry beyond, and they will become impatient of any barrier or impediment in the way of what they consider a grand outlet of our empire. Should any circumstance, therefore, unfortunately occur to disturb the present harmony of the two nations, this ill-adjusted question, which now lies dormant, may suddenly start up into one of belligerent import, and Astoria become the watchword in a contest for dominion on the shores of the Pacific.

APPENDIX

APPENDIX

Draught of a petition to Congress, sent by Mr. Astor in 1812

To the honorable the Senate and House of Representatives of the
United States, in congress assembled,

The petition of the American Fur Company respectfully sheweth:

That the trade with the several Indian tribes of North America, has,
for many years past, been almost exclusively carried on by the merchants
of Canada; who, having formed powerful and extensive associations for
that purpose, being aided by British capital, and being encouraged by
the favor and protection of the British government, could not be
opposed, with any prospect of success by individuals of the United
States.

That by means of the above trade, thus systematically pursued, not
only the inhabitants of the United States have been deprived of commercial profits and advantages, to which they appear to have just and
natural pretensions, but a great and dangerous influence has been
established over the Indian tribes, difficult to be counteracted, and
capable of being exerted at critical periods, to the great injury and
annoyance of our frontier settlements.

That in order to obtain at least a part of the above trade, and more
particularly that which is within the boundaries of the United States,
your petitioners, in the year 1808, obtained an act of incorporation from
the state of New York, whereby they are enabled, with a competent
capital, to carry on the said trade with the Indians in such manner as

may be conformable to the laws and regulations of the United States, in relation to such commerce.

That the capital mentioned in the said act, amounting to one million of dollars, having been duly formed, your petitioners entered with zeal and alacrity into those large and important arrangements, which were necessary for, or conducive to, the object of their incorporation; and, among other things, purchased a great part of the stock in trade, and trading establishments, of the Michilimackinac Company of Canada. —Your petitioners also, with the expectation of great public and private advantage from the use of the said establishments, ordered, during the spring and summer of 1810, an assortment of goods from England, suitable for the Indian trade; which, in consequence of the president's proclamation of November of that year, were shipped to Canada instead of New York, and have been transported, under a very heavy expense, into the interior of the country. But as they could not legally be brought into the Indian country within the boundaries of the United States, they have been stored on the island of St. Joseph, in lake Huron, where they now remain.

Your petitioners, with great deference and implicit submission to the wisdom of the national legislature, beg leave to suggest for consideration, whether they have not some claim to national attention and encouragement, from the nature and importance of their undertaking; which, though hazardous and uncertain as it concerns their private emolument, must, at any rate, redound to the public security and advantage. If their undertaking shall appear to be of the description given, they would further suggest to your honorable bodies, that unless they can procure a regular supply for the trade in which they are engaged, it may languish, and be finally abandoned by American citizens; when it will revert to its former channel, with additional, and perhaps with irresistible, power.

Under these circumstances, and upon all those considerations of public policy which will present themselves to your honorable bodies, in connexion with those already mentioned, your petitioners respectfully pray that a law may be passed to enable the president, or any of the heads of departments acting under his authority, to grant permits for the introduction of goods necessary for the supply of the Indians, into the Indian country that is within the boundaries of the United States, under such regulations, and with such restrictions, as may secure the public revenue and promote the public welfare.

And your petitioners shall ever pray, &c.

In witness whereof, the common seal of the American Fur Company is hereunto affixed, the   day of March, 1812.

By order of the Corporation.

AN ACT to enable the American Fur Company, and other citizens, to introduce goods necessary for the Indian trade into the territories within the boundaries of the United States.

WHEREAS, the public peace and welfare require that the native Indian tribes, residing within the boundaries of the United States, should receive their necessary supplies under the authority and from the citizens of the United States: Therefore, be it enacted by the Senate and House of Representatives of the United States, in congress assembled, that it shall be lawful for the president of the United States, or any of the heads of departments, thereunto by him duly authorized, from time to time to grant permits to the American Fur Company, their agents or factors, or any other citizens of the United States engaged in the Indian trade, to introduce into the Indian country, within the boundaries of the United States, such goods, wares, and merchandise, as may be necessary for the said trade, under such regulations and restrictions as the said president or heads of departments may judge proper; any law or regulation to the contrary, in anywise, notwithstanding.

=======

Letter from Mr. Gallatin to Mr. Astor, dated

NEW YORK, *August* 5, 1835.

Dear Sir,—

In compliance with your request, I will state such facts as I recollect, touching the subjects mentioned in your letter of 28th ult. I may be mistaken respecting dates and details, and will only relate general facts, which I well remember.

In conformity with the treaty of 1794 with Great Britain, the citizens and subjects of each country were permitted to trade wih the Indians residing in the territories of the other party. The reciprocity was altogether nominal. Since the conquest of Canada, the British had inherited from the French the whole fur trade, through the great lakes and their communications, with all the western Indians, whether residing in the British dominions or the United States. They kept the important western posts on those lakes till about the year 1797. And the defensive Indian war, which the United States had to sustain from 1776 to 1795, had still more alienated the Indians, and secured to the British their exclusive trade, carried through the lakes, wherever the Indians in that quarter lived. No American could, without imminent danger of property and life, carry on that trade, even within the United States, by the way of either Michilimackinac or St. Mary's. And independent of the loss of commerce, Great Britain was enabled to preserve a most dangerous influence over our Indians.

It was under these circumstances that you communicated to our government the prospect you had to be able, and your intention, to purchase one half of the interest of the Canadian Fur Company, engaged in trade by the way of Michilimackinac with our own Indians. You wished to know whether the plan met with the approbation of government, and how far you could rely on its protection and encouragement. This overture was received with great satisfaction by the administration, and Mr. Jefferson, then president, wrote you to that effect. I was also directed, as secretary of the treasury, to write to you an official letter to the same purpose. On investigating the subject, it was found that the executive had no authority to give you any direct aid; and I believe that you received nothing more than an entire approbation of your plan, and general assurances of the protection due to every citizen engaged in lawful and useful pursuits.

You did effect the contemplated purchase, but in what year I do not recollect. Immediately before the war, you represented that a large quantity of merchandise, intended for the Indian trade, and including arms and munitions of war, belonging to that concern of which you owned one half, was deposited at a post on lake Huron, within the British dominions; that, in order to prevent their ultimately falling into the hands of Indians who might prove hostile, you were desirous to try to have them conveyed into the United States; but that you were prevented by the then existing law of non-intercourse with the British dominions.

The executive could not annul the provisions of that law. But I was directed to instruct the collectors on the lakes, in case you or your agents should voluntarily bring in and deliver to them any parts of the goods above mentioned, to receive and keep them in their guard, and not to commence prosecutions until further instructions: the intention being then to apply to congress for an act remitting the forfeiture and penalties. I wrote accordingly, to that effect, to the collectors of Detroit and Michilimackinac.

The attempt to obtain the goods did not, however, succeed; and I cannot say how far the failure injured you. But the war proved fatal to another much more extensive and important enterprise.

Previous to that time, but I also forget the year, you had undertaken to carry on a trade on your own account, though I believe under the New York charter of the American Fur Company, with the Indians west of the Rocky mountains. This project was also communicated to government, and met, of course, with its full approbation, and best wishes for your success. You carried it on, on the most extensive scale, sending several ships to the mouth of the Columbia river, and a large party by land across the mountains, and finally founding the establishment of Astoria.

This unfortunately fell into the hands of the enemy during the war, from circumstances with which I am but imperfectly acquainted—being then absent on a foreign mission. I returned in September, 1815, and sailed again on a mission to France in June, 1816. During that period I visited Washington twice—in October or November, 1815, and in March, 1816. On one of those two occasions, and I believe on the last, you mentioned to me that you were disposed once more to renew the attempt, and to re-establish Astoria, provided you had the protection of the American flag; for which purpose, a lieutenant's command would be sufficient to you. You requested me to mention this to the president, which I did. Mr. Madison said he would consider the subject, and, although he did not commit himself, I thought that he received the proposal favorably. The message was verbal, and I do not know whether the application was ever renewed in a more formal manner. I sailed soon after for Europe, and was seven years absent. I never had the pleasure, since 1816, to see Mr. Madison, and never heard again any thing concerning the subject in question.

I remain, dear sir, very respectfully,
Your obedient servant,
ALBERT GALLATIN.

John Jacob Astor, Esq.,
New York.

Notices of the present state of the Fur Trade, chiefly extracted from an article published in Silliman's Journal for January, 1834.

The North-west Company did not long enjoy the sway they had acquired over the trading regions of the Columbia. A competition, ruinous in its expenses, which had long existed between them and the Hudson's Bay Company, ended in their downfall and the ruin of most of the partners. The relics of the company became merged in the rival association, and the whole business was conducted under the name of the Hudson's Bay Company.

This coalition took place in 1821. They then abandoned Astoria, and built a large establishment sixty miles up the river, on the right bank, which they called Fort Vancouver. This was in a neighborhood where provisions could be more readily procured, and where there was less danger from molestation by any naval force. The company are said to carry on an active and prosperous trade, and to give great encouragement to settlers. They are extremely jealous, however, of any interference or participation in their trade, and monopolize it from the coast of the Pacific to the mountains, and for a considerable extent north and south. The American traders and trappers who venture across the mountains, instead of enjoying the participation in the trade of the river and its tributaries, that had been stipulated by treaty, are obliged to keep to the south, out of the track of the Hudson's Bay parties.

Mr. Astor has withdrawn entirely from the American Fur Company, as he has, in fact, from active business of every kind. That company is now headed by Mr. Ramsay Crooks; its principal establishment is at Michilimackinac, and it receives its furs from the posts depending on that station, and from those on the Mississippi, Missouri, and Yellow Stone rivers, and the great range of country extending thence to the Rocky mountains. This company has steamboats in its employ, with which it ascends the rivers, and penetrates to a vast distance into the bosom of those regions formerly so painfully explored in keel-boats and barges, or by weary parties on horseback and on foot. The first irruption of steamboats into the heart of these vast wildernesses is said to have caused the utmost astonishment and affright among their savage inhabitants.

In addition to the main companies already mentioned, minor associations have been formed, which push their way in the most intrepid manner to the remote parts of the far west, and beyond the mountain barriers. One of the most noted of these is Ashley's company, from St. Louis, who trap for themselves, and drive an extensive trade with the Indians. The spirit, enterprise, and hardihood of Ashley, are themes of the highest eulogy in the far west, and his adventures and exploits furnish abundance of frontier stories.

Another company of one hundred and fifty persons from New York, formed in 1831, and headed by Captain Bonneville of the United States army, has pushed its enterprises into tracts before but little known, and has brought considerable quantities of furs from the region between the Rocky mountains and the coasts of Monterey and Upper California, on the Buenaventura and Timpanogos rivers.

The fur countries, from the Pacific, east to the Rocky mountains, are now occupied (exclusive of private combinations and individual trappers and traders) by the Russians; on the north-west, from Bhering's Strait to Queen Charlotte's Island, in north latitude fifty-three degrees, and by the Hudson's Bay Company thence, south of the Columbia river; while Ashley's company, and that under Captain Bonneville, take the remainder of the region to California. Indeed, the whole compass from the Mississippi to the Pacific Ocean is traversed in every direction. The mountains and forests, from the Arctic Sea to the Gulf of Mexico, are threaded, through every maze, by the hunter. Every river and tributary stream, from the Columbia to the mouth of the Rio del Norte, and from the M'Kenzie to the Colorado of the West, from their head springs to their junction, are searched and trapped for beaver. Almost all the American furs, which do not belong to the Hudson's Bay Company, find their way to New York, and are either distributed thence for home consumption, or sent to foreign markets.

The Hudson's Bay Company ship their furs from their factories of York fort and from Moose river, on Hudson's Bay; their collection from Grand river, &c., they ship from Canada; and the collection from Columbia goes to London. None of their furs come to the United States, except through the London market.

The export trade of furs from the United States is chiefly to London. Some quantities have been sent to Canton, and some few to Hamburgh; and an increasing export trade in beaver, otter, nutria, and vicunia wool, prepared for the hatter's use, is carried on in Mexico. Some furs are exported from Baltimore, Philadelphia, and Boston; but the principal shipments from the United States are from New York to London, from whence they are sent to Leipsic, a well-known mart for furs, where they are disposed of during the great fair in that city, and distributed to every part of the continent.

The United States import from South America, nutria, vicunia, chinchilla, and a few deer skins; also fur seals from the Lobos islands, off the river Plate. A quantity of beaver, otter, &c., are brought annually from Santa Fé. Dressed furs for edgings, linings, caps, muffs, &c., such as squirrel, genet, fitch skins, and blue rabbit, are received from the north of Europe; also coney and hare's fur; but the largest importations are from London, where is concentrated nearly the whole of the North American fur trade.

Such is the present state of the fur trade, by which it will appear that the extended sway of the Hudson's Bay Company, and its monopoly of the region of which Astoria was the key, has operated to turn the main current of this opulent trade into the coffers of Great Britain, and to render London the emporium instead of New York, as Mr. Astor had intended.

We will subjoin a few observations on the animals sought after in this traffic, extracted from the same intelligent source with the preceding remarks.

Of the fur-bearing animals, "the precious ermine," so called by way of pre-eminence, is found, of the best quality, only in the cold regions of Europe and Asia.* Its fur is of the most perfect whiteness, except the tip of its tail, which is of a brilliant shining black. With these black tips tacked on the skins, they are beautifully spotted, producing an effect often imitated, but never equalled in other furs. The ermine is of the genus mustela, (weasel,) and resembles the common weasel in its form; is from fourteen to sixteen inches from the tip of the nose to the end of the tail. The body is from ten to twelve inches long. It lives in hollow trees, river banks, and especially in beech forests; preys on small birds, is very shy, sleeping during the day, and employing the night in search of food. The fur of the older animals is preferred to the younger. It is taken by snares and traps, and sometimes shot with blunt arrows. Attempts have been made to domesticate it; but it is extremely wild, and has been found untameable.

The sable can scarcely be called second to the ermine. It is a native of northern Europe and Siberia, and is also of the genus mustela. In Samoieda, Yakutsk, Kamschatka, and Russian Lapland, it is found of the richest quality, and darkest color. In its habits, it resembles the ermine. It preys on small squirrels and birds, sleeps by day, and prowls for food during the night. It is so like the marten in every particular except its size, and the dark shade of its color, that naturalists have not decided whether it is the richest and finest of the marten tribe, or a variety of

* An animal called the stoat, a kind of ermine, is said to be found in North America, but very inferior to the European and Asiatic.

that species.* It varies in dimensions from eighteen to twenty inches.

The rich dark shades of the sable, and the snowy whiteness of the ermine, the great depth, and the peculiar, almost flowing softness of their skins and fur, have combined to gain them a preference in all countries, and in all ages of the world. In this age, they maintain the same relative estimate in regard to other furs, as when they marked the rank of the proud crusader, and were emblazoned in heraldry: but in most European nations, they are now worn promiscuously by the opulent.

The martens from Northern Asia and the mountains of Kamschatka are much superior to the American, though in every pack of American marten skins there are a certain number which are beautifully shaded, and of a dark brown olive color, of great depth and richness.

Next these in value, for ornament and utility, are the sea otter, the mink, and the fiery fox.

The fiery fox is the bright red of Asia; is more brilliantly colored and of finer fur than any other of the genus. It is highly valued for the splendor of its red color and the fineness of its fur. It is the standard of value on the north-eastern coast of Asia.

The sea otter, which was first introduced into commerce in 1725, from the Aleutian and Kurile islands, is an exceedingly fine, soft, close fur, jet black in winter with a silken gloss. The fur of the young animal is of a beautiful brown color. It is met with in great abundance in Bhering's island, Kamschatka, Aleutian and Fox islands, and is also taken on the opposite coasts of North America. It is sometimes taken with nets, but more frequently with clubs and spears. Their food is principally lobster and other shell-fish.

In 1780 furs had become so scarce in Siberia, that the supply was insufficient for the demand in the Asiatic countries. It was at this time that the sea otter was introduced into the markets for China. The skins brought such incredible prices, as to originate immediately several American and British expeditions to the northern islands of the Pacific, to Nootka Sound, and the north-west coast of America; but the Russians already had possession of the tract which they now hold, and had arranged a trade for the sea otter with the Koudek tribes. They do not engross the trade, however; the American north-west trading ships procure them, all along the coast, from the Indians.

At one period, the fur seals formed no inconsiderable item in the trade. South Georgia, in south latitude fifty-five degrees, discovered in 1675, was explored by Captain Cook in 1771. The Americans immedi-

* The finest fur and the darkest color are most esteemed; and whether the difference arises from the age of the animal, or from some peculiarity of location, is not known. They do not vary more from the common marten, than the Arabian horse from the shaggy Canadian.

ately commenced carrying seal skins thence to China, where they obtained the most exorbitant prices. One million two hundred thousand skins have been taken from that island alone, and nearly an equal number from the island of Desolation, since they were first resorted to for the purposes of commerce.

The discovery of the South Shetlands, sixty-three degrees south latitude, in 1818, added surprisingly to the trade in fur seals. The number taken from the South Shetlands in 1821 and 1822 amounted to three hundred and twenty thousand. This valuable animal is now almost extinct in all these islands, owing to the exterminating system adopted by the hunters. They are still taken on the Lobos islands, where the provident government of Montevideo restrict the fishery, or hunting, within certain limits, which insures an annual return of the seals. At certain seasons these amphibia, for the purpose of renewing their coat, come up on the dark frowning rocks and precipices, where there is not a trace of vegetation. In the middle of January, the islands are partially cleared of snow, where a few patches of short straggling grass spring up in favorable situations; but the seals do not resort to it for food. They remain on the rocks not less than two months, without any sustenance, when they return much emaciated to the sea.

Bears of various species and colors, many varieties of the fox, the wolf, the beaver, the otter, the marten, the raccoon, the badger, the wolverine, the mink, the lynx, the muskrat, the woodchuck, the rabbit, the hare, and the squirrel, are natives of North America.

The beaver, otter, lynx, fisher, hare, and raccoon, are used principally for hats; while the bears of several varieties furnish an excellent material for sleigh linings, for cavalry caps, and other military equipments. The fur of the black fox is the most valuable of any of the American varieties; and next to that the red, which is exported to China and Smyrna. In China, the red is employed for trimmings, linings, and robes; the latter being variegated, by adding the black fur of the paws, in spots or waves. There are many other varieties of American fox, such as the gray, the white, the cross, the silver, and the dun-colored. The silver fox is a rare animal, a native of the woody country below the falls of the Columbia river. It has a long, thick, deep lead-colored fur, intermingled with long hairs, invariably white at the top, forming a bright lustrous silver gray, esteemed by some more beautiful than any other kind of fox.

The skins of the buffalo, of the Rocky mountain sheep, of various deer, and of the antelope, are included in the fur trade with the Indians and trappers of the north and west.

Fox and seal skins are sent from Greenland to Denmark. The white fur of the arctic fox and polar bear is sometimes found in the packs brought to the traders by the most northern tribes of Indians, but is not particularly valuable. The silver-tipped rabbit is peculiar to England,

and is sent thence to Russia and China.

Other furs are employed and valued according to the caprices of fashion, as well in those countries where they are needed for defences against the severity of the seasons, as among the inhabitants of milder climates, who, being of Tartar or Sclavonian descent, are said to inherit an attachment to furred clothing. Such are the inhabitants of Poland, of Southern Russia, of China, of Persia, of Turkey, and all the nations of Gothic origin in the middle and western parts of Europe. Under the burning suns of Syria and Egypt, and the mild climes of Bucharia and Independent Tartary, there is also a constant demand, and a great consumption, where there exists no physical necessity. In our own temperate latitudes, besides their use in the arts, they are in request for ornament and warmth during the winter, and large quantities are annually consumed for both purposes in the United States.

From the foregoing statements, it appears that the fur trade must henceforward decline. The advanced state of geographical science shows that no new countries remain to be explored. In North America, the animals are slowly decreasing, from the persevering efforts and the indiscriminate slaughter practised by the hunters, and by the appropriation to the uses of man of those forests and rivers which have afforded them food and protection. They recede with the aborigines, before the tide of civilization; but a diminished supply will remain in the mountains and uncultivated tracts of this and other countries, if the avidity of the hunter can be restrained within proper limitations.

Height of the Rocky Mountains.

Various estimates have been made of the height of the Rocky mountains, but it is doubtful whether any have, as yet, done justice to their real altitude, which promises to place them only second to the highest mountains of the known world. Their height has been diminished to the eye by the great elevation of the plains from which they rise. They consist, according to Long, of ridges, knobs, and peaks, variously disposed. The more elevated parts are covered with perpetual snows, which contribute to give them a luminous, and, at a great distance, even a brilliant appearance; whence they derived, among some of the first discoverers, the name of the Shining mountains.

James's Peak has generally been cited as the highest of the chain; and its elevation above the common level has been ascertained, by a trigonometrical measurement, to be about eight thousand five hundred feet. Mr. Long, however, judged, from the position of the snow near the summits of other peaks and ridges at no great distance from it, that they were much higher. Having heard Professor Renwick, of New York, express an opinion of the altitude of these mountains far beyond what had usually been ascribed to them, we applied to him for the authority on which he grounded his observation, and here subjoin his reply:—

COLUMBIA COLLEGE, NEW YORK, *February* 23, 1836.

Dear Sir,—

In compliance with your request, I have to communicate some facts in relation to the heights of the Rocky mountains, and the sources whence I obtained the information.

In conversation with Simon M'Gillivray, Esq., a partner of the Northwest Company, he stated to me his impression, that the mountains in the vicinity of the route pursued by the traders of that company were nearly as high as the Himalayas. He had himself crossed by this route, seen the snowy summits of the peaks, and experienced a degree of cold which required a spirit thermometer to indicate it. His authority for the estimate of the heights was a gentleman who had been employed for several years as surveyor of that company. This conversation occurred about sixteen years since.

A year or two afterwards, I had the pleasure of dining, at Major Delafield's, with Mr. Thompson, the gentleman referred to by Mr. M'Gillivray. I inquired of him in relation to the circumstances mentioned by

Mr. M'Gillivray, and he stated, that, by the joint means of the barometer and trigonometric measurement, he had ascertained the height of one of the peaks to be about twenty-five thousand feet, and there were others of nearly the same height in the vicinity.

I am, dear Sir,
Yours truly,
JAMES RENWICK.

To W. IRVING, Esq.

Suggestions with respect to the Indian tribes, and the protection of our Trade.

In the course of this work, a few general remarks have been hazarded respecting the Indian tribes of the prairies, and the dangers to be apprehended from them in future times to our trade beyond the Rocky mountains and with the Spanish frontiers. Since writing those remarks, we have met with some excellent observations and suggestions, in manuscript, on the same subject, written by Captain Bonneville, of the United States army, who has lately returned from a long residence among the tribes of the Rocky mountains. Captain B. approves highly of the plan recently adopted by the United States government for the organization of a regiment of dragoons for the protection of our western frontier, and the trade across the prairies. "No other species of military force," he observes, "is at all competent to cope with these restless and wandering hordes, who require to be opposed with swiftness quite as much as with strength; and the consciousness that a troop, uniting these qualifications, is always on the alert to avenge their outrages upon the settlers and traders, will go very far towards restraining them from the perpetration of those thefts and murders which they have heretofore committed with impunity, whenever stratagem or superiority of force has given them the advantage. Their interest already has done something towards their pacification with our countrymen. From the traders among them, they receive their supplies in the greatest abundance, and upon very equitable terms; and when it is remembered that a very considerable amount of property is yearly distributed among them by the government, as presents, it will readily be perceived that they are greatly dependant upon us for their most valued resources. If, superadded to this inducement, a frequent display of military power be made in their territories, there can be little doubt that the desired security and peace will be speedily afforded to our own people. But the idea of establishing a permanent amity and concord amongst the various east and west tribes themselves, seems to me, if not wholly impracticable, at least infinitely more difficult than many excellent philanthropists have hoped and believed. Those nations which have so lately emigrated from the midst of our settlements to live upon our western borders, and have made some progress in agriculture and the arts of civilization, have, in the property they have acquired, and the protection and aid extended to them, too many advantages to be induced readily to take up arms against us, particularly if they can be brought to the full conviction that their new homes will be permanent and undisturbed; and there is every reason and motive, in policy as well as humanity, for our ameliorating their condition by every means in our power. But the case is far different with regard to the Osages, the Kanzas, the Pawnees, and other roving hordes beyond the frontiers of the settlements. Wild and restless in their character and habits, they are by no means so susceptible of control or civilization; and they are urged by strong, and, to them, irresistible causes in their situation and necessities, to the daily perpetration of violence and fraud. Their permanent subsistence, for example, is derived from the buffalo hunting grounds, which lie a great distance from their towns. Twice a year they are obliged to make long and dangerous expeditions, to procure the necessary provisions for themselves and their families. For this purpose, horses are absolutely requisite, for their own comfort and safety, as well as for the transportation of their food, and their little stock of valuables; and without them they would be reduced, during a great portion of the year, to a state of abject misery and privation. They have no brood mares, nor any trade sufficiently valuable to supply their yearly losses, and endeavor to keep up their stock by stealing horses from the other tribes to the west and south-west. Our own people, and the tribes immediately upon our borders, may indeed be protected from their depredations; and the Kanzas, Osages, Pawnees, and others, may be induced to remain at peace among themselves, so long as they are permitted to pursue the old custom of levying upon the Camanches and other remote nations for their complement of steeds for the warriors, and pack-horses for their transportations to and from the hunting ground. But the instant they are forced to maintain a peaceful and inoffensive demeanor towards the tribes along the Mexican border, and find that every violation of their rights is followed by the avenging arm of our government, the result must be, that, reduced to a wretchedness and want which they can ill brook, and feeling the certainty of punishment for every attempt to ameliorate their condition in the only way they as yet comprehend, they will abandon their unfruitful territory, and remove to the neighborhood of the Mexican lands, and there carry on a vigorous predatory warfare indiscriminately upon the Mexicans and our own people trading or travelling in that quarter.

"The Indians of the prairies are almost innumerable. Their superior horsemanship, which, in my opinion, far exceeds that of any other people on the face of the earth, their daring bravery, their cunning and skill in the warfare of the wilderness, and the astonishing rapidity and secre   with which they are accustomed to move in their martial expeditions, will always render them most dangerous and vexatious neighbors, when their necessities or their discontents may drive them to hostility with our frontiers. Their mode and principles of warfare will always protect them from final and irretrievable defeat, and secure their families from participating in any blow, however severe, which our retribution might deal out to them.

"The Camanches lay the Mexicans under contribution for horses and mules, which they are always engaged in stealing from them in incredible numbers; and from the Camanches, all the roving tribes of the far west, by a similar exertion of skill and daring, supply themselves in turn. It seems to me, therefore, under all these circumstances, that the apparent futility of any philanthropic schemes for the benefit of these nations, and a regard for our own protection, concur in recommending that we remain satisfied with maintaining peace upon our own immediate borders, and leave the Mexicans and the Camanches, and all the tribes hostile to these last, to settle their differences and difficulties in their own way.

"In order to give full security and protection to our trading parties circulating in all directions through the great prairies, I am under the impression, that a few judicious measures on the part of the government, involving a very limited expense, would be sufficient. And, in attaining this end, which of itself has already become an object of public interest and import, another, of much greater consequence, might be brought about, viz., the securing to the states a most valuable and increasing trade, now carried on by caravans directly to Santa Fé.

"As to the first desideratum: the Indians can only be made to respect the lives and property of the American parties, by rendering them dependant upon us for their supplies; which can alone be done with complete effect by the establishment of a trading post, with resident traders, at some point which will unite a sufficient number of advantages to attract the several tribes to itself, in preference to their present places of resort for that purpose; for it is a well known fact, that the Indians will always protect their trader, and those in whom he is interested, so long as they derive benefits from him. The alternative presented to those at the north, by the residence of the agents of the Hudson's Bay Company amongst them, renders the condition of our people in that quarter less secure; but I think it will appear, at once, upon the most cursory examination, that no such opposition further south could be maintained, so as to weaken the benefits of such an establishment as is here suggested.

"In considering this matter, the first question which presents itself is, where do these tribes now make their exchanges, and obtain their necessary supplies? They resort almost exclusively to the Mexicans, who, themselves, purchase from us whatever the Indians most seek for. In this point of view, therefore, *cæteris paribus*, it would be an easy matter for us to monopolize the whole traffic. All that is wanting is some location more convenient for the natives than that offered by the Mexicans, to give us the undisputed superiority; and the selection of such a point requires but a knowledge of the single fact, that these nations invariably winter upon the head waters of the Arkansas, and there prepare all their buffalo robes for trade. These robes are heavy, and, to the Indian, very difficult of transportation. Nothing but necessity induces them to travel any great distance with such inconvenient baggage. A post, therefore, established upon the head waters of the Arkansas, must infallibly secure an uncontested preference over that of the Mexicans, even at their prices and rates of barter. Then let the dragoons occasionally move about among these people in large parties, impressing them with the proper estimate of our power to protect and to punish, and at once we have complete and assured security for all citizens whose enterprise may lead them beyond the border, and an end to the outrages and depredations which now dog the footsteps of the traveller in the prairies, and arrest and repress the most advantageous commerce. Such a post need not be stronger than fifty men; twenty-five to be employed as hunters, to supply the garrison, and the residue as a defence against any hostility. Situated here upon the good lands of the Arkansas, in the midst of abundance of timber, while it might be kept up at a most inconsiderable expense, such an establishment within ninety miles of Santa Fé or Tous would be more than justified by the other and more important advantage before alluded to, leaving the protection of the traders with the Indian tribes entirely out of the question.

"This great trade, carried on by caravans to Santa Fé, annually loads one hundred wagons with merchandise, which is bartered in the northern provinces or Mexico for cash and for beaver furs. The numerous articles excluded as contraband, and the exorbitant duties laid upon all those that are admitted by the Mexican government, present so many obstacles to commerce, that I am well persuaded, that if a post, such as is here suggested, should be established on the Arkansas, it would become the place of deposite, not only for the present trade, but for one infinitely more extended. Here the Mexicans might purchase their supplies, and might well afford to sell them at prices which would silence all competition from any other quarter.

"These two trades, with the Mexicans and the Indians, centring at this post, would give rise to a large village of traders and laborers, and would undoubtedly be hailed, by all that section of country, as a permanent and invaluable advantage. A few pack-horses would carry all the clothing and ammunition necessary for the post during the first year, and two light field-pieces would be all the artillery required for its defence. Afterwards, all the horses required for the use of the establishment might be purchased from the Mexicans at the low price of ten dollars each; and, at the same time, whatever animals might be needed to supply the losses among the dragoons traversing the neighborhood, could be readily procured. The Upper Missouri Indians can furnish horses, at very cheap rates, to any number of the same troops who might be detailed for the defence of the northern frontier; and, in other respects, a very limited outlay of money would suffice to maintain a post in that section of the country.

"From these considerations, and my own personal observation, I am, therefore, disposed to believe, that two posts established by the government, one at the mouth of the Yellow Stone river, and one on the Arkansas, would completely protect all our people in every section of the great wilderness of the west; while other advantages, at least with regard to one of them, confirm and urge the suggestion. A fort at the mouth of Yellow Stone, garrisoned by fifty men, would be perfectly safe. The establishment might be constructed simply with a view to the stores, stables for the dragoons' horses, and quarters for the regular garrison; the rest being provided with sheds or lodges, erected in the vicinity, for their residence during the winter months."

END OF VOLUME II